Hush Puppy

**Center Point
Large Print**

Also by Laurien Berenson and available from Center Point Large Print:

Doggie Day Care Murder
Unleashed

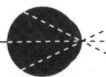

**This Large Print Book carries the
Seal of Approval of N.A.V.H.**

Hush Puppy

A Melanie Travis Mystery

Laurien Berenson

CENTER POINT LARGE PRINT
THORNDIKE, MAINE

This Center Point Large Print edition is published in the year 2011 by arrangement with Kensington Publishing Corp.

The text of this Large Print edition is unabridged. In other aspects, this book may vary from the original edition. Printed in the United States of America. Set in 16-point Times New Roman type.

ISBN: 978-1-60285-995-1

Library of Congress Cataloging-in-Publication Data

Berenson, Laurien.
 Hush puppy : a Melanie Travis mystery / Laurien Berenson. —
Center Point large print ed.
 p. cm.
 ISBN 978-1-60285-995-1 (lib. bdg. : alk. paper)
 1. Travis, Melanie (Fictitious character)—Fiction.
  2. Women private investigators—Connecticut—Fiction.
  3. Women dog owners—Fiction.
  4. Older men—Crimes against—Fiction.
  5. Large type books. I. Title.
PS3552.E6963H87 2011
813′.54—dc22
                                              2010042737

Since moving to Georgia,
it has been my good fortune to be surrounded
by strong Southern women.
This book is gratefully dedicated to
five of the best:

Joanna Wilburn, Ruth Wilburn, DVM,
and Sally Ross Davis—three terrific sisters
whose kindness made a dream come true

And to Laura Mulvaney and Jenny Troyer,
who make each day at Ivy Manor Farm
such a joy

For fellow dog lovers everywhere, here's a treat that your dogs will adore. I don't know the origin of this recipe, but dog show exhibitors have been using it for years. These brownies make wonderful bait in the show ring, or a terrific reward for a great dog anytime.

Dog Brownies

Ingredients:

1 lb. liver
1 C flour
2 C cornmeal
2 eggs
½ C chicken broth or milk
garlic powder (to taste—my dogs like a lot!)

Puree liver in blender or food processor. Add pureed liver (and juices) to dry ingredients in mixing bowl. Stir together well, adding liquid as necessary. Pour mixture into a greased brownie pan and bake for 25 minutes at 350 degrees.

Cool, cut, and enjoy!

In order not to spoil, these brownies must be refrigerated. They can also be frozen and thawed as needed, but in my house, with six dogs who recognize the aroma of baking brownies and wait anxiously in the kitchen for them to cool, this is rarely an option.

❧ One ❧

My mother always told me never to open a door unless I knew what lay behind it.

Sound advice, perhaps, but a rule I had trouble adhering to. As an adult, I'd come to realize she'd been speaking metaphorically, attempting to temper my natural enthusiasm with a bit of useful caution. No matter; by then the habit of throwing open doors and rushing gleefully onward was already deeply ingrained.

Being an optimist, I was always certain that whatever lay beyond each new portal would be a happy surprise, and the few bumps and scrapes I'd suffered along the way had done nothing to diminish that belief. Nevertheless, on that soggy March afternoon, as I hurried through the Howard Academy auditorium, climbed the half flight of steps, and went backstage to the prop room, I wasn't expecting any surprises at all. Much less the one I found.

I'd been sent to find an oil painting of Honoria Howard, sister of early-twentieth-century robber baron, Joshua Howard, and cofounder of the school. Commissioned portraits of the pair hung side by side in the front hall of the stone mansion that formed the nucleus of the private academy. This painting, said to be of lesser quality, apparently also suffered the secondary sin of being monstrously unflattering. It had been relegated to storage and eventually found its way to the prop room, where it was hauled out on occasion when a set required period atmosphere.

Having seen the portrait Honoria favored, indeed having passed by it daily since taking the job as special needs tutor at Howard Academy the previous September, I was privately of the opinion that the woman had been lucky to find an artist who'd been able to record her countenance for posterity without flinching. If that painting featured her good side, I could readily understand why no one had wanted to find wall space for this one.

If I hadn't been in such a hurry, the sound of voices, arguing loudly, might have given me pause. As it was, I'd already opened the door before I realized I might be intruding.

Eugene Krebbs, the school's elderly caretaker, stood in the middle of the small, cluttered room. Wearing his customary overalls and hangdog expression, he was holding a broom in one hand and gesturing forcefully with the other.

He wasn't a big man, and his clothes hung on him as if chosen to suit a larger frame. I judged him to be in his late sixties, though older wouldn't have surprised me. His soft, fleshy features and watery brown eyes gave him a look of amiability that was at odds with a perpetually grumpy disposition.

Before coming to Howard Academy, I'd worked in the Connecticut public-school system for half a dozen years. There, the rules had been stringent, the budget adhered to, the paperwork endless. And a man like Krebbs would have long since been retired. Here he was only one of many private-school eccentricities I'd encountered in the last semester and a half.

His custodial skills were totally outdated—the broom he brandished was evidence of that—and a support staff seemed to do much of the actual work. I'd been told Krebbs had been a fixture at the school for decades. Everyone seemed to take his presence for granted, and though he never seemed to accomplish much, he was often to be found hovering glumly in the background.

I'd never had occasion to speak with Krebbs before; in fact, I wasn't sure I'd ever heard him do more than mutter or mumble. Certainly I'd never heard him yell.

"You don't belong here." Krebbs shook the broom to reinforce his message. "Now take your butt and get out before I decide to turn you in."

The object of his wrath was a girl. Standing beside an old couch, tangled in a jumble of moth-eaten velvet curtains, she looked barely half his size. The expression on her face was all angry defiance.

"You just try it!" she said with a sneer.

A student? I wondered, trying to place her. She looked about ten, which meant fifth grade. In my position as tutor, I taught a cross section of pupils from throughout the school, but this girl didn't look familiar. She had short dark hair, a skinny build, and, I noted absently, remarkably dirty hands. Rather than wearing the school uniform, she was dressed in jeans and a sweatshirt. I was quite sure I'd never seen her before.

"Excuse me," I said loudly. "Is there a problem here?"

Krebbs turned and glared. The girl moved swiftly. Slithering past him, she bolted for the door.

I blocked her path and held out my arms to catch her. Even though I was braced, she nearly knocked me down. Close up, she was tiny. Her chin barely came to the middle of my chest, and when my hand circled her arm, I felt only the bulky material of her sweatshirt, not the bone and sinew underneath.

"Not so fast," I said. "Who are you? What's your name?"

"What's it to you?"

"See?" said Krebbs "Like I said, she don't belong here. She don't even have a name."

Surprisingly, his words seemed to wound the girl; or maybe it was the derision in his tone. "I do too have a name."

"What is it?" I asked, looking back and forth between them. I wondered what she was doing in this musty, out-of-the-way room. And what she could possibly have done to make Krebbs so angry.

"Jane," the girl said softly.

"Jane Doe, I'll bet," spat Krebbs.

I ignored him and said, "I'm Ms. Travis. Are you a student here?"

Jane tossed her head, the gesture looking oddly out of place on the small, elfin girl. "Not exactly."

"She means no," said Krebbs. "Look at her. Her clothes are dirty. *She's* dirty—"

"Do you mind?" I snapped. There was no way Jane was going to talk to me in the face of the caretaker's open hostility. He closed his mouth and stared at me sullenly.

It was too late. With a quick wrench, Jane pulled her arm free and raced out the door. Already several steps behind, I followed her across the stage and watched helplessly as she bounded down the steps, pushed open a side door, and was gone.

Frowning, I turned back. Krebbs had ambled out onto the stage and was sweeping listlessly, his broom seeming to disperse as much dust as it gathered.

"What was that all about?"

I had to ask the question twice. The first time,

either Krebbs didn't hear me or else he chose to ignore it. The second, I walked around in front of him and planted myself in his path.

"Eh?" he said.

"Who was that girl and why were you yelling at her?"

"I weren't yelling. I thought about hitting her with the broom, though." Krebbs smiled slightly, as though he found the notion satisfying.

"Why?"

"Trying to get rid of her. I been trying for a week, maybe more."

"Where does she come from?"

"Heck if I know. She just showed up one day. Found her in the dining hall, snatching cookies out of the cupboard. She's a thief, pure and simple. I ran her off, and I thought that was the end of it. But she came back, all right. Probably casing the place, with some kind of robbery in mind."

The thought of that tiny slip of a girl master-minding a robbery was ludicrous. Krebbs seemed perfectly serious, though.

"Have you spoken to Mr. Hanover about her?"

Russell Hanover II was Howard Academy's headmaster. Popular with parents and alumni alike, he was conservative, dedicated to the education of young minds, and starched stiffer than a nun's habit. I couldn't imagine he'd condone the caretaker's heavy-handed tactics.

"Why would I do a thing like that?" asked Krebbs. "It's my job to take care of the school, and that's what I was doing. I would have gotten rid of her for good this time if you hadn't of come along.

"You're new around here." His rheumy glare made the words sound like an accusation. "Maybe you don't know how things work yet."

"I know that you don't go around chasing young girls with a broom. Nor trying to scare them half to death either." I could see why Jane had felt the need to yell at this man. I was half-tempted myself.

"Things are different here than they are in public school," Krebbs said with a snort. "People are different. You'd be a far sight better off if you took the time to figure that out before poking your nose into where it don't belong."

I pulled myself up, and said with dignity, "I am a teacher here, Mr. Krebbs. And as such, I am entitled to seek answers when I see a situation that strikes me as unusual. Why were you in the prop room?"

He shrugged and ducked his head. I was reminded of a dog indicating submission to a dominant male. In Krebbs's case, however, I suspected the obeisance was all for show.

"Just doing my job. I came up onstage to sweep up and noticed that the door was open.

Shouldn't have been anyone in there this time of day, so I went and had a look."

"What was Jane doing in there?"

Krebbs mumbled something under his breath.

"Pardon me?"

"Looked like maybe she was sleeping. She had some of them velvet curtains down and was using them for a blanket."

Sleeping? Curiouser and curiouser. "And there was something about her demeanor that made you suspect she was dreaming of robbing the school?"

Maybe I shouldn't have been so sarcastic. Certainly, Krebbs's baleful look indicated as much. He picked up his broom and shuffled away across the stage.

I headed in the other direction and returned to the prop room. I hadn't taken the time to look around before; now I did. The place was a mess. Old furniture, knickknacks, bits of costume and scenery were all piled haphazardly in the cramped space.

Howard Academy had hired a new drama coach at the end of January. Until then, the position had been handled in a perfunctory manner by the music teacher, who also ran the glee club. It was easy to see that her abilities had been overtaxed by both jobs. The prop room looked like it hadn't been cleaned or organized in years. It was probably possible to trace the history of shows performed by moving each

14

successive layer of junk to see what lay beneath.

A thick coating of dust covered fabric and upholstery alike, and the heavy burgundy curtains Jane had been using as a blanket were beginning to mildew as well. I lifted the drapes off the couch and shook them out. There was a small thump as something square and solid landed on my foot. A book had been nestled between the folds of material.

Setting the curtains aside, I reached down to see what Jane had been reading. The paperback had a bright, cheery cover: Shakespeare's *Much Ado About Nothing*. A stamp on the flyleaf proclaimed the book to be "Property of Howard Academy Library." Judging by the crease in the spine, Jane had been about halfway through the play.

I wondered if she'd been enjoying it. Shakespeare was one of my favorites, but I'd been considerably older than ten when I'd started reading him. Even now, I was tutoring eighth graders who wouldn't have dreamed of approaching the bard's work without the comfort of a Cliffs Notes edition close at hand.

I folded the curtains and set them aside. The book I left on the couch where I'd found it. What little I knew about the elusive Jane had intrigued me. I hoped Krebbs hadn't succeeded in scaring her off; I was looking forward to the opportunity of getting to know her better.

🐾 TWO 🐾

Thank goodness the prop room was small or I might have been there all afternoon. As it was, it took me twenty minutes to find Honoria's portrait and another ten to pry it out from behind the cupboard where it had been wedged. The oil painting was of medium size, and encased in a massive gilt frame whose faded gold color did nothing to lighten the portrait's somber tone.

For some reason, the artist had painted primarily in shades of brown and gray. Perhaps he'd decided that livelier colors didn't suit his subject, for he'd portrayed Honoria, seated in a straight-backed chair, as a woman with rigid posture and stern, unbending features. Her eyes were small and deep-set and seemed to stare directly at the viewer. Her mouth was fixed in a line of permanent disgruntlement.

One of Honoria's hands lay fisted in her lap. The other dangled at her side, its fingers twined through the topknot of a medium-sized gray dog. A Poodle, I realized, moving the portrait out into the light and taking a closer look, either a large Miniature or a small Standard. When I wiped away a decade's worth of accumulated grime, the dog's lion clip was clearly visible, identifying it as

16

a relative, albeit distant, of Faith, my own Standard Poodle at home.

A small brass plaque screwed to the bottom of the frame read, "Honoria Howard and Poupee. 1936." Honoria's inclusion of the dog's name along with her own made me smile. I knew very little about the school's cofounder, but already I liked her better than I had a few minutes ago.

"There you are!"

I jumped slightly. The painting, propped on the floor but still heavy, swayed in my grasp. Michael Durant, the new drama coach, hurried to grab the other side of the frame. He was tall and slender, his build almost storklike, but there must have been strength in his arms because he held the portrait upright easily. He brushed back the dark brown hair that was long enough to curl around his collar and studied the painting with his usual intense gaze.

"I see you found the old witch. My God, she's a handful, isn't she? No wonder you didn't bring the painting back. We were all wondering where you'd gotten to."

By "all" he meant the rest of our newly formed Spring Pageant Committee. Six weeks earlier, Russell Hanover had come up with the idea of putting together a lavish drama production to celebrate the lives of Howard Academy's founding family. In honor of this first-time endeavor,

Michael had been added to the staff, and plans were now supposed to be taking shape.

The only problem was that although Russell's idea seemed good in theory, nobody could quite figure out what the play was supposed to be about. By all accounts, Joshua Howard had been a shipping magnate whose methods had stopped just short of larceny. He was also rumored to have dabbled in bootlegging. And while I thought such topics would make for a lively and entertaining production, I could also understand why Russell felt the need to highlight other aspects of our esteemed founder's life. If only someone could come up with any.

The week before, our somewhat desperate headmaster had formed an ad hoc committee, and, to my chagrin, I'd found my name at the bottom of the list. Our first meeting had taken place the previous Friday. In a frenzy of creativity befitting a bevy of educators, we'd brainstormed wildly. Everyone had thrown out ideas, and nothing had been settled.

This week when we met again, we were still at square one. It had been Sally Minor's idea to dig up Honoria's portrait and hang it in the teachers' lounge where we were meeting in the hope that it might prove to be an inspiration. Sally had been at Howard Academy for more than a decade and was a prime source for all sorts of interesting snippets of past history.

"It's just a ratty old painting," she said. "I'm sure nobody'd care if we borrowed it and stuck it up in here."

"Except maybe the other teachers who'd have to look at it all day." Ed Weinstein smirked. He taught upper-school English and always seemed to be laughing at some private joke that he declined to share with the rest of us.

"I don't think anyone would mind." Rita Kinney was shy and soft-spoken, possessing a quiet beauty that she did nothing to enhance. She taught fourth through sixth grade history, and this was the first time she'd volunteered a thought. "I vote for giving it a try. It can't hurt."

Being the newest staff member in the group besides Michael, our leader, I'd been dispatched to hunt down the painting. "There was a bit of a problem," I said.

"I guess there would be. I've never seen so much junk." Michael lifted the painting free and laid it back against the couch. "This place is a pit, isn't it? Your basic testament to the excesses of private education. Do you suppose they ever threw anything out? Or even thought of using it twice?"

He picked up the burgundy-velvet curtains I'd folded and tossed the heavy bundle on top of a similar pair in a faded shade of hunter green. A cloud of dust rose, then settled, around them. "Russell promised me free rein with the drama department, such as it is. I can see the first order of business better be cleaning this room."

"After we come up with a theme for the pageant," I said firmly. "Did the committee think of anything after I left?"

"Lots of things, none of them useful. We did manage to pass a rule prohibiting smoking at the meetings."

"Ed?" I ventured.

"Ed. He seemed to think that if he stood next to the window when he lit up, nobody would mind. Sally changed his mind about that pretty quickly."

"She would." I grinned. "Do you really think we ought to take this monstrosity back and hang it up?"

"The committee voted for it." Michael squatted down in front of the painting. "I'm happy to bow to majority rule. Who's the artist anyway? Is there a signature?"

"Just initials." I'd already looked. "R.W.H., whoever that is."

"Maybe an artist with too much taste to want his name associated with the finished product? Hey, what's this?" Michael read the plaque on the bottom of the frame, then looked at the dog in the lower corner of the picture. "Poupee? Silly name for a rather silly looking dog."

"It's a Poodle," I told him. "Probably a small Standard. Even though they were originally bred in Germany, lots of people still think of them as French Poodles. I would imagine that's how he got the name. As to the silly looking trim, that's not his fault. In those days, it was called a lion trim. Now we use a variation called a continental in the show ring."

Michael stood up and dusted off his hands. "How do you know so much about it?"

"I have a Poodle at home that looks quite a bit like that one. My aunt breeds Standard Poodles. She's shown them for years, and now she's got me doing it, too."

"I have to admit it's a pretty distinctive look, with the hair long on the front and all shaved off in back. Maybe we could use your dog in the pageant."

"Doing what?" I asked, surprised.

"She could play the part of Poupee." Michael saw the expression on my face and grinned. "Hey, don't knock it. That's probably the best idea we've come up with all week."

Somehow, that wasn't a comforting thought.

By the time we got back to the teachers' lounge, the rest of the committee had grown tired of waiting for us and gone home. Meetings held at the end of the day on Friday are never popular, especially as Howard Academy has early dis-mis-sal so that everyone can get a jump on their weekend plans. Some of my students would be heading north with their parents to ski; others, south, in search of sun. At least one had theater tickets for Broadway and another was planning to go fox hunting.

As for me, I was heading home to let out the dog and meet my six-year-old son, Davey's, school bus. We'd have milk and cookies together, and he'd tell me about his day. After that, I had to give Faith a bath as she was entered in a dog show that weekend where I had high hopes of picking up some much-needed points toward her championship. I wouldn't have traded places with anyone.

As always, Faith was waiting by the door when I got home. She whined softly as I fitted the key to the lock, then launched herself into the air in a frenzy of greeting as the door swung open. Standards are the largest of the three varieties of Poodles. Faith stands twenty-four inches at the shoulder and weighs more than forty pounds. Catching her in full flight requires both strength and dexterity, but I was used to the task by now.

Margaret Turnbull, Faith's breeder and my Aunt Peg, would have been horrified to see one of her dogs exhibit such a lack of manners. The Cedar Crest Standard Poodles are an illustrious line, well-known throughout the dog show world for producing generation after generation of eye-catching champions. Each of Aunt Peg's dogs is impeccably trained, and she never allows anything less than the best behavior.

Unfortunately for me, it's a standard she also applies to her relatives.

Since Aunt Peg wasn't around to see, however, I gave Faith a hug and ruffled my hands through the long black mane coat on the front half of her body. Poodles have long been one of the most popular breeds in the world and, as an admittedly biased owner, it wasn't hard for me to see why. Beneath the highly stylized show clip, Faith was a dog of uncommon intelligence and dignity. She understood my moods and most of what I said, and had a marvelous sense of humor. In short, she was the perfect companion.

It didn't surprise me that Honoria Howard had chosen to include her Poodle when she'd had her portrait painted. Poodle owners tend to think of their pets as members of the family. No doubt she'd felt the same way about Poupee as I did about Faith.

I'd just let the dog out into the fenced backyard when the squeal of air brakes signaled the arrival of Davey's bus. My son never does anything at half speed. As I headed toward the front of the house, I could already hear the front door opening.

"Hey!" called Davey, slamming the door behind him. "Where is everyone?"

I reached the hall and saw my son standing

just inside the door. He looked like he'd grown an inch since I'd sent him to school that morning. A new gap had appeared between the hem of his jeans and the tops of his sneakers. Luckily for the sake of warmth, it was filled by gym socks, currently an indeterminate shade of muddy brown. They'd been white when he'd left.

Davey dropped his backpack and jacket on the floor. "Where's Faith?" he asked. She was usually the first to greet him.

"Outside in back. I just got home. Do I get a hug?"

He shied away and made a face. Six years old and already cynical.

"Pick up your backpack," I said. "And hang your jacket in the closet where it belongs."

"I should have hugged you." Davey sighed. "It would have been easier."

I've always been a sucker for logic like that. I held out my arms. "There's still time to change your mind."

"Okay." He allowed a brief embrace. Thank goodness Aunt Peg wasn't there; no doubt she'd have complained about the way I was training my dog *and* my child.

Not that I tend to pay much attention to things like that. For most of Davey's life, I've been a single mother. Though Davey's father had recently reappeared, and we were now on good terms (albeit from opposite ends of the country), I was still accustomed to doing things my own way.

All that was due to change soon; several months earlier I'd gotten engaged. Sam Driver and I have known each other for nearly two years. Not unexpectedly, we'd met over a dog, a stolen Standard Poodle that each of us was pursuing for a different reason. By the time we got things sorted out, it was clear to both of us that our initial attraction was also worth investigating.

Sam's the kind of man women fantasize about but never expect to find. I had no idea how I'd gotten so lucky, but I wasn't about to question my good fortune, especially as Davey and Sam adored each other. Even the notoriously picky Aunt Peg approved, though the fact that he was a fellow Standard Poodle breeder had obviously swayed things in his favor. We'd be seeing Sam and his new puppy, Tar, at the show the next day.

I brought Faith in from outside, gave her a biscuit and put out a glass of milk and plate of cookies for Davey. While they were both munching, I set up Faith's grooming table and hair dryer in preparation for her bath. Showing a Standard Poodle is no small undertaking, and Faith was now nearly two years old and in full bloom. Her correctly textured coat was long and dense; the bath and blow-dry that followed would take several hours to complete.

Faith's continental trim is one of two approved show clips for adult Poodles, and the one in which the majority are shown. The previous evening I'd clipped her face, feet, and most of her hindquarter and legs. In addition to her mane coat, she had pom pons on her hips, legs, and at the end of her tail, all of which needed to be carefully scissored.

The job is an exacting one requiring an educated eye and a steady hand. Fortunately, I'd be able to count on Aunt Peg's help at the show the next day to pull everything together. For much of Faith's show career, Peg and I had been competing against each other as she'd kept Faith's sister, Hope, from the same litter. Thanks to my aunt's experience and superior handling skills, however, her Standard Poodle had sailed through the process, completing the requirements for her championship before Christmas. Hope was now retired from the show ring, and Peg had promised me her expert assistance.

With that in mind, I allowed myself to hurry through Faith's blow-dry. After her bath, I blotted the excess water from her hair with several big, fluffy towels, then didn't redampen the areas of her coat that had air-dried before I was able to work my way around to them—a cardinal sin among people who show Poodles professionally.

Then again, I reminded myself, the pros were paid to do this job. I was a mother first, a teacher second, and a Poodle exhibitor third. And sometimes, something had to give. I brushed quickly through Faith's now crinkly bracelets, and declared the job done.

The Poodle seemed pleased by my speedy performance. I know I was. I packed up my grooming equipment, leaving it ready to go to the show in the morning, then went upstairs and fixed dinner for my son.

Saturday's show was in New York, just on the other side of the Hudson River. Over the years, it has become harder and harder to find locations suitable for holding dog shows; and any venue which proves to be both practical and profitable tends to see a lot of action. Rockland Community College was one such site, and I'd been there several times over the last year.

About a third of the large room where the show was being held had been set aside for grooming. Each entry, from the smooth coated hounds to the labor intensive wire haired terriers, would have been bathed, clipped, plucked, and brushed to the point of perfection. But despite the preparations that were done at home beforehand, there was always something left to do just before entering the ring.

The professional handlers, who travel with

strings of dogs and work from dawn 'til dark on show days, had already staked out their space. Aisles were defined by their stacked crates and rows of grooming tables. Making our way through the congestion, Davey and I looked for familiar faces. Usually, Aunt Peg saves me a spot, but today she wasn't showing a dog. Sam was, but I wasn't sure he'd be there yet.

"Look!" cried Davey, waving enthusiastically. "There's Terry."

Terry Denunzio was assistant to prominent professional handler Crawford Langley. He'd been a part of the dog show scene for less than a year, but he and I were already buddies. I changed course and headed in his direction.

"Air kiss," Terry said, offering his cheek for a smooch. "I don't want to mess your makeup."

"Nor yours." I cocked a brow. Terry was gay and deliciously good looking. He knew it and he flaunted it.

"Nasty, nasty. Are you looking for the hunk?"

Terry calls them like he sees them, and that was his pet name for Sam. Sam hated it. I thought it was kind of cute.

"Yes, is he here yet?"

"Just unloaded, and went to park his car. That's his stuff." Terry pointed to a table and crate at the end of the row. "I'm sure you can squeeze right in next to him. Especially since the two of you like to be cozy."

"Thanks," I said, ignoring the innuendo because I knew Terry was dying for me not to.

I set up my things, put Faith in her crate, left Davey under Terry's watchful eye, and went back outside to park my car. When I returned a few minutes later, Sam was back as well and Aunt Peg had arrived. In my absence, she'd taken the liberty of releasing Faith from her crate and putting the Standard Poodle up on the grooming table.

"Did you actually use a hair dryer on this bitch last night?" Peg asked. "Or did you just blow on her a few times and hope for the best?"

I didn't even try to mount a defense. Aunt Peg hated excuses, even good ones, which I didn't exactly have. She'd celebrated her sixtieth birthday in the fall and, to nobody's surprise, outlasted all of us on the dance floor. She was brash and blunt, and knew everything there was to know about dogs.

"Good morning to you, too," I said instead.

Aunt Peg harrumphed and gestured toward Sam's nine-month-old Standard Poodle puppy, who was standing on his table. "Look at Tar. There isn't a single curl in his coat."

She was right, there wasn't. Not much I could do about that. Tuning out the complaint, I walked past Peg and greeted Sam with a kiss.

I had to stand up on my toes because, at six-foot-two, he's a good eight inches taller than I am. He's broad through the shoulders, but his chest and hips taper, giving the impression of strength, not bulk. His eyes are cornflower blue, and they crinkle at the edges when he smiles, like he was doing now.

"Maybe Sam had more time," I said over my shoulder.

"Maybe I had more patience," said Sam, who knows perfectly well how frustrated I get with the process of correctly straightening the Poodle's coat with a blow-dryer.

I'd taken a step back, but his hands were still resting lightly on my shoulders, so I felt his reaction when Sam's body stiffened. He was staring off into the crowd gathered at ringside with the oddest expression on his face.

"What's the matter?" I asked, turning to have a look.

"Sheila." The word slipped out on an indrawn breath. I wasn't sure if it was a prayer or a curse.

By this time, Aunt Peg was frowning, too. Even Terry had tuned back into our conversation. I scanned the faces in the crowd but still had no idea who might cause such a reaction.

"Who's Sheila?" I asked.

Sam swallowed heavily before answering. "My ex-wife."

❧ Three ❧

Ex-wife?

I must have heard wrong, I thought. Sam didn't have an ex-wife, at least not one that I'd ever heard about. And considering the length and depth of our relationship, it seemed rather late for a tidbit of information like that to be popping up.

"Ex-wife?" I repeated the words aloud to see what sort of reaction they'd bring. I was half hoping I'd get a denial. It didn't happen. Indeed, Sam didn't even seem to hear me.

"Sam?"

He glanced at me fleetingly. "Excuse me a minute, would you?" He strode away, cutting quickly through the crowd.

Left behind, Tar paced unhappily on the top of his table. All show Poodles are trained at an early age to stay when placed on a grooming table, but Tar was a puppy, just beginning his career. The combination of his master leaving without a reassuring word and the swirl of activity around him made him nervous.

I wanted to watch Sam and see what happened next. Instead, I found myself catching an armful of flying Poodle when Tar launched himself into the air and attempted to follow Sam into the

31

crowd. Puppy or not, Tar was nearly full grown, and packed with muscle. I staggered backward into a crate and spit out a hank of dense black hair. For his age, Tar had a topknot to be proud of.

"Here," said Terry, whisking the puppy out of my arms and putting him back where he belonged. "I'll take care of him. You go do what you need to do."

Much as I appreciated the thought, I realized I had no idea what to do next. Should I storm after Sam and demand an explanation? Maybe introduce myself to Sheila and invite her to our wedding? Or should I stay here and start brushing Faith as if nothing was wrong and let Sam come back and tell me what was going on when he was ready?

When he was ready? Hah! With news like this he should have been ready a long time ago.

I decided to stay put and picked up a pin brush and comb. Terry looked disappointed; no doubt he'd been hoping for fireworks. I did, however, sneak a peek at Sheila as I laid Faith on her side and started to brush.

Sam's ex-wife was tiny, so petite I could only see her as the ringside crowd shifted and eddied. She had shiny dark hair bobbed just below chin length and pale, flawless skin. Her full lips were outlined in a rosy shade of pink that matched the one on her long fingernails. As she spoke, she waved a hand gracefully in the air.

Whatever she was saying, Sam seemed mesmerized. I felt my stomach muscles clench. The coffee I'd drunk earlier was suddenly burning a hole in my gut.

"Who's that?" asked Davey, watching the proceedings avidly from his high perch on top of Faith's crate.

"An old friend of Sam's. Someone we haven't met yet."

"She looks like a nice lady."

"I'm sure she is," Aunt Peg said.

She'd taken custody of Tar from Terry and was now standing by the puppy's table. Though I knew for a fact that Peg was one of the most curious people on the face of the earth, she'd barely glanced in Sheila's direction. That alone was enough to make me suspicious.

"How sure?" I asked.

"What?" Peg said innocently.

"You knew about this," I accused.

She didn't deny it.

"I can't believe it!"

"Melanie, don't be melodramatic. Sheila Vaughn has been showing Pugs for years. Of course, I know who she is. She lives somewhere in the Midwest. Illinois, I believe."

Knowing Aunt Peg, next she'd start telling me the names of Sheila's dogs. "Did you know she was Sam's ex-wife?" I hissed the words out under my breath. Davey had gone back to coloring in his book, and I'd just as soon he didn't tune back in to our conversation.

Aunt Peg opened Sam's tack box and started unloading Tar's grooming supplies. "I imagine the topic may have come up at some point."

"And you never felt the need to mention it to me?" I asked incredulously.

"Why should I? It wasn't any of my business. Something like that was between Sam and you. For all I knew, he'd told you himself."

Aunt Peg was a master at minding everyone's business but her own. Fine time she'd chosen to keep her thoughts to herself. "Well, he hadn't," I grumbled.

"So I see." Peg picked up a slicker and began to brush Tar's legs. "I wonder why not."

"So do I."

Now that the initial shock had passed, my anger seemed to be evaporating with it. Instead I felt numb. How could Sam have something as important as a previous marriage in his past and never feel the need to tell me about it? He knew all about my ex-husband, Bob; the two of them had even met. And if he'd never bothered to mention Sheila, what other kinds of secrets might he also be hiding?

Brushing a Poodle is a mindless job. The fingers work by rote, parting the hair and smoothing it upward, teasing out the occasional snarl with a wide-toothed comb. Your hands

34

are busy, but your thoughts can be elsewhere.

By the time I had Faith fully brushed out, I'd pictured Sam with a trio of ex-wives, a gaggle of screaming children, and a felony warrant outstanding for his arrest. I kept trying to see the bright side, but the absurdity of the situation didn't make me feel any better at all.

When Sam returned, I had Faith standing up on her table and was scissoring a finish on her trim. Aunt Peg was supposed to be helping me, remember? Instead, with Sam gone, she was working on getting Tar ready. Losing her expert assistance was just one more thing to be annoyed about.

"Sorry about that," said Sam, slipping in between the tables and taking the brush and comb from Peg. "I didn't think it would take so long."

Sorry about that? That's the kind of thing you say when you sneeze, or stumble, or forget to call; not when you get caught hiding a secret that might alter the plans someone thought she'd made for the rest of her life.

"So that's Sheila." I smiled politely. "You didn't want to bring her over and introduce her?"

Sam looked confused. Was he wondering why I wasn't screaming? Funny, so was I.

"She was in a hurry," he said. Which did nothing to explain why she'd stopped and talked to him for half an hour. "I'll tell you about it later."

"Yes," I said. "You will."

Since Sam had taken over Tar's grooming, Aunt Peg came to stand beside Faith's table. She reached around the Poodle and took the scissors out of my hand. "Just a precautionary measure," she said pleasantly.

"If you're going to hold them, you may as well make yourself useful." Keeping hold of Faith's nose to maintain her position, I stepped back out of the way and let Aunt Peg go to work.

Rockland County was a mid-sized show but the entry in Standard Poodles was strong. Many factors influence the size of an entry, but the most important is the judge. Each arbiter brings his own set of preferences and life experiences to the ring; and the best an exhibitor can hope for is a fair and unbiased appraisal by an experienced hand. Based on what Aunt Peg had told me, Rockland's judge was such a man.

Tony Rondella had been a part of the Poodle scene for many years, first as a professional handler, later as a judge. His opinion was highly valued by those who cared about the breed. A win under Tony, usually hard-fought in tough competition, was an event to be celebrated.

As she worked, Aunt Peg let her gaze roam over the Standard Poodles in Crawford's setup. There were four, two blacks, a white, and a brown, all waiting on their tables in various stages of readiness. Since Crawford was often the one to beat, I looked up the Poodles in the catalogue and assessed Faith's chances.

Two were males, one already a finished champion and there to compete for Best of Variety. The other was an Open dog. That made him Sam's problem, not mine; until the Best of Variety judging, the classes would be divided by sex. I read Aunt Peg the listings for the two bitches.

"The puppy's no threat," she said. "She's barely seven months, and a brown besides. That won't help."

Though in theory judging is supposed to be color-blind, in reality it seldom is. In Poodles, certain colors are easier to win with than others. Judges' prejudice plays a part, as does the fact that those colors are more apt to produce a quality dog. In Standards, blacks and whites reap the majority of the wins.

"What about the Open Bitch? Dantanna's Glory Bee?"

Aunt Peg chuckled. "Glory be, that's what her owners will be saying if Crawford ever manages to finish that bitch. She's not a great one. She's needed her second major for six months at least. Crawford must be feeling desperate to bring her here under Tony."

"At least it's a major," I said. "That gives her a shot."

In order to become an A.K.C. champion, a dog

must accumulate fifteen points under several different judges. Major wins, two of which are necessary to attain a championship, are wins of three points or more at a single show, which means that a substantial amount of competition must be present. Only a certain number of dog shows will offer majors in any given year. Which ones will is often determined by the caliber of the judge that's been hired. Have someone popular on your panel, and the exhibitors will enter in droves. Hire a lesser judge and suffer the consequences.

In the time that I'd been showing Faith, she'd managed to accumulate seven points. Technically she was halfway to her championship. In reality, however, she had yet to win either of her majors, and the need to do so loomed before me like a major stumbling block. Many factors—time of year, dearth of good judges, dwindling entries—often combined to leave a dog "stuck for majors" for months at a time. The sooner I could get at least one of Faith's big wins out of the way, the better I'd feel.

"Nervous yet?" asked Sam.

I shot him a look. Tar had his topknot in, and Sam was spraying up his neck hair. The puppy really looked good. I was glad I wouldn't have to compete against him.

"No," I said coolly. I was lying, and we both knew it. "You?"

Sam shook his head. "Tony's not the easiest person to show under, but as long as Tar behaves himself, we'll be okay."

"What do you mean, he's not easy?" I asked. Usually Aunt Peg made sure I was informed in advance about judges' idiosyncrasies. She'd been vague about what I should expect from Tony Rondella, however. Now I wondered why.

"He used to handle Poodles himself," said Sam. "And he was one of the best. There's nothing that annoys him more than seeing a good dog incompetently presented. He's been known to take a leash out of an exhibitor's hand and give a handling lesson in the ring."

"Great." I moaned. Someone like Tony Rondella would probably make mincemeat out of my technique. "Maybe he won't notice me."

"He'll notice you," Aunt Peg said firmly. She poked me with the tip of the scissors, hard. "He'll notice Faith the minute she walks in the ring. She's a very pretty bitch, and just his type. This is the chance you've been looking for, so don't blow it."

That was Aunt Peg's version of a pep talk. It did nothing to quiet the butterflies that were beginning to leap in my stomach. "You might have warned me," I mentioned.

"Pish," said Peg. "Then you'd have only started getting nervous sooner."

"Trust me," said Sam. "There's no way to

prepare for Tony. You're better off if his judging comes as a surprise."

"Thanks, but I've had quite enough surprises for one day," I said pointedly.

That shut Sam up.

Good, I thought. It was meant to.

As I sprayed up Faith's topknot and neck hair, Aunt Peg took Davey up to the ring to pick up our numbered armbands. All too soon, they were back, and it was time to go.

From ringside, Tony Rondella didn't look too imposing, but I knew how quickly impressions could change once the judging started. The steward called the Puppy Dog class into the ring and Sam walked Tar to the head of the line.

"He looks good," I commented.

"He should look good," said Aunt Peg. She was Tar's breeder, and admittedly biased since he came from her Cedar Crest line. But Peg was fair when it came to her Poodles. If she didn't like the way one had turned out, she would be equally quick to admit that, too. "Fortunately Tar has inherited the best traits from both his parents. You always hope for that, but you don't often see it happen. He's young yet, but that won't matter today. Tony should love him."

Her prediction proved prophetic. Tar was quickly awarded the blue ribbon in the puppy class and when he went back in the ring a few minutes later to vie with the other class winners for the award of Winners Dog, he easily won that, too.

"Just two points," said Peg, consulting her catalogue. "The major broke. There are a lot more bitches entered, though. It will hold there."

I nodded, but I wasn't listening. The Puppy Bitch class was in the ring, which meant that it was almost Faith's turn. I pulled a comb out of my pocket and flicked it through her topknot.

Now that Faith was nearly two years old and fully mature, I had started entering her in the Open class. Open is usually the biggest class and the hardest to win. The professional handlers show there with their best dogs.

Faith had picked up her previous points at smaller shows. Today, with a major on the line, nearly a dozen Standard Poodle bitches were standing ready at the gate. If Faith were to have a chance of winning in competition this strong, I would have to pull out all the stops.

"Stop fussing," said Aunt Peg, batting away my hand. "You're knocking everything down. Faith looks fine."

"No she doesn't," I babbled. "She needs more hair. Look at Crawford's bitch."

"She could stand to be trimmed back," Aunt Peg said, considering. "Of course Crawford doesn't dare. The best thing about that bitch is her coat. He's using it to cover a multitude of sins. Tony won't be fooled. He's not only seen every grooming trick in the book; I think he invented most of them. I imagine Faith will beat Glory Bee quite handily."

Easy for her to say. She wasn't judging.

"In you go," Peg said briskly, as the steward called the Open bitches into the ring. "Have fun, dear!"

Have fun? I thought grimly as I found a place toward the end of the line. Who was she kidding? This wasn't fun, it was torture. I had to be crazy. That was the only explanation for how I'd let Aunt Peg talk me into this.

Tony lifted his hands and motioned for the line of bitches to gait around the big ring. That was relatively easy. All I had to do was keep Faith moving in a straight line and not fall down. Keeping one eye on where I was going and the other on the judge, I watched Tony skim his gaze down the line. It paused a moment when it came to Faith, then moved on. Good, I thought, we'd been noticed.

I might have been nervous, but Faith wasn't. She'd been in the show ring a number of times by now and knew what was expected of her. Poodles are very fast learners. Add to that a natural tendency to show off and play to the crowd, and you have all the makings of a first-class show dog.

When Faith's turn came to be individually examined, she stood like a statue. Tony liked

42

her head, I could tell. And he lingered happily on her front end assembly. When he reached her hind-quarter, I saw the first glimmering of dissatisfaction. He lifted both her hind legs and repositioned them, then had another look.

So far, so good. There weren't any deductions for handler error; the only thing that mattered was the quality of the dog.

The judge finished his examination and asked me to move Faith down and back. I thought she gaited well as we trotted across the ring on the diagonal mat, but before we'd even made it back, Tony Rondella was already shaking his head. "You're going too fast," he said. "Take it slower. And I'd like to see her on a loose lead."

We tried again. And again after that. No matter what I did, I couldn't seem to make Tony happy. Finally, in utter frustration, I all but dropped the leash and let Faith find her own way. Amazingly, this time when we returned, he was smiling.

"Fine," he said. "Now take her around to the end of the line."

Tony quickly examined the rest of the entrants. That done, he walked straight to Faith, pulled her out of line, and sent us to the other side of the ring. The other Poodles he liked followed. "Once around," he said, then quickly pointed.

I assume he said, "One, two, three, four,"

because they always do, but in truth I'd stopped listening after the first word, because Faith was at the head of the line and his finger was pointing her way. I took the blue ribbon, tucked it in my pocket, and quickly restacked Faith on the mat. She still had to beat the winners of the earlier bitch classes in order to win the major.

Once again, Faith was great. Since the judge had asked for a loose leash earlier, I continued to let Faith guide herself, offering only minimum input. Clearly she was up to the task, and clearly Tony Rondella appreciated everything she had to offer. He wasted no time in awarding her Winners Bitch.

"Well done," Peg whispered in my ear, as I stepped out the gate while reserve winners bitch was judged. "That's four points. Don't forget, Sam can use the major, too. Tony prides himself on actually judging the dogs. He doesn't always share."

Sharing the majors is a time-honored tradition, frowned on by the American Kennel Club and beloved of exhibitors everywhere. Since the number of points awarded is dependent upon the number of competitors defeated, it often happens that Winners Dog and Winners Bitch within the same breed will be awarded a different number of points.

When Best of Variety is judged, the Winners

Dog and Winners Bitch also compete against the champions as they have yet to be defeated on the day. In addition, these two are judged against each other for Best of Winners. The one chosen BOW receives the higher number of points awarded.

Especially when a major is involved, most judges can be counted on to share the points, thus making sure that both entrants end up with the coveted win. Likewise most exhibitors, having already secured the major for themselves, don't mind holding their dogs back so as to make their competitor look better.

All I would have had to do to make sure that Tar got the extra points was handle Faith badly. In my case, it wouldn't even have been a stretch. Tar was a pretty puppy; he deserved to win a major. But on that day, he didn't get one.

Sam smiled at me as we filed into the ring. That wonderful, knowing smile that reminded me of all the things we'd shared. He looked like a man who didn't have a care in the world, and I felt like a woman betrayed.

I set my shoulders and didn't smile back, and when Tony Rondella compared his two winners, Faith and I put on a dazzling show. Tar was a beautiful Standard Poodle, but Faith had him beaten cold on maturity and conditioning. At nine months of age, there was simply nothing the puppy could do about that.

Tony judged dogs, and he didn't share the major. I accepted the blue-and-white ribbon with a greedy grin that probably revealed volumes about my own maturity level and strode out of the ring without looking back.

❧ Four ❧

"I guess we need to talk," Sam said when he'd caught up to me back at the crates.

"I guess we do," I agreed.

The satisfaction I'd felt had been short-lived; already I was beginning to regret my childish display of pique. Even with a good dog, majors were never easy to come by. No matter how annoyed I was at Sam, I shouldn't have responded by depriving Tar of his shot.

"So talk," I said.

All right, I admit it. I was dying to hear what he had to say. Besides, we even had a modicum of privacy, as Davey and Aunt Peg had gone off together from ringside. It would have been nice to think that Peg was being discreet; but knowing her, it was more likely they'd gone to search for food, preferably something sweet.

"Sheila is part of my past," said Sam.

"I guess so, if she's your ex-wife."

He looked exasperated. "We're not going to get anywhere if you won't listen."

"I've been listening for two years, and apparently it didn't help because Sheila never came up."

I knew I sounded snippy. Worse, I wasn't even sorry. I hopped Faith up onto her table, let her lie

47

down, and began the process of taking apart her elaborate show ring hairdo. Across the aisle, Sam was doing the same with Tar. I could see him take several deep breaths before speaking again.

"I don't know what you're so upset about," he said finally.

He had to be kidding. I peered at him closely. He looked serious enough. I took that as a bad sign.

"I'm upset because you lied to me."

"No, I didn't. I've never lied to you about anything."

"Why didn't you tell me about Sheila?"

"She wasn't important." Sam shrugged. "It always seemed like we had better things to talk about."

"She was important enough for you to have married her," I pointed out.

"That was a long time ago."

Spraying conditioner into Tar's topknot, Sam angled his body away so I couldn't see his expression. Was it my imagination or did his tone sound wistful? "Tell me about her," I said.

Any woman in the world would have known better than to head into those treacherous waters. Not Sam; he plunged right in.

"Sheila was a firecracker," he said. "She had mercurial ups and mercurial downs. When she liked something, she was passionately devoted to it. When something didn't please her, she wanted

48

no part of it. I was twenty-three when we met, and I'd never known anyone like her."

I'm human, okay? I was waiting to hear something uncomplimentary. Hearing Sam call his ex-wife a passionate firecracker wasn't exactly what I'd had in mind. My eyes narrowed. Come to think of it, he'd never complimented me on my passion.

"How did the two of you meet?"

"In business school. Second year. She was majoring in marketing, and it wasn't hard to figure out why. She could sell dog collars at a cat convention."

I nodded in what I hoped was an encouraging way. I wished he'd hurry up and get to the part about the disagreements, the acrimony, the divorce.

"So we got married," said Sam. "Big wedding, huge cathedral, white dress, the whole works."

I waited—it wasn't like I wasn't busy—a full five minutes for him to continue. Surely that couldn't be where he intended to end the story.

"That's *it?*" I asked finally.

"Pretty much." Sam nodded. Tar had less hair than Faith, and he was almost finished.

What about lawyers, and papers, and divvying up assets? I wondered. What about sleepless nights and assigning the blames? Obviously Sam had a talent for glossing over major details.

"You *did* get divorced, didn't you?"

49

"Of course. It happened six years ago. Like I said, it's all in the past. None of it has any relevance to my life now."

Right. Sheila had had enough relevance to make him drop what he was doing—which, as I recalled, was talking to me—and run across the room to see her. And the story he'd told about their life together had holes big enough to drive a truck through.

"Look what we got!" Davey came skipping down the aisle. He was holding up a sugar-coated doughnut.

"What about lunch?" I asked. Noon had come and gone while we'd been in the Poodle ring.

"This is my lunch," Davey informed me. "I've had two already. Aunt Peg said I could."

I gazed at Peg, who smiled benignly. "I guess you haven't read any of those studies about the effects of good nutrition on growing children."

"Pish," she said. "He'll grow. I've always had a taste for sweets and look at me." Nearing six feet tall and built along the sleek lines of a Borzoi, Peg was a glowing advertisement for good health. Something only an idiot would have attributed to her diet. "Did you and Sam manage to get things sorted out?"

"No," I said firmly, just as Sam answered, "Yes."

"Pity about that major," Aunt Peg mentioned, just to throw some gas on the fire.

"There'll be others." Sam seemed remarkably composed about the loss. Peevishly, I wondered if that was because his mind was on other things.

"We met Mrs. Vaughn," said Davey. "She's nice."

I dropped my comb. It landed on the floor with a clatter. "You did? When?"

"Just now. Aunt Peg and I went over to say hello."

"Welcome to the East Coast," said Aunt Peg. "That sort of thing."

I bent down to pick up my comb. Knowing Peg, a what-are-you-doing-here sort of inquisition seemed more likely.

"I think that should be Ms. Vaughn," I corrected Davey. "Unless she's gotten married again?"

"Nope," Davey said cheerfully. "Aunt Peg asked."

She would, I thought. For once, my aunt's curiosity seemed like an endearing trait. I waited avidly for my son to continue.

"She told me to call her Mrs. Vaughn. She said she liked being a missus." Davey studied all sides of his doughnut before finding one he liked and taking a big bite. Blithely he talked and chewed at the same time. "Mrs. Vaughn said we'll probably see her at some of the other shows around here because she's working in New York until summer."

"Really?" I pushed the words out with effort. "How nice."

51

"She has Pugs. Their faces are all wrinkly, and sometimes they snort. She let me pet one. Her name was Tulip."

It was a good thing Davey was in a talkative mood because all the adults in our little group seemed to have been struck dumb.

Sam was busy with Tar. Having finished working on his hair, he stood the big puppy up, let him shake, then put him in his crate. Aunt Peg was munching on a brownie. No one else but me seemed unduly concerned about this sudden turn my life had taken.

"I guess you've known about this for a while," I said to Sam.

"What?" he asked over his shoulder as he tossed equipment in his tack box.

So help me, I wanted to smack him. Could he possibly have any doubt what we were talking about?

"Sheila. Her job in New York. You know . . ." I finished vaguely. It seemed like a better idea than outlining the specifics, like the fact that Miss Fourth of July was about to be living in our backyard.

"No, I had no idea until I saw her here this morning. Sheila and I haven't kept in touch." He said this last part slowly, as if I were a small child, and he wanted to make sure I understood.

My hands moved methodically as I continued to work on Faith's coat by rote. All at once, I found myself wondering if Sheila had divorced him for patronizing her.

"Where will she be staying?" asked Aunt Peg.

"She's leased a house in North Salem," said Sam. "As I'm sure you can understand, she needed space for her dogs. She's just settling in, and there are some minor repairs she's been struggling with. I told her I'd stop by this afternoon after the show and have a look."

"This afternoon?" my voice squeaked. Faith, who'd been lying quietly on the grooming table, lifted her head and looked at me. It's a pity when your dog is better at sensing your feelings than your fiancé.

"Sure. That's okay, isn't it? I didn't think we had anything planned."

He was right, we didn't. But by now our lives were so intertwined that we didn't usually bother to make plans. Since both of us were busy during the week, we'd fallen into the routine of spending most of our weekends together. Even though Sam and I hadn't spoken about it, I'd just assumed that he'd be coming home with us after the show.

"You're right," I said brightly. My smile felt as phony as a nine inch topknot on a six-month-old puppy. "We didn't have any plans."

"Good." Sam nodded. "This shouldn't take long. Sheila mentioned something about a piece of fence that's sagging and a faucet that drips all night. How about if I call you when I'm done?"

"Good idea," I said, as he loaded his crate, table, and tack box onto a dolly and prepared to leave. "You do that."

Aunt Peg, the buttinsky who'd brought us together in the first place, was surveying the situation with a worried frown. If Sam had had any sense, he'd have been worried, too. But obviously he was too intent on his upcoming rendezvous with Sheila to hear the chill in my tone.

"See you later, sport." Sam gave Davey a hug. "You take good care of your mom, okay?"

"Okay," Davey echoed. "See you later."

Ah, the innocence of youth.

"Sagging fence, my fanny," I said when Sam was gone. "The woman owns Pugs. Pugs! Have you ever seen a Pug jump?"

"Actually I have—" Peg began. One look at my face was enough to silence her.

"You know what I mean."

"Yes, I do," said Peg. "But I think you're over-reacting. So Sam spends an afternoon with his ex-wife, so what? As I recall, you spent several weeks with your ex-husband last spring."

"That was different. For starters, I didn't have any choice in the matter. Bob came to see Davey, remember?"

"And Sheila came to the Northeast for a job.

The move is only a temporary one, and it has nothing to do with the fact that Sam is here."

"Maybe not," I grumbled. "But did he have to look so happy to see her? He called her mercurial and passionate. He said she could sell dog collars at a cat convention."

"Why would one want to—? Never mind." Aunt Peg choked off that thought. "What do you suppose caused them to divorce?"

"Sam didn't say. He seemed to think it wasn't relevant."

"He's a man," said Peg, as if that it explained everything. Actually, it pretty much did.

While we'd been talking, I'd been breaking down Faith's tight, show ring topknot and replacing it with the looser banding she would wear at home. Now I finished fixing the last of the protective wraps around her ear hair. We were ready to pack up and go.

"Maybe Sam will explain everything when he calls you," said Peg.

"Like how a woman who was never even important enough to mention is suddenly worth devoting his free time to?"

"Something like that." Peg sighed.

Perhaps Sam might have been able to come up with a good reason for the way he was acting, but as it happened, he never got the chance. Davey and I found so many things to do over

55

the next two days that we were never home to answer the phone if indeed it had rung. When we got back from the show, we went out to the mall, then followed that excursion with dinner and a movie.

Sunday we devoted to yard work. March is the perfect time to pick up the mess that winter has left behind, and we were outside nearly all day. Once Davey thought he heard the phone ringing; but by the time he and Faith made it up the steps and into the house, the caller had given up. I guess it was just Sam's bad luck that I'd taken the tape out of the answering machine and forgotten to replace it.

All in all we were so busy that neither Davey nor I had any time to spend wondering what Sam might have been up to on that pretty spring weekend.

Yeah, right.

By Monday morning, I'd spent two hectic days and two semisleepless nights, and my butt was dragging. It seems to be a fact of life that when I get to school on time nobody notices; and when I come barreling in the back door a few minutes late, inevitably I get caught. Luckily when you're a teacher, you're too old to get detention. Unfortunately that doesn't make it any easier to meet up with the headmaster.

Shedding my coat as I dashed down the hallway, I whipped around a corner and ran smack into Russell Hanover II. "Ah, Ms. Travis," he said, reaching out a hand to steady me. "The very person I was looking for. In a hurry, are we?"

"Just a bit," I said, reaching up a hand to run my fingers through my hair.

In truth I didn't look disheveled, it's just that Russell always makes me feel that way. Both his tailoring and his deportment are impeccable. I've never seen a wrinkle in his clothing, and though hc's in his late forties, his face is still remarkably smooth. That's probably due to thc usual lack of expression on his bland features. Russell's hair is medium brown and thinning along his temples. He wears it short and combed straight back, and the severc cut suits him wcll.

"I'm told you've signed on as a member of our Spring Pageant Committee," he said.

Actually I hadn't actually signed on, I'd been conscripted. Though I suspected Russell himself had monitored the selections, I nodded as though the whole thing had been my idea.

"Excellent. Mr. Durant tells me the committee is having a bit of a problem coming up with a suitable program. Since your schedule tends to have more flexibility than some of the others, I thought you might have the time to take a look through some of our archives in the basement."

"I'd be happy to," I said. This was the first I'd heard of such a collection.

"It seems Honoria Howard was a bit of a

pack rat." Russell frowned slightly, as if he couldn't quite believe he'd described one of the school's illustrious founders in such unflattering terms. "There are several dozen boxes stored in a rather shabby little room downstairs. I've never had occasion to sort through them myself, but I understand they contain all manner of records: correspondence, invoices, and perhaps even some photographs that pertain to the academy's early years. I was hoping you might come across something that would hasten the committee on its way."

Hasten? I thought. Was that what he'd said? I knew the word existed, but I'd never actually heard it used in conversation before. Just for kicks, I tried it out myself.

"I'd be delighted to hasten things along any way I can."

"Good." Russell reached in his pocket and produced a key. "There are a number of entrances to the lower level. You'll find the most convenient one in the front hall, tucked in the back beneath the stairs. The storeroom you're looking for is beneath the southwest corner of the building.

"I'm told there's a table in the room, and there should be ample lighting for your purposes. Of course, you may feel free to bring anything upstairs that you wish to examine further. Krebbs informs me that the door is customarily kept locked, so I've had an extra key made. You may return it to me at your leisure when the project is finished."

I pocketed the key and turned to leave. Russell, however, remained where he was. "Is there something else?" I asked.

The headmaster's frown had returned. "First bell rings for assembly at precisely eight-forty-five. Not unreasonably, we expect our teachers to be in their classrooms, with their coats off and their day planned by then."

"Yes sir," I said without a trace of sarcasm. First bell had been ringing as I'd come through the back door. Now I could hear the sound of the students beginning to fill the upper hallway. Assembly had just let out. I tucked my coat behind my back. "That's not a problem."

"Quite right," Russell agreed mildly. He turned and walked away down the hall.

This is my first year teaching at Howard Academy and, so far, it's been an interesting experience. The students are different than those I'd encountered in the public-school system, and their problems sometimes make me feel as though I've stepped into the setting of a Jane Austen novel. Asked to have a substandard test signed by a parent and returned the next day, I was given a choice between accepting the nanny's signature or receiving a fax from the parents who were vacationing in Bruges. What the hell, I thought, and opted for the fax. It was probably as close as I was going to get to Belgium anytime soon.

I'm a tutor, not a classroom teacher, so by the time a student gets shifted into my special help program a problem has already been identified. Usually it's something simple and a bit of extra attention is all it takes to get things back on track. Because the needs of the children change constantly, so does my schedule, and I enjoy the freedom that gives me.

Russell had been entirely correct. I often have periods during the school day when nothing is scheduled. That morning I had one at ten-thirty. Curious now about what I might find, I used it to head down to the basement.

The main building at Howard Academy is a turn-of-the-century stone mansion, built in opulent times by a man to whom money was no object. Over the years, the salons and drawing rooms have been converted to more functional classrooms, but much of the charm of the mansion remains. This is especially true in the front entrance hall with its burnished hardwood floor, dramatic split staircase, and hand-rubbed antique furniture.

My first sight of the entrance hall had left me gasping in pleasure. Now I scarcely noticed it as I hurried through, intent on my quest. Twin portraits of Joshua and Honoria Howard hung side by side above a mahogany console holding a vase filled with fresh, fragrant flowers. Their eyes seemed to be on me as I found the door just where Russell had said it would be in the darkened recess beneath the stairs.

I half expected the door to creak open, revealing rickety stairs and dim lighting, but I couldn't have been more wrong. Like everything else at Howard Academy, the basement was in excellent shape. There was a switch plate next to the door, and when I flipped on the lights, I could easily see my way down the solid wooden stairway.

The lower level was huge, mirroring the house above it; and only part of it had been finished. Though several rooms had been partitioned off along one wall, it was clear that the basement's major function over the years had been as a depository for excess supplies and equipment. I walked past wooden packing crates, stacks of old textbooks, and several rusty appliances on my way to the other side. Nearly everything was overlaid with a thick coating of dust.

The door to the first room stood partly open, and I glanced inside as I went by. Judging by the racks that lined the back wall, it had, once upon a time, served as a wine cellar. Now nothing remained of that bygone era but a torn label on the floor and a musty aroma. I was about to move on when a fleeting flash of color caught my eye.

I stepped back and heard the quiet shuffle of footsteps from within. At least I hoped it was footsteps. If not, Eugene Krebbs was going to have to deal with some rather large rats.

"Who's there?" I demanded.

Five

"Who wants to know?" a voice came back, equally sharp.

I smiled in relief. "Jane, is that you?"

"No." Now she sounded sullen.

I stepped into the doorway and turned on the light. Jane was standing in the corner of the small room, looking much as she had the last time I'd seen her. In fact she didn't look as though she'd changed her clothes since. Aware of my scrutiny, she jutted out her chin and stared at me defiantly.

"What are you doing here?" I asked.

"What's it to you? And how do you know my name anyway?"

"We met last week, remember? Upstairs, in the prop room behind the stage."

"I guess." Jane hooked her thumbs in the pockets of her grimy jeans. "You were with that nasty old guy, Krebbs."

"Actually, *you* were the one with Krebbs." Casually, I took a step closer. The room was empty; I couldn't see any reason why Jane would have been in there. "As I recall, he was asking you to leave."

"Yeah, well I did, didn't I?"

"But you came back."

"Obviously. With smarts like that, I guess it's no wonder you're a teacher."

"And with an attitude like that, I guess it's no wonder Krebbs figured you for trouble. Were you enjoying the play?"

Jane stared at me suspiciously. "What play?"

"*Much Ado About Nothing.* I found it on the couch in the prop room after you'd left."

"That wasn't mine." Her answer was quick and defensive. "I don't know anything about it."

"Too bad. Shakespeare's one of my favorite writers. I thought maybe we could talk about him sometime."

"Why?"

Despite the sharpness of her tone, Jane appeared genuinely puzzled, as if no one had ever taken the time to seek her opinions and she couldn't imagine why anyone would.

"Why not?" I asked. "That's what people do. They talk about the things they enjoy."

"Well, I don't."

"How come?"

I looked around for a place to sit. Jane seemed to be relaxing a little. Maybe if I did the same, she might hang around long enough for me to get some answers. There weren't any chairs or boxes; I ended up leaning against a shelf.

" 'Cause it's nobody's business what I like," she said.

"Surely it's somebody's business," I said gently. "What about your parents?"

"That's nobody's business either!" Jane strode past me toward the doorway. "I gotta go."

"Where?"

"Where what?" She paused.

"Where are you in such a hurry to get to?"

"Away from here."

I followed her out into the main room of the basement. Jane was heading toward a door in the far wall that led outside. "Hey!" I called after her. "Are you hungry?"

Her steps slowed, then she spun around angrily. "What's the matter with you, anyway? How come you keep asking so many questions? Why don't you just leave me alone?"

"Because I can't," I said honestly.

Jane made a disgusted sound and waved a hand through the air. She shoved the back door open, bolted through, and disappeared.

Who was she? I wondered. Not a student, yet she obviously knew her way around the campus. But if she didn't belong in a classroom at Howard Academy, why wasn't she in school somewhere else?

It was the question about her parents that had made her run, I thought. She had to have a family somewhere. Did anyone know where she was during the day? Didn't anyone care?

I'd tried not to come on too strong so I wouldn't

scare her off; it hadn't seemed to help. Next time we met, I'd probably be better off grabbing her and holding on until I had some answers.

Two doors down from the wine cellar was the room where the archives had been stored. It was easy enough to find; that was the only door with a lock on it. Though I used the key Russell Hanover had given me, the gesture seemed superfluous. The lock rattled in its casing and the door fell open easily. A child with a bobby pin could have picked it.

Most of the other rooms in the basement had been empty. This one was crammed full, stacked from floor to ceiling with crates and trunks. The light fixture looked only slightly younger than Edison, but its hundred-watt bulb illuminated the space easily. As Russell had promised, there was a table. Though old, it was made of wood and looked sturdy enough. It had to be, to hold the boxes stacked on top of it.

Looking around, I realized for the first time the enormity of the job Russell had handed me. I wondered if he'd had any idea. I walked over and lifted the top of the closest box. A yellowing piece of paper caught my eye.

Bill of Sale. Purchased this day, July 19, 1923, by Joshua A. Howard for the sum of eight dollars, forty cents. Twenty chickens. Good brood hens. Signed Raymond H. Floyd.

Smiling, I lifted the paper and read the one beneath it. It was a receipt for roof repair to a barn, dated four years later. Below that was a playbill from the 1960s, *Camelot*, starring Julie Andrews and Robert Goulet.

I thumbed through the rest of the box, skimming through odds and ends that didn't seem to be organized by date or function. Reaching the bottom, I straightened and gazed slowly around. Howard Academy had been founded in the 1920s. Basically, what was stored in this room was three-quarters of a century's worth of debris.

I looked at my watch and sighed. Though I'd barely begun to look through the records, my free period was just about over. Students were due in my classroom in ten minutes.

I shoved the top box aside and picked up the one beneath. I might as well take it upstairs with me. That way, I could sort through it during the rest of the day.

Lunchtime at Howard Academy is a carefully scripted event. Students are seated at large, round tables, set with tablecloths and linen napkins. A member of the faculty presides at each one. The kitchen staff serves the food, which is usually hot and always delicious. Conversation is quiet and respectful.

Teachers take turns eating with the students. Those who are free usually sit together at the end of the dining room. Michael had scheduled another committee meeting over lunch period, however, so I fixed myself a tray in the kitchen and carried it down the hall to the teachers' lounge.

I was the first to arrive, but Sally Minor walked through the door a moment later. She was an ample woman in her early fifties, who had the privilege of being highly respected by both students and administration alike. She was sharp, canny, and fiercely committed to the educational process. I didn't know her well, but I liked her a lot.

"Grab a seat at the table while you still can," she said, staking out one end for herself. "Let Ed balance his lunch on his knees. Maybe that will slow him down enough to keep him from arguing too much."

"What's the matter now?" I walked over to the sideboard and poured a cup of coffee from the pot. "He can't still be upset about that smoking thing. The whole building's nonsmoking, he's always had to walk outside when he wants a cigarette."

"Or sneak into the boys' room," Sally muttered.

"He really does that?"

"Does it? He makes a habit of it. What kind of example do you think that sets for the kids?"

I added a dollop of milk to my cup, carried it over, and sat down. "Why doesn't Mr. Hanover stop him?"

"Maybe he doesn't know. Maybe he doesn't care. Anyway, the newest problem had nothing to do with that. After you left the last meeting . . ." Sally's eyes flickered up toward Honoria's portrait, now gazing down upon us from the east wall. ". . . we all just started throwing out ideas. Everyone was feeling pretty desperate by then."

I nodded, remembering. I'd been just as happy to escape.

"Anyway, Ed started talking about how Joshua Howard was rumored to have made some of his money bootlegging during Prohibition. He seemed to know a little bit about liquor being brought in from Canada across the Great Lakes and somehow he managed to parlay that into the notion that the pageant ought to be a play about pirates."

"Pirates?" I laughed. "Joshua Howard was no saint, but I don't think he was a pirate."

"Of course he wasn't a pirate! Everybody knows that. This is just another one of his hare-brained schemes."

"You must be talking about Ed." Rita Kinney opened the door and carried her tray inside.

"How can you tell?"

"For one thing your face is all red." She came and sat down beside us. "That's pretty much your usual reaction whenever he's around. And speaking of which, he's right behind me so watch what you say."

"I'll say whatever I please," Sally said firmly. "Ed's the one who can watch out."

"Ah, Sally." The door pushed open once more and Ed Weinstein appeared. He held his tray in front of him like a shield, and the thick, black mustache that adorned his upper lip was twitching like a rabbit's nose. "Is that your tender voice I hear, or is there a foghorn blowing on the Sound?"

"Oh stuff it, Ed. Now that Melanie's back, you can consider your pirate idea voted down. She didn't like it any better than the rest of us did."

"Fine. Be that way." Ed pushed Rita's tray to one side and made a place for himself at the table. "I don't see you coming up with anything better. At least the pirate idea had potential. I don't know what we're killing ourselves for, anyway. It's not like this is a big tradition or anything. There's never even been a spring pageant before. I'm beginning to think maybe we should just scrap the whole idea."

"Good thought," Sally said sarcastically. "Do you want to be the one to tell Mr. Hanover his pet project's been abandoned, or should I?"

"Everybody here? Excellent!" Michael Durant was the last to arrive. He entered the room on the run and went straight to the coffeepot to pour himself a cup. "How're we doing, people? Who's got something great for me?"

"I'm sure Sally must," Ed said snidely. "Since

she seems to think that all my ideas are unworthy."

Michael hadn't brought his lunch with him, and he didn't join us at the table. Instead he paced around the room, coffee cup in hand, a study in frenetic energy. "Sally? Thoughts?"

"The chicken's excellent," she said.

At this rate, the spring pageant was never going to take place.

"I have an idea," I said. "It's not a great one, but at least it's something we could discuss."

"Go on," Michael prompted, training his intense gaze my way.

"What if, instead of aiming for a huge theme, we tried doing something smaller? A slice of life kind of thing. There's a whole storeroom full of records in the basement. I was down there looking at them this morning."

Ed was already shaking his head, but Michael ignored him. "What kinds of records?"

"So far, I've hardly done anything more than open the first box. It was filled with pretty mundane things, a couple of receipts, a bill of sale for some chickens."

"Chickens!" Ed snorted. "And you thought my pirate idea was bad."

"I'm not saying we should build the pageant around the chickens." I decided to ignore him, too. "Just that we might find something useful there. And barring that, we might find enough

71

information about how Joshua and Honoria lived in the early years of this century to reconstruct a day in their lives. I think the kids might enjoy that."

"Speaking as their history teacher, I think that's an interesting idea," Rita said. "Students are always asking why it's important to study the past. This could be a way to make a piece of that past come alive."

Sally's no pushover when it comes to her kids, but even she was nodding. She was probably afraid that a "no" vote might have us all talking to parrots and sewing eye patches come spring. "The idea's got potential," she agreed. "You say there's a whole room filled with records?"

I nodded. "Mr. Hanover gave me the key this morning. So far, I've only looked at one box—"

Outside the room, someone ran past the door and down the hall, the tread of their footsteps echoing loudly. As teachers, it was our duty to punish such infractions. We all glanced toward the door, but nobody got up. A moment later, a second set of footsteps, sounding equally hurried, followed. I wondered what was going on.

Michael turned back to me. "Do you have any idea what's in the rest of the boxes?"

"No," I admitted. "Judging by what I've already seen, I doubt that it's anything earthshaking. Still, I imagine we'll be able to reconstruct quite a bit of information about the early years of the school."

Michael walked over and perched on the edge of the table. "I think Melanie has something here. Unless anyone objects, I say we go with it. A Day in the Life of Joshua and Honoria Howard."

Broadway would never come calling, but for our purposes, it just might do the trick.

"Who's going to write the script?" I asked.

"That's my job," said Michael. "And I'd like to get started as soon as possible. Keep me informed of everything you find that you think I might be able to use. In fact, I might just go down and have a look around myself."

As he finished speaking, the class bell rang, long and loud, in the hallway outside.

"That was quick." Sally sniffed the last bite of crumb cake into her mouth. "Have we been here that long?"

I looked at the wall clock. "No, it's early. We should have fifteen more minutes."

"That's odd," said Ed. "You don't suppose one of the little pranksters has sneaked into the office—"

"And rung the bell that would call them back to class early?" Rita asked skeptically. "I doubt it."

We all heard the sirens at the same time. Automatically, our heads turned toward the window, but since the teachers' lounge was in the back of the building, facing the parking lot, there was nothing to be seen.

"Fire?" asked Michael.

"No alarm." I got up and opened the door. "If there were a fire, someone would pull that first thing to get the kids out of the building."

Across the hallway, I could see into the classroom beyond and out its wide windows. A silvery blue police car was speeding up the long driveway, followed by an ambulance from Greenwich Hospital. Leanne Honeywell, the sixth grade math teacher, was hurrying down the hallway toward her room.

"What's going on?" I asked.

She stopped, glanced around, then whispered, "I'm not really sure, but whatever it is, Mr. Hanover looked like he was going to have a stroke when he heard about it. He told us all to stay calm, go to our classrooms, and keep the kids inside. He was heading down the hill to the caretaker's cottage.

"All I can think is that something terrible must have happened."

❧ Six ❧

The faculty lounge emptied faster than you can say Kibbles 'N Bits.

Ed, Sally, and Rita went straight to their class-rooms. Not having students to attend to, Michael and I volunteered to clean up and return the lunch trays to the dining room. When that was done, there was a certain sense of inevitability to the way we found ourselves standing next to the back door.

"We ought to go see what's happening," said Michael. My kind of guy.

"Maybe we can help," I said.

"After the police and an ambulance crew have already arrived? Don't bet on it." His steps matched mine as I hurried out the door and down the stairs. "I just want to see what all the fuss is about."

The caretaker's cottage was a euphemistic name for an old wooden shed that stood next to the soccer field and housed most of the tools used by Krebbs and the groundskeeping crew. Erected at the same time as the original house, it had obviously suffered periods of neglect and haphazard repair. Two of its windows had broken panes, and the back wall tilted alarmingly. Though I'd passed by the building numerous times on my way to the sports fields, I'd never had occasion to go inside.

From the top of the hill, we could already see a knot of people gathered around the door to the cottage. Police and EMTs were bustling in and out. Russell Hanover was standing off to one side, looking deeply troubled. Michael and I headed his way.

"What is it?" Michael asked. "What's happened?"

The headmaster wasn't pleased to see us. "I asked everyone to stay inside. I don't want the children alarmed in any way. Please go straight back to your classes."

"We don't have any classes," I said. "Michael and I were working on the pageant. Is there anything we can do to help?"

Russell considered his answer for a long moment. This was the first time I'd seen his composure shaken. He looked like a man who had no idea what to do next.

"We seem to have all the help we need," he said finally. "I've been asked to stay out of the way, and I suggest that both of you do the same."

Michael craned his head around the group, trying to see inside the shed. "What's going on in there?"

"Apparently there's been an accident. Mr. Krebbs has suffered an injury, and the authorities are seeing to him now. I'm sure everything will be fine."

Looking at what was happening around us, I didn't share his confidence. Though I couldn't see into the building, none of the emergency personnel seemed too concerned about the condition of Eugene Krebbs. He hadn't been brought out, and nobody was rushing to his aid. Instead another patrol car had arrived, and an officer with a video camera had begun to tape the proceedings.

Having had the misfortune to be present at the scene of several murders over the last few years, I was pretty sure this sort of activity meant that Krebbs was anything but fine. The arrival of a dark blue sedan containing Detective Thomas Shertz, whom I'd met when a member of Aunt Peg's kennel club had been murdered the year before, only confirmed my suspicions. He parked his car at the edge of the field and climbed out, his topcoat flapping around him in the wind.

If Detective Shertz had been born a dog, he'd have been a Chow. The attributes were all there: squat build, bushy hair, pugnacious features. Once I'd gotten the image in my mind, it was almost a disappointment to find that he didn't have the requisite black tongue. The detective conferred with the officers at the scene, then came over to speak with Russell.

He introduced himself, then pulled out a small pad of paper and began to take notes. "I understand you've identified the man in the shed as Eugene Krebbs."

"That's correct. He's the school's caretaker. Krebbs has been employed at Howard Academy for decades. Longer than anyone else, I think." Russell's voice choked. "Is he . . .?"

"Dead?" Shertz said. "I'm afraid so."

"How did he die?" I asked.

"He appears to have been stabbed. Most likely with the pitchfork we found lying next to him." Belatedly, Shertz's gaze swung in my direction. He frowned slightly, as if trying to place me. "You would be?"

"Melanie Travis. I'm a teacher here. You and I met last year when Monica Freedman was murdered."

He thought for a moment, then said, "The kennel club case?"

I nodded.

Beside me, Russell Hanover had grown pale. "Murder? Are you trying to tell me that Eugene Krebbs was *murdered?*"

"At the moment, it looks that way."

"But that isn't possible! Not here. Not at Howard Academy. . . !"

Shertz mustered a sympathetic expression; but his posture—shoulders thrust forward, chin jutted—radiated determination. No doubt he'd heard similar protests before. "I'm going to have to ask you some questions."

"Of course," Russell agreed. "We'll cooperate in any way we can. Let me explain something, however. Some of the most prominent people in Greenwich entrust the care of their children to Howard Academy, and I have no intention of breaching that trust. My students' welfare is my highest priority. I must have your assurance that their needs will come first."

"What comes first is finding a murderer," Shertz said implacably. "I understand your concerns, and I'll do everything in my power to take them into consideration. But I won't allow my investigation to be compromised in any way. Is that clear?"

Russell nodded curtly. He was much more accustomed to giving orders than taking them, and it showed.

"Who found the body?" asked Detective Shertz. He looked over at Michael, the one member of our party he hadn't heard from yet.

The drama coach shook his head. "Melanie and I were inside in a meeting when the bell rang and we saw the commotion out here."

"Mr. Hanover?"

"I don't know," Russell admitted. "I received a call from Mrs. Plimpton in the kitchen. I was in my office, and Harriet passed her right through. She was terribly flustered, and it took a minute before I could even understand what she was trying to tell me. She said she'd been told there was a body in the caretaker's cottage. Of course, I was sure she was mistaken. I thought perhaps someone was playing a prank."

"Is that the kind of thing that would pass for funny around here?" Shertz asked humorlessly. Even in a town as upscale as Greenwich, Howard Academy was considered a bastion of privilege. The detective wouldn't be the first person, who couldn't afford to send his children to the school, to assume that those who did attend were willful, shallow, and overindulged.

"Hardly," Russell snapped. "However, at the time I didn't see any other possible explanation."

"Did Mrs. Plimpton tell you who'd given her that information?"

"Not that I recall. Our conversation was rather brief. I came directly outside to see what was going on."

"And when you got here . . . ?"

"I immediately went into the shed."

"You couldn't see Mr. Krebbs from the doorway?"

"No, it was dark. I turned on the light. Of course, then I saw Krebbs lying on the ground."

"Did you approach the body?"

"I'm not sure." Russell shivered slightly, and I wondered whether his reaction was due to the chilly March air or the memory of what he'd seen. "I think so. Yes, I believe I must have. I thought he was unconscious. I certainly didn't realize he was dead." His cheeks grew pink. "I knew I had to go get help. I went right back up the hill to the school and called the police."

Shertz flipped his pad over to a clean page. "Did you touch anything in the shed while you were there? Maybe pick something up or move a piece of equipment out of the way?"

"No, nothing," Russell said firmly.

"You touched the light switch," I pointed out. Shertz glanced in my direction, then back to the headmaster.

"Maybe I did." Russell exhaled loudly. "I'm afraid I wasn't paying any attention to details like that. As I'm sure you can imagine, this has all been a most distressing experience."

"We're going to need to get your fingerprints," said the detective. "Who else has access to the building?"

Russell was silent, staring down at his hands as if imagining the ignominy of being finger-printed. "I think pretty much everyone around here does," I answered for him. "I've never seen the door locked, and during the day, when Krebbs and his crew are out working, it's often sitting open."

Shertz pursed his lips and made a note. "I'd also like to speak to the woman who called your office. Mrs. Plimpton, right? Where would I find her?"

"She runs our food services." Russell gestured up the hill toward the main building.

Standing where we were, it was easy to see that if someone had left the caretaker's cottage and gone for assistance, the nearest door would have led directly into the kitchen. But who had sounded the alarm? I wondered. And why hadn't that person stayed around to help?

"I don't understand any of this," said Russell. "It makes no sense. Why would anyone want to do such a thing?"

"That's what we're going to find out." Shertz flipped his pad closed and put it away. "Was anything of value stored in this shed?"

"As far as I know, just some tools and equipment. To tell you the truth, until this afternoon I'd never been inside. Krebbs was in charge of the caretaker's cottage. I had no reason to question his stewardship."

"Do you think he might have interrupted a burglary?" Michael asked.

"It's a possibility," said Shertz. "Until we know more, we're not ruling anything out."

"Detective?" one of the officers called from the doorway of the shed. "Could you come over here?"

"Excuse me," said Shertz. "I'll be back in a minute."

"What an ungodly mess," Russell muttered under his breath. "Once the parents get wind of this, all hell will break loose."

Trust Russell to be more worried about the school's reputation than the fact that Krebbs was dead. Then again, considering the tenor of my recent dealings with the caretaker, I wasn't exactly overwhelmed with grief myself. Michael, meanwhile, had tagged along after Detective Shertz and was taking in the scene as avidly as a sightseer at a prime tourist attraction.

"The sooner the police get this wrapped up the better," Russell said, turning to me. "Perhaps you could run up to the kitchen and fetch Mrs. Plimpton? I'm sure the detective won't mind speaking with her down here."

And even if he did, Russell probably wouldn't allow him much choice. Already the headmaster was working to control the spin and distance the school from what had happened. If he could arrange for Shertz to conduct his interviews off school grounds, I was sure that would have pleased Russell even more.

Mrs. Plimpton was a motherly figure with soft, gray hair and a fondness for frilly aprons and support hose. The fact that her kitchen ran like a well-oiled machine, however, made me suspect that there was a core of steel beneath the cream puff exterior. As soon as I opened the back door, Mrs. Plimpton accosted me. Clearly she'd been watching the proceedings out the window.

"Well?" she demanded.

"It's Eugene Krebbs," I said.

"Oh Lord," she whispered, crossing herself. "How bad?"

"He's dead."

"Dead?" The shriek came from the other side of the large kitchen, where two of her helpers were standing behind a stainless-steel counter. Mrs. Plimpton sent a glare in their direction.

"The police would like to speak with you," I said.

"With me? Why?"

"They think he was murdered." I'd lowered my voice, but it didn't seem to matter. Another scream sounded, louder than the first.

"Murdered on the job!" cried a woman with the voice of Minnie Mouse. "What's this world coming to? Who's going to be next?"

"You are, if you don't stop that wailing," Mrs. Plimpton said sharply, before turning back to me. "I don't know anything to tell the police. Why do they want to talk to me?"

"Mr. Hanover said you were the one who called him . . ."

"He's in charge. Someone tells me something like that, I figure it's up to him to see to it."

"You did the right thing," I said reassuringly. "I'm sure that's all the police want to ask you about. Mr. Hanover asked me to come and get you so you could talk to the detective."

"Outside?" From her tone, you'd think I'd suggested we take a dip in Long Island Sound.

"Mr. Hanover thinks it will be easier."

"I'll have to get my coat. I'm certainly not going out there like this, and catch my death of cold."

I waited while she went into a back room. The kitchen help passed the time by standing around staring at me. If they had work to do, they weren't in any hurry to get to it. One, a skinny young woman with buckteeth and a nervous smile, edged closer around the counter.

"Was there a lot of blood?" she whispered.

"I don't know. I didn't go inside the cottage."

"I'll bet it looks just awful in there," said the other. From her voice, I recognized her as the shrieker. "I bet there's blood and guts everywhere, just like in the movies. I wonder who they're going to get to clean it up. They better not be asking me!"

"It's a crime scene, stupid," said the first. "Ain't nobody going to be cleaning in there while the police are still looking for clues."

"Krebbs, murdered." The shrieker shook her head. "I always knew that man was up to no good."

"Really?" I asked. "What makes you say that?"

"Just the way he acted. He gave me the willies, always skulking around and showing up places where you didn't expect him to be. How old was that man, anyway? A hundred? What was he still doing working? This school gives me benefits. You better believe when I get to be his age, I won't be working no more."

"Wonder if he'll turn himself into a ghost," mused Buckteeth. "He was ugly enough for it. Big old house like this ought to have a ghost, you know?" She laughed at the thought. "Just a little something to threaten the kids with when they get out of line."

"There're no such thing as ghosts," Mrs. Plimpton said firmly, striding back in. She'd put a long wool coat on over her dress and tied a plaid, fringed muffler around her neck. "So don't you be starting any rumors about a thing like that. That's the kind of trouble that's likely to come right back around and bite you in the butt."

We headed out the door and down the steps. "You don't suppose the police think I had anything to do with what happened?" Mrs. Plimpton asked, sounding suddenly nervous. "I couldn't have, you know. I was in the kitchen working all morning. Shawna and Bobbi can back me up on that."

"I'm sure you're not a suspect. The police just want to know who found the body."

"It was a girl. I don't know her name. She came running up the back stairs and pounded on the door. It wasn't even locked, I don't know what she was knocking for. She was all out of breath and agitated like crazy. I guess she just felt the need to make some noise."

"One of the students?" I asked.

"She must be, I don't know where else she would have come from." Mrs. Plimpton frowned. "Though I don't recall ever seeing her in the dining room. Usually I have a pretty good memory for faces. Maybe she's new. Her clothes were kind of strange though."

"Strange?" I gulped.

"Well, she wasn't in uniform, for one thing. And though she was wearing a sweatshirt, she wasn't in gym clothes either. I remember thinking, maybe that's a costume for a play. Around this school, you don't see many little girls running around in blue jeans."

The knot in my stomach grew. "Did she have short dark hair and big brown eyes?"

"That's right, she did. Do you know her?"

"I'm afraid I do," I said.

Jane.

❤ Seven ❤

By the time Mrs. Plimpton and I reached the bottom of the hill, Russell and Michael had disappeared, and Detective Shertz was waiting for us. I performed the introductions, then started to tell the detective about Jane.

"Thanks for your help," he said brusquely. "I can take things from here. I'd prefer to speak with Mrs. Plimpton privately."

"Yes, I know, but—"

He held up a hand. My voice stilled.

"I'm sure you're interested in what happened, but my investigation will proceed much more smoothly without your interference."

"I wasn't trying to interfere—"

"Maybe you don't understand, Ms. Travis. This is police business."

Any idiot could understand that. Of course, that was exactly what Detective Shertz's patronizing tone implied: that I was an idiot who wanted to meddle in his case for no good reason.

"Fine," I said, aware that I had a tutoring session in ten minutes. "I'll get back to my kids."

Predictably, all afternoon my students were full of questions. Mindful of Russell's dictum, I merely said that there'd been an accident in the caretaker's cottage and that the police were looking into it. They could have figured out that much by looking out the window, so I didn't feel I was betraying any confidences.

By midafternoon, much of the activity around the cottage had died down. The door was shut and padlocked. Though the building was festooned with bright yellow crime-scene tape, most of the police crew had moved on.

That didn't stop the rumors that had begun to circulate among the students, however. None of the stories approached the truth, but they did make for fascinating listening. If Russell had thought he could insulate the kids from what had happened, he'd better think again. In the absence of facts, they were busy concocting tales that were even more gruesome than the truth.

As soon as I had a free minute, I headed over to the headmaster's office. His secretary, Harriet, sat behind a desk in the small anteroom outside. Normally, she has the placid look of a Labrador Retriever with a full stomach. Today, her expression was pinched and wary. Like Russell, she seemed poised to expect the worst.

"Is he in?" I asked when she looked up.

Harriet nodded.

"Do you think he can spare me a few minutes?"

"I doubt it, the way things have been going today, but I'll check."

Harriet stood up and walked over to the door, opened it, and stuck her head inside. Though

Russell wasn't visible from where I stood, I could hear their conversation clearly. He must have realized that, because a moment later he appeared in the doorway.

"Is it important?" he asked.

"Yes."

He waved a hand, ushering me in.

"Do you want me to hold your calls?" asked Harriet.

"If it's the detective, pass it through. Otherwise, take a message. If anyone else from the media calls, just tell them we have no comment at this time."

I followed him into the inner sanctum. Russell's office was a large room, beautifully decorated with some of the furniture that had originally graced Joshua Howard's own library. There was a wide bay window with a cushioned window seat, and floor-to-ceiling bookshelves. The hardwood floor was covered by a slightly worn Persian rug. I'm sure the intent was to make Howard Academy's wealthy parents feel right at home, and I imagine it succeeded admirably.

Today, the headmaster looked far too distracted to notice, much less appreciate, the luxury of his surroundings. "I hope you don't mind if we keep this short," he said. "I'm afraid I have a dozen other things I should be doing."

"Not at all. Is there anything I can do to help?"

Russell sat down in the plush leather chair behind his desk. I chose one opposite him and did the same. "There doesn't seem to be much anyone can do right now, except wait and see what the police are able to find out.

"Unfortunately, the fact that this school has been linked to a murder investigation seems to have sent the media into a frenzy. Already, I've fielded calls from as far away as Philadelphia, and there's currently a New York news van shooting footage from the end of the driveway."

"The police won't do anything to stop them?"

"Detective Shertz's men were kind enough to escort them off the property when they arrived. The news team is now set up on a public road, however, so there's nothing else we can do." The headmaster smiled wanly. "Under other circumstances, I might even be among the first to tell you that the public has a right to know."

"Easier to say when it's not your business they're interested in."

"Quite so," Russell agreed. He leaned his elbows on the arms of his chair and steepled his fingers in front of his lower face. "What can I do for you, Ms. Travis?"

"I was wondering if you'd spoken with Detective Shertz since he interviewed Mrs. Plimpton?"

"Only briefly. Apparently she supplied him with the description of a student, and we're having some difficulty tracking down just whom she meant . . ."

"That's what I wanted to see you about. Mrs. Plimpton mentioned the girl to me, too. I've seen her several times myself and I believe her name is Jane. I'm fairly certain she isn't a student."

"I don't understand," said Russell.

"Actually, neither do I. Unfortunately, the person who seemed to have known the most about her was Eugene Krebbs."

"Krebbs?"

"The two of them were together the first time I met her. We were in the prop room behind the stage, and after she ran away, Krebbs indicated that he'd seen her hanging around before. He said she didn't belong here."

Russell was frowning now. "Maybe you'd better start at the beginning."

"I'm afraid that is the beginning. It happened just last week. I asked Krebbs at the time if he'd spoken to you about her, and he told me he was planning to take care of the problem himself."

"What problem? Who was she?"

"I don't know. At first, I assumed she was a student, too, but Krebbs said she wasn't. And she certainly seems to come and go as she pleases . . ."

"You mean you've seen her again?"

"Just this morning. After we spoke, I went down to the basement."

"The archives."

I nodded. "There's a room down there that looks as though it might once have been a wine cellar. Jane was in there."

Russell was looking more perplexed by the moment. "Doing what?"

"I don't know. She ran off again as soon as I saw her. Krebbs thought she'd been sleeping in the prop room, and he mentioned something about her stealing food."

"A runaway, perhaps?" Russell mused. "I wonder how long this has been going on. Is it possible she's been living here and nobody knew?"

"It's a big campus. Still, I would think that if she were actually making a home here, we'd have seen more signs of her occupancy. I was wondering if maybe she lives in the neighborhood and comes over here during the day when she's supposed to be in school."

"Why would she do something like that?"

I had no answer, so I didn't offer one.

After a moment, Russell said, "You say she calls herself Jane? Any idea of a last name?"

"None. Krebbs laughed when she told me her name was Jane. He seemed to think she was making it up."

"They'd met before, then."

"Apparently so. Krebbs was yelling at her when I came across them. I gathered it wasn't

93

the first time they'd had a confrontation." Even though the man was dead, I didn't try very hard to hide my annoyance, and Russell picked up on my tone.

"Krebbs wasn't always the easiest man to get along with," he said wearily.

It wasn't my place to question the headmaster's policies, but good sense has never stopped me from blurting out a question before. "Then why did you keep him on? From what I could see, the man hardly did any work."

"I had no choice in the matter. Nor did either of the headmasters before me. Krebbs had preceded all of us, and his job was guaranteed by the school for as long as he chose to work. Whether I agreed with the terms of Krebbs's employment or not, there was nothing I could do about the situation but make the best of it."

I sat back in my chair, letting my body relax along the curve of the warm leather. "That sounds like an unusual arrangement."

"In the public-school sector, perhaps. But not here. You have to remember what things were like when Howard Academy was founded. Joshua and Honoria lived a life of great wealth and privilege. Often such families employed large numbers of servants, and it wasn't unusual for valued retainers to hold a position for life."

I quickly counted back the decades and shook my head. "I know Krebbs was old, but—"

Russell smiled slightly. "It was his father, Arthur Krebbs, who worked for the estate as Joshua's butler. I gather Krebbs grew up on the Howard family compound in the company of Joshua's children. I suppose it seemed only natural that he, too, would go to work for the family. As far as I know, Krebbs has always been a fixture here."

"I guess that explains his attitude," I said under my breath.

"You and he had problems?"

"No," I said quickly. "We'd never even spoken before last week. But I didn't like the way he treated Jane, and I told him so. He said *I* was the one who didn't understand how things worked."

Russell's mouth flattened into a straight line. "You might have come to me about that."

"I wish I had. Then maybe none of this would have happened."

"Are you saying that you think the girl might have had something to do with Krebbs's death?"

Until the headmaster voiced the thought, I hadn't allowed myself to think it. But it did make a certain sort of sense. I knew that Jane and Krebbs had argued, probably more than once. I'd also seen him threaten her. I knew she'd been on the school grounds earlier in the day, and she'd been the one to report the caretaker's death.

Mrs. Plimpton had described Jane as breathless and agitated. Had the girl's state been due to the shock of stumbling over a dead body, or could it have been caused by the even greater shock of having just committed murder?

"No," I said fiercely. I wasn't sure which one of us I was trying to convince. "She's only a child. She hardly looked more than ten. She couldn't have done something so awful . . ."

"Even so, you need to tell this to the detective. Have you spoken with him?"

"I tried, but he didn't want to hear about it."

"Try again," Russell said firmly, rising from his seat. "The sooner the police figure out what happened, the sooner we'll all be able to get back to normal. I've issued a memo on the subject, it's probably sitting in your mailbox right now. Everyone is to cooperate with the authorities to the fullest extent of their abilities."

"Of course," I said, standing as well.

"I've called an afternoon assembly. You'll hear the bell shortly. The students know perfectly well that something happened. Keeping silent on the subject will only encourage more of the rampant speculation that already seems to be sweeping through the school. At this point, they're much better off having the facts.

"I will also announce that we'll be holding a small memorial service for Eugene Krebbs this weekend. As far as I know, we at Howard

Academy were his only family. My wife, Bitsy, is already working at putting things together. We're hoping to find some alumni who might be able to provide remembrances and anyone who would like to take part is more than welcome."

"That's very nice of you," I said.

"It's the least we could do. Eugene Krebbs committed his life to the service of the Howard family and their vision of education. We have no intention of forgetting his contribution now that he's gone." The headmaster tapped his finger on the face of his watch and walked out from behind his desk. We headed to the door together.

I'd done my duty by reporting what I knew; now it was time to satisfy my curiosity. "Krebbs seems like a rather unlikely murder victim to me. Do you have any idea why someone might have wanted to kill him?"

"None," Russell said firmly.

The subject was closed.

❧ Eight ❧

Most afternoons Davey rode the school bus home from Hunting Ridge Elementary, a public school in the town of Stamford and my former place of employment. Though my son enjoyed school, I had the impression that he thought riding back and forth in the big yellow bus was the best part of his educational experience. He always emerged in front of our house in high spirits.

Today, though, Davey didn't come flying down the steps with his usual exuberance. Even when Faith bounded across the yard to greet him, he seemed distracted. Usually, he lets her chase him around the yard. Now he simply patted her head and stood, staring at our empty driveway.

"What's up?" I asked, looping my arms around Faith's neck as a precaution as the school bus pulled away.

"Where's Sam?"

"Sam?" My brow furrowed. That wasn't the topic I'd been expecting. "I imagine he's working. You know we hardly ever get to see him during the week."

"That's why we spend the weekends together," said Davey. "Except this weekend we didn't."

"We saw him at the dog show." I unhooked

Davey's backpack from his shoulders and slipped it off, carrying it myself as we went inside.

"That was hardly any time at all. He was supposed to be here this afternoon. He said he'd come."

"When?" I thought back, but couldn't remember any such promise.

"This morning."

I glanced over at Davey. His expression was smug, and I wondered what he knew that I didn't.

That morning I'd overslept, awakening only when Faith—whose internal alarm clock was more reliable than the digital model next to my bed which I'd forgotten to set—had licked my face so I'd get up and let her out. The next half hour had been a blur as I'd rushed to make up for lost time and never quite succeeded.

For the most part, Davey had been left to his own devices. He'd dressed himself, packed his backpack, and fixed his own breakfast. Beyond that, I had no idea what he'd been up to.

"Sam and I talked this morning," he told me now. "I called him on the telephone. I used the speed dial," he added proudly. "Sam said there must have been something wrong with our phone all weekend because he called and called and never got us."

"Really?" I muttered. "What else did he say?"

"That he was hoping we'd have a chance to get together real soon. So I invited him over."

Just like that. I sighed. Nothing like having a six-year-old social secretary to toss a spanner into the works. How could I throw a decent snit when Davey was working behind my back to patch things up?

Faith lifted her head and looked toward the door, which I'd just closed behind us. She woofed softly, then jumped up to press her nose on the window beside it.

"That must be him!" Davey threw open the door and boy and dog went flying out.

I followed more slowly. Sam was indeed pulling his blue Blazer into the driveway. Tar was riding shotgun on the passenger seat, his muzzle wedged into the slit of open window Sam had left for him at the top.

The puppy made snuffling noises, and, as the car rolled to a stop, Faith jumped up and planted her paws on the door. Mud from the half-melted, early-spring yard left a trail of paw prints on the clean window.

Sam didn't seem to notice as he came around to open the car door and let the puppy out. "Hi," he said, smiling when he saw me on the steps. "What happened this weekend? I tried to call, but I couldn't even get your machine. Was your phone out of order?"

"Something like that."

Davey and the two Poodles rushed past me into the house. Sam came up the steps behind them. His body blocked the chilly air, and felt warm and wonderfully solid against mine. I slipped my hands around his sides and rested my head on his chest.

"I missed you." Sam's lips brushed a kiss across the top of my head.

I almost told him I'd missed him, too. Instead, I found myself straightening and pushing away. "How was your afternoon with Sheila?" I asked as we went inside.

"Fine."

If he thought he was going to get way with offering *that* as an answer, he'd better think again. "Just fine?"

Sam shrugged. "I propped up her fence and put a new washer on her faucet. It was no big deal."

Not to him, perhaps; but I'd have been willing to bet Faith's first major that Sheila hadn't been so blasé.

Maybe I'd get more information by beating around the bush. "Does she have a nice place?"

"It's a pretty piece of land, but the house is nothing special. It's also not in very good shape. Sheila will probably spend the whole time she's here making repairs."

"Why'd she take it then?"

"I doubt she had much choice. Not many

landlords are looking to rent to someone with five dogs. You pretty much have to take what you can get and be thankful for it."

We'd reached the kitchen and found the back door standing open. Davey and the two Poodles were outside in the fenced yard, playing catch. I pushed the door shut to cut off the influx of cold air, then went to the refrigerator and got out a couple of beers. "Was it nice seeing Sheila again after all this time?"

Sam accepted the can I offered him and looked at me warily. "Is that a trick question?"

"No, I'd really like to know."

"Yeah, it was," Sam said thoughtfully. "We had a chance to talk. We haven't done that in years. When we broke up, every decision seemed to turn into a major hassle. Now it's just not all that important anymore. Not worth arguing over, anyway. It's a lot nicer to remember the good times."

Because it was easier to talk about this while my mind was half-occupied elsewhere, I opened a bag of nacho chips, shook them out onto a plate, covered them with cheese and jalapeño peppers and put them in the microwave. "How long were you and Sheila married?"

"Five years and five months."

Funny that he should remember so precisely. "Whose idea was the divorce?"

"Hers."

He hadn't even hesitated. Damn it.

"How come?"

The microwave beeped. I removed the plate of steaming nachos, set it down in the middle of the table, then took a seat opposite. Sam looked at the plate for a long moment before finally choosing a piece from the edge. "Why are you so interested in all this?"

"Are you kidding?"

Sam didn't answer, so I guessed he wasn't. "Sheila is your *ex-wife*."

"So?"

"So she's someone who was once very important to you, someone you thought you'd be spending the rest of your life with."

"Yeah, well." Sam chewed and slowly swallowed. "I was wrong. It doesn't matter now anyway, does it? Sheila is my past. You're my present and my future. You and Davey both."

Though his words warmed me, I couldn't help but wonder. If Sheila had been put as firmly behind him as he claimed, why was Sam so reluctant to discuss her? And how come he'd been so happy to see her on Saturday?

"Enough about me," said Sam. "How was your day?"

I gulped, choked on a nacho, and grabbed for a sip of beer. I wasn't at all ready to change the subject; and even if I had been, this wasn't the direction I'd have gone. Sam accepted the fact that I'd been involved in several murder investigations, but I knew he wasn't entirely comfortable with the notion that it might happen again.

"You okay?" He watched me recover.

"Just fine." I decided to lead into things slowly. "There was a bit of a problem at school this afternoon."

"What kind of problem?"

"Nothing that concerns me, really."

"That's nice." Now he was growing suspicious. "What kind of problem?"

"The school caretaker died. The police seem to think he was murdered."

"Murdered?" Sam paled slightly. "What happened?"

I glanced out to the backyard, making sure that Davey was still happily occupied with the dogs. "Krebbs was stabbed with a pitchfork. It happened out in the cottage where all the equipment is stored. He was an elderly man who'd been a fixture around the school for decades. I can't imagine why anyone would have wanted to hurt him."

"Could it have been an accident?"

"The police don't think so. Detective Shertz is heading up the investigation. I'm going to talk to him tomorrow."

Sam helped himself to another chip. "About what?"

"There's a girl named Jane who's been hanging around the school. She was the one who found the body, and may also have been one of the last people to see him alive. I've only met her twice, but I seem to know more about her than anyone else."

Sam nodded, and we both let the silence stretch. I suspected there was more he wanted to say, but he didn't offer, and I didn't ask. Considering how I felt about Sheila's unexpected presence in our lives, I figured that made us even.

"Warm front's supposed to be coming through tonight," Sam said. "Tomorrow might hit sixty."

"Great!" I said, as my heart sank. We weren't even married yet and already we'd been reduced to discussing the weather? That didn't bode well for the future.

I'd planned on driving down to the Greenwich police station after school on Tuesday, but that turned out not to be necessary. Detective Shertz was back at Howard Academy, and when he'd finished meeting with Russell, the headmaster suggested he have a word with me.

The detective arrived, unannounced, in my classroom at ten-thirty. I had a fourth grader doing math problems on the blackboard and another student due in twenty minutes. Neither of these facts made an impression on Shertz, who simply walked into the room and planted himself beside my desk.

"Ms. Travis," he said. "I understand we need to talk."

Wendy Jennings looked around nervously. She was a shy child, given to writing so lightly on her papers that the teachers had trouble reading her work. That was why I had her standing at the board. Along with the math, we'd been working on making bold, broad strokes with the chalk.

"Wendy, do you think you can continue for a moment by yourself?"

She nodded, and I saw her swallow heavily. Though the detective wasn't in uniform, he still carried himself with an air of authority. Even his stare seemed to intimidate the small girl.

"We'll talk out in the hall," I said, heading for the door.

"Here is better." Shertz pulled out a chair and sat down. "I'd just as soon not have the whole school listening in."

"And I'd just as soon not have you scaring my students half to death," I whispered.

Shertz glanced in Wendy's direction. Her back was to us, but I could see the slight tremor in her shoulders. In the space of a single problem, her strokes had gone from strong to nearly invisible.

"She looks okay to me."

She didn't to me. "Wendy, could you come here a moment, please?"

"Yes, Ms. Travis." She put down her chalk and

approached us reluctantly. Rather than look at Detective Shertz, the girl focused her gaze on the ground. Good thing, because now he was frowning, and it didn't make him look any friendlier.

"You heard about what happened yesterday, didn't you?" I asked gently.

Wendy managed to nod without looking up. "Mr. Hanover told us in the assembly and then my parents talked to me about it last night. They told me not to leave the school building and not to talk to anyone I didn't know."

"Did they tell you that the police are already working hard to find out what happened?"

"Yes."

"Policemen are our friends, right? They take care of us when things go wrong. Wendy, this is Detective Shertz. He's the policeman in charge of the whole investigation. He's the one who's going to find out what happened to Mr. Krebbs. I know he looks scary, but he's here to help us."

Seeing what I was trying to do, Shertz had lightened his expression. Until I got to the part about him looking scary, that is; then his glare returned. I slid my foot over and kicked him in the ankle just as Wendy finally raised her eyes. She saw him flinch, but it was better than the scowl he'd been wearing.

Like most of the students at Howard Academy, Wendy had beautiful manners. She held out a small, delicate hand, and said, "I'm pleased to meet you, Detective Shertz."

Shertz looked surprised, but quickly recovered. His large hand reached out and swallowed hers. I was pleased to see he didn't pump it too heartily. The detective even managed a smile.

"I'm pleased to meet you, too, Wendy. I apologize for interrupting your class, but Ms. Travis and I have some things we need to talk about. Will it bother you if we do it here?"

"No, sir. I have some work I can do at the board." She started to walk away, then paused and turned back. "Are you going to arrest the person that killed Mr. Krebbs?"

"Yes, I am. As soon as we're sure we have the right person, we're going to do just that."

"Good." Satisfied, Wendy went back to her math problems.

"Nice kid," said Shertz, when she was out of earshot.

"They're all nice kids." I pulled out a chair beside him and sat down. "They don't deserve to have something like this happen at their school. This is a place where they ought to be able to feel safe."

"You don't have to lecture me." Shertz's momentary goodwill faded. "Believe me, the police department is doing everything it can to get to the bottom of this. I understand you have some information about the girl we're looking for, the one who found Krebbs's body."

I nodded. "I believe her name is Jane, and I'm almost certain she's not a student here. I've run into her several times recently. She's like a shadow, always slipping in and out of places unexpectedly."

"Do you know where we can find her now?"

"No, she seems to come and go as she pleases. I suspect she lives somewhere in the neighborhood and comes here to amuse herself when she should be at school."

"Just Jane?" Shertz frowned again. It seemed to be his habitual expression. "That's the only name you have?"

"It's the one she gave me. Krebbs seemed to think she might have been lying about that."

"She'd lied to him about other things?"

"I don't know, I only saw them together once. At the time, they were arguing pretty strenuously."

"About what?"

"Jane's right to be here, I think. Krebbs had found her sleeping in the prop room behind the stage and was trying to chase her off with a broom."

Shertz reflected on what I'd said. "Would you have characterized Eugene Krebbs as a violent man?" he asked finally.

"I have no idea, I barely knew him. Some of the other teachers who've been here longer can probably answer that question better. I will say, however, that I was appalled by the way he treated Jane."

"Any thoughts on how we might be able to get in touch with her?"

"No, although I'd probably start by looking around the neighborhood, maybe checking the public-school records for absentees."

"We'll do that." Shertz stood. "One last thing. Why didn't you tell me this yesterday?"

"When we first spoke, I didn't realize it was Jane who'd found the body. Then when I knew, you didn't want to listen."

The detective looked exasperated. "I'm listening now. Anything else you think I ought to know?"

"No."

"Too bad."

I thought so, too. He left the room, and I went back to work.

❀ Nine ❀

With all that had happened the day before, I'd never had a chance to go through the box of records I'd brought upstairs from the basement. With two free periods in a row after lunch, I decided to use the time to take a look. I was certain I'd left the cardboard carton pushed against the wall behind my desk, but now it wasn't there.

Perplexed, I checked beneath the tables and looked in the storage closet. The box was gone. Considering its musty, dilapidated condition, I guessed it was possible that the cleaning crew had thought it was garbage and thrown it out when they came through the night before.

Terrific, I thought. Russell had entrusted me with the Howard Academy archives, and the first thing I'd managed to do was lose some of them. I'd never even opened the carton; there was no way of knowing what it might have contained. Hopefully, it hadn't been anything valuable.

Fishing the key to the storeroom out of my purse, I headed back down to the basement. Though the lock on the door seemed looser than ever, it opened easily enough. I turned on the overhead lights, picked another box, and began to sift through the papers.

Like the first carton I'd tackled, this one was filled with a random selection of remnants from the early years of the school. Some of the papers were mildly interesting; others, totally mundane. I found invoices for textbooks and dining-room linens jumbled in with a kitchen shopping list and a pamphlet extolling the virtues of *Doctor Elliott's Miracle Cold and Influenza Cure.*

Near the bottom, a sheaf of correspondence had been clipped together: letters from Honoria to her brother. That looked promising. I pulled them out, sat down at the table, and began to read.

Within minutes, I'd been transported back to the world of the early 1930s. It was the height of the Depression, but neither Joshua and Honoria nor Howard Academy seemed to be feeling the pinch. Joshua's wife, Mabel, had died the year before, and he was off traveling "the Continent," and trying to put his sorrows behind him. His six children, though mostly grown by that point, had been entrusted to the watchful care of his sister.

Honoria began her letter by assuring her brother that the family was well. Josh's eldest daughter, Agnes, was expecting her second baby; the pregnancy was proceeding nicely. James, a middle child, and one of only two boys, was concentrating on his studies at college—a good thing in Honoria's opinion as the boy was somewhat lacking in aptitude. Ruth, the youngest, had apparently inherited her mother's appreciation for art. She'd asked for a set of oil paints for her birthday and was showing signs of real talent.

As to the school, Honoria's chief concern was the fact that the fledgling Howard Academy curriculum was lacking a course in Greek. Though Latin was a required subject, she felt their students were not being offered a thorough enough grounding in the classics, an opinion that Joshua didn't seem to share. Their argument, carried on through several months' worth of letters, was lively and interesting, and I was so caught up in trying to decipher the handwritten correspondence I never even heard the door to the storeroom open.

The first clue I had that I was no longer alone came when a shadow fell across the table. I started and looked up.

"Sorry," said Michael Durant. He laid a hand on my shoulder and leaned over to see what I was reading. "I knocked, but I guess you didn't hear me. That must be interesting stuff."

"It is. Letters between Honoria and Joshua." I shuffled the papers back into a bundle.

Michael pulled up the other chair in the room, dusted off the wooden seat, and sat down. "Anything we can use for the pageant?"

"Probably not, even though it is fascinating.

When these letters were written, Joshua was touring Europe while Honoria kept things running here. They were arguing about whether or not Greek should be added to the school curriculum."

Michael fingered the edge of the top letter, glancing at Honoria's cramped script. "It was certainly a different way of life. Joshua Howard had quite a large family, didn't he?"

"Six children, four girls and two boys. His wife died relatively young, and apparently Honoria stepped in to take her place, looking after the family as well as the school."

Michael nodded, seeming lost in thought.

"Is there something I can do for you?" I asked after a moment.

"Hmm?" He looked up.

"I was wondering what you were doing down here. Is there something you need?"

"You, actually." Michael smiled. "I was looking for you. Two things. First, I wanted to let you know we're having another pageant committee meeting tomorrow morning before first bell. Any and all scintillating ideas will be gratefully accepted."

"Okay." A memo in my mailbox could have covered that. "And?"

Michael hesitated. "I guess I was wondering if you were all right," he said finally.

"All right?"

"You know, after yesterday. That was pretty creepy."

"It was certainly a shock," I agreed. "I barely knew Krebbs, but still, to have him die like that—"

"Not just dead, murdered!" Michael shuddered. "It could have been any one of us."

I hadn't thought of things that way, and I wondered if Michael was right. Had someone deliberately set out to murder Krebbs, or had he simply had the bad luck to be in the wrong place at the wrong time?

"I guess maybe you're used to that kind of thing," Michael said slowly. "Rumor has it you've been involved in a couple of murders yourself."

"Only by accident." Howard Academy was the type of institution that preferred its teachers to keep a low profile, and I'd tried my best to adhere to that policy.

"But you solved them, didn't you?" When I didn't answer right away, Michael leaned closer across the table, his expression eager. "So now what?"

"What do you mean?"

"What's your next step?"

"Me? No way." I held up a hand, as if to ward off even the suggestion that I might get involved. "I don't have a next step, except maybe to open another one of these boxes and keep reading."

"Oh."

He slumped back in his chair, looking deflated, and I felt myself taking pity on him. "How come you're so curious?"

"Who wouldn't be, under the circumstances? Maybe this kind of thing is old hat for you, but I think it's pretty interesting."

"I doubt that Krebbs would feel that way." My tone was sharper than I'd intended, but Michael didn't look chastened.

"I've only been here a couple of months," he said, "so it's not like I knew the man. Besides, if you discount all the administration hysteria over how the murder is going to affect the school's reputation and social standing, nobody around here seems very broken up. My guess is, once the initial furor dies down, nobody's going to miss the guy at all."

The sad thing was, he had a point. Though Russell had said Krebbs's only family was the school, I hadn't heard a single person profess any real grief at the man's passing. Instead, everyone seemed more concerned about their own agendas.

Michael stood. "I guess I'll be heading back upstairs. Don't forget. Tomorrow, eight A.M. We'll meet in the faculty lounge again."

"Got it," I said. "I'll see you there."

Now that I'd lost my train of thought, it was hard to get reinvolved in the Howards' problems from half a century earlier. I was scanning the top letter desultorily when the door to the room pushed open again and a slender girl slipped inside.

"It's about time," said Jane. "I thought he'd never leave."

"Is that what you do?" I asked. "Spy on people?"

"When I need to."

She strode over to the chair Michael had recently vacated and sat down, immediately tilting it back to balance on its rear legs. Her blue jeans were ripped across both knees, and only one of her sneakers was tied. Today she was wearing a T-shirt whose slogan proclaimed, *"Beer it's not just for breakfast anymore."*

Everything about Jane radiated defiance, and I had to wonder how she'd managed to become so hard, so young. She looked scarcely older than Wendy, but the two girls were worlds apart.

"Done looking yet?" Jane wiggled her foot against the table's edge, and her chair rocked precariously.

"I guess." Matching her mood, I sat back and crossed my arms over my chest, "What are you doing here?"

"You asked me if I was hungry. Well, I am."

Just like that, I thought. As if there hadn't been twenty-four hours and a dead body between question and answer.

"I imagine I can find you some food. What are you going to give me in return?"

"You want money?" Jane snorted. "That's a laugh. Everyone around here is rich."

Not entirely true, though I could see how she might perceive things that way. I pulled out an apple I'd saved from lunch out of the pocket of my blazer, and tossed it to her across the table. Jane snagged the fruit one-handed and bit into it immediately. I wondered if she'd had any breakfast that morning; or, come to think of it, dinner the night before.

"I wasn't thinking of money," I said. "How about information. Do you know the police are looking for you?"

"Big deal." She tried to sound tough, but her gaze shifted away.

"They want to talk to you about what happened yesterday—"

Jane's chair thumped to the floor. Abruptly she stood. "Don't tell me they think I whacked that old guy?"

Before I could answer, she was already backing toward the door. "I'm not going to chase you," I said. "But I wish you wouldn't leave. The police just want to talk to you, that's all. You were the one who found Krebbs, weren't you?"

"So what if I was? It doesn't mean I killed him."

"Of course not," I agreed. "It must have been

terrible for you, finding him lying there like that."

"Yeah, I guess." She stepped back toward the table. Having made short work of the apple, Jane was now gnawing on the core. "Got anything else?"

Clearly she didn't want to talk about what she'd seen. I couldn't say that I blamed her. "I don't have any more food down here, but I bet we could get something from the kitchen."

"You mean steal it?"

"No." I almost laughed. "I was thinking more in terms of asking for something politely." Jane didn't look convinced. "We had meat loaf for lunch. Maybe the staff could find us some leftovers."

"Why should they?"

"Why not?" I walked out from behind the table and headed for the door. "Coming?"

"Maybe I'll wait here. You could bring something back."

"And take the chance that you'll disappear while I'm gone? I don't think so."

Jane grinned. "I guess you're not as dumb as you look."

"And I guess you're not as hungry as you said you were; otherwise, you wouldn't be wasting my time arguing."

I turned off the light, then waited until she'd walked through the doorway and pulled the

119

door shut. When I took out the key, Jane shook her head.

"I don't know why you bother," she said. "A three-year-old could pick that lock."

"Probably." The door jiggled loosely as I flipped the bolt. "Have you tried it?"

"Yeah, sure."

"Why?"

"Because it's the only door down here that's locked. Right away, that made it the most interesting place to be."

That made sense. "Did you get in?"

"Less than a minute," Jane told me proudly.

"So how come you keep hanging around here? Shouldn't you be in school?"

Jane followed me up the stairs. "In case you hadn't noticed, we *are* in school."

"I mean one where you're enrolled, where you take classes with other kids your age and learn things."

"School's boring. Besides, I already know plenty."

I didn't doubt that for a minute. I'd been leading the way, but as we neared the dining room, Jane skipped past me and went on ahead. She seemed to know the hallways and passages of the old building just as well as I did.

She bypassed the door leading to the large, formal dining room and scooted down a narrow alleyway that angled back to the kitchen. "Come *on,*" she said. "If we don't get there soon, they might throw everything out."

The kitchen was quiet and nearly empty when we got there. The only person in sight was one of the servingwomen I'd met the day before. She took one look at Jane and screamed. The sound ricocheted loudly off the gleaming appliances and tiled floor.

"You're back!" she said, pointing a finger at Jane and looking as if she'd seen a ghost. "Don't tell me somebody else is dead."

"Nobody's dead," I said firmly. Afraid she'd slip back out the door, I grasped Jane's hand. It was cold as ice. "We're looking for something to eat."

"Eugene Krebbs is dead. Don't try and tell me he's not. I saw the whole story on the evening news. Shawna, I said to myself, girl, that is one dangerous place to work, when spirits be loose in the hallways and even an old man isn't safe."

Jane glanced at me and rolled her eyes. I was glad to see she wasn't taking Shawna's performance to heart.

"Maybe we should just help ourselves," I said.

Shawna didn't try to stop me, so I took that as assent. Two big subzero refrigerators filled one wall. I found the leftover meat loaf on the top shelf of the first one I opened. Several loaves of whole wheat bread were stored beneath it.

"Sandwiches?" I asked Jane.

"Is there ketchup?"

An industrial-sized jar was in the pantry. While I cut two thick slabs off the wedge of meat loaf, Jane found a glass and filled it to the top with milk. She drank the first glassful down and filled it again while waiting for me to finish.

Shawna, meanwhile, tended to business on the other side of the room and studiously ignored us. I was probably the first teacher she'd ever seen raid the kitchen, but she didn't say a word.

Carrying the plate and a stack of napkins, I led the way to a corner table in the dining room. Jane reached for the first sandwich as she slid into her chair and quickly wolfed it down. Ignoring the napkins, she licked the ketchup off her fingers and went for the second. At this rate, we'd be back in the kitchen in no time.

Two minutes later, the second sandwich was also gone. As Jane took a deep breath and followed it with a sip of milk, I asked, "Better?"

"Yeah." She wiggled in her chair and glanced back toward the kitchen. If she were like my son, she was thinking about dessert. "Thanks."

"You're welcome. When was the last time you ate?"

She shot me a look. "Yesterday, I guess."

"Nobody at your house fixes meals?"

"Yeah, there are meals. I just don't always eat them."

Maybe, I thought. Maybe not. I kept my tone casual. "Where do you live?"

"Right," Jane sniffed. "I tell you that, and you'll take me home."

"Not necessarily. You seem to spend a great deal of time here. I'm thinking there's probably a good reason for that."

Jane didn't answer. Instead, she reached for her milk and finished it off. Getting information from her was like trying to pry a bone from the jaws of a pit bull.

"Dessert?" I asked. The girl's eyes widened fractionally. "I bet we can find some cookies."

"Even better, I bet we can make Shawna scream again."

I smiled with her. "Let's go for it."

To Jane's disappointment, this time the kitchen was empty. I rinsed off the plate in the sink while she rifled through the pantry. When she thought I wasn't looking, she slipped a box of unsweetened chocolate into her pocket. I pretended not to notice; the chocolate's bitter taste would probably be punishment enough.

Jane emerged from the pantry a moment later with a bag of iced oatmeal cookies that looked good enough to make my own stomach rumble. This time, we poured two glasses of milk

"You're going to have to talk to the police," I said as we munched. "They think Krebbs was murdered, and since you were the first person to get there after he died, whether you realize it or not, you may have some valuable information for them."

Jane shook her head. Her mouth was filled with cookie, but she pushed a word out around it. "No."

"There's no point in arguing—"

"I'm not," Jane protested, when she'd finally swallowed. "But you're wrong. I didn't find Krebbs after he died. When I got there, he was still alive."

# Ten

"Alive?" I gasped. That possibility hadn't even occurred to me. "Are you sure?"

"His fingers were moving," said Jane, her face clouding over. "That was the first thing I saw. That, and the blood."

I wanted to reach over and put my arms around her, but I didn't dare. I was afraid she'd stop talking, or worse, run away again. Instead, I simply listened.

"I was just passing by the shed. There was a wheelbarrow sitting next to the door. I'd seen Krebbs with it earlier, so I figured he was inside. I always liked to keep track of where he was . . ." Jane glanced in my direction. "You know?"

Remembering their encounter in the prop room, I nodded.

"I didn't hear anything, so I figured I'd have a look, maybe sneak up on him so he wouldn't even know I was there. He always thought he was so smart." She shook her head in disgust. "Half the time, he had no idea what was going on.

"But when I looked inside the shed, he was lying on the floor. At first I thought he'd tripped and fallen. Then I saw his face. His eyes were just staring off into space. It was really spooky."

"Did you go into the shed?"

"I didn't mean to," Jane said quickly. "I didn't even realize what I was doing. I just kind of kept walking. Krebbs's fingers were twitching, and his lips were moving. I thought he was trying to talk to me, except I didn't want to get close enough to hear what he was saying. Part of me thought it was a trick. You know, like he'd set this up to scare me and any second he was going to jump up and grab me?"

Even in the retelling, I could feel Jane's terror. I slid my arm around her shoulders, and she didn't pull away.

"He didn't get up, though. And I only heard him say one word. Jason. At least that's what it sounded like. That made me think of those old horror movies. You know, like *Friday the Thirteenth*? I just turned and ran."

"You were very brave," I said, giving her shoulder a squeeze.

"I was scared shitless."

The teacher in me wanted to correct her vocabulary. The mother in me won out; I just kept holding on. "That's when you went to get Mrs. Plimpton?"

"Right. I wasn't looking for her in particular. I just wanted to get help. I knew Krebbs was in bad shape, but I didn't think he was going to die. I thought an ambulance could come and save him."

"Jane," I said gently. "You're going to have to talk to the police about this. Detective Shertz is the man in charge of the investigation. You need to tell him what you saw."

"I didn't see anything," Jane said firmly. "Just what I've told you."

"I know, but sometimes when the police ask questions you remember things you didn't realize you knew. It's important for you to tell them everything so they can find out who did this."

"Jason did it. That's what Krebbs said."

I turned the name over in my mind. It wasn't an unpopular one, and I could think of several students who were called that. However, I couldn't imagine why any of them would have wanted to murder Eugene Krebbs. "Do you know who he meant?"

"No." Jane shook her head emphatically as she twisted out of my grasp. "That's what I've been trying to tell you. I don't *know* anything. And I don't want to talk to the police."

I gazed at her sadly. Such a small girl, with such a large burden. And I wasn't making things any easier for her. "Are you afraid they might find out something about you? Like where you live, or that you don't go to school?"

"It's none of their business. It's nobody's business!" She put down her glass and started to walk away.

"Running won't help," I called after her. "Detective Shertz will find you. He has to, it's his job. You might as well give in and talk to him willingly."

Jane whirled to face me. "You're a real pain, you know that?"

"Only when I have to be."

Grudgingly she walked back and took the cookie I held out. "I hate teachers."

"I'll try not to take it personally."

Jane was silent for a moment. "Will you be there?" she asked finally.

"Where?"

"When I talk to the detective, will you come with me?"

"Is that what you want?"

"What I want is to be left alone." She sighed. "But it doesn't look like that's going to happen. So I guess you may as well call the guy and tell him I'll see him."

"Detective Shertz was here earlier. He might still be here now. What about your parents?"

"What about them?" Jane looked annoyed.

"Wouldn't you like them to be here, too?"

"My father's dead," she said shortly. The bald announcement carried not the slightest shred of emotion. "My mother's in Boston. She wouldn't come down here for something like this."

"You ought to ask her—"

"I don't know how to reach her. No one does.

I think she's living on the street. She doesn't carry a cell phone, okay?"

"Okay," I said softly, wishing I could ease her hostility, longing to put my arms around her once more. "Who takes care of you?"

"I live with my grandmother. My mom's mom. She's okay."

Okay was a relative term, I thought, considering that I was talking to a child who wasn't in school, was dressed in dirty clothes, and hadn't eaten since the day before.

"Does she know where you are?" I asked.

"Sure." Jane smiled slightly. "She thinks I'm in school. And I am. So everything works out fine."

Right. "I imagine the police will want to speak with her, too," I said, thinking aloud.

"If you try to call her, I'll walk."

Clearly I'd pushed her as far as she was going to go. "The only person I'm going to call is Detective Shertz. It's up to him to decide what to do after that."

I checked with Russell's secretary. Harriet informed me that the detective had left before lunch and was not expected back on campus for the rest of the day. My next call was to the police department. I was certain Shertz wasn't the only person working on the case, but he was the one I knew. When he proved unavailable, I left a message, setting up an appointment at the school for the next day.

"You will come back, won't you?" I asked Jane, fully aware that I had no way to ensure her compliance.

"I guess."

"Promise?"

"I told you I'll be here," Jane said, frowning. "Isn't that good enough?"

It had to be. It was all the assurance I was going to get.

Howard Academy is situated just north of downtown Greenwich, on the edge of a residential area. As you drive out of town, compact, older homes quickly give way to stately mansions. Within a mile, you're well into estate territory. Beautiful houses, each worth more than I will earn in my lifetime, line the country roads.

Aunt Peg lives in backcountry Greenwich. Her home is a rambling farmhouse set in the midst of a tree-fringed meadow. In the summer, wildflowers abound. In the winter, deer leave tracks beneath her windows. She and her husband, Max, bought the house forty years earlier, before the price of Greenwich real estate skyrocketed.

Max and Peg had never had any children, but they had raised glorious dogs. Over the decades, the Cedar Crest line of Standard Poodles had become known worldwide for its beauty, health, and good temperament. Faith was a Cedar Crest Standard Poodle, and to my mind she embodied everything that was wonderful about the breed. Thanks to Aunt Peg, I now had two children, and I couldn't imagine living without either one.

Max Turnbull had died several years earlier and now that he was gone, Peg was beginning to scale down. Though there was a trim kennel building in the backyard, these days it seldom housed more than a handful of Poodles. The other dogs, those who had already finished their championships and no longer wore the elaborate clip required for the show ring, lived in the house with Aunt Peg.

Currently, the indoor herd numbered five. After school, when I'd swung by home and picked up Faith, gotten Davey off the bus, then driven to Aunt Peg's house for a visit, the Poodles announced our arrival as soon as we turned in the driveway. That was business as usual. Faith functions as a combination burglar alarm/personal greeter at my house, too.

When Peg opened the front door, the Standard Poodles spilled down the steps and across the yard. All were black, and each wore the same no-muss, no-fuss kennel trim, with closely clipped face and feet, pom pon on the end of the tail, and a short blanket of hair covering the rest of their bodies. As Faith leapt from the car to join them, I found myself envying, not for the first time, the trim, sporty look of her sleeker cousins.

"This is a pleasant surprise," said Aunt Peg, following the group down the stairs. "And might I add, it's about time."

"Time for what?" asked Davey. He was already rolling on the ground with the Poodles, who tended to treat him as a smaller, less hairy, litter-mate. "We just got here."

"Time for you to go inside and see if you want a snack. I've got angel food cake and fresh raspberries." As Davey scampered inside, Peg turned her attention to me. "Fine niece you are. A murder takes place right under your nose, and you don't even have the decency to call. I had to read about it in the morning paper just like everyone else."

Sweets are only one of Peg's vices; curiosity is another. Her interest didn't surprise me; nor did the rebuke.

"I'm here now, aren't I? Besides, there isn't that much to tell. I'd barely met Eugene Krebbs, nobody seems to know why anyone would want to murder him, and the police are investigating."

Peg did a quick nose count, making sure that all the Poodles were with us as we walked inside, then closed the door. "There has to be more to it than that. You're in a perfect position to have all sorts of inside information, so don't think you're going to get away with giving me short shrift."

Davey was waiting for us impatiently in the

kitchen. Aunt Peg and I took a few minutes out from our conversation to get him set up with a plate of cake and berries and a glass of milk. Peg fixed another plate for herself, only larger. I settled for a small bowl of raspberries.

"There's heavy cream in the refrigerator," Peg offered as she dug into her cake. She must be the only person on earth who thinks of heavy cream as a staple. Check out my refrigerator and you'll find yogurt and 1% whole milk.

"I'm fine," I said.

"Good. Then you can tell me all about what's been happening at my alma mater."

I lifted my head and stared. "Your *what?*"

"My old school. Really, Melanie, is your education so lacking—"

"I know what the term means," I broke in. "But I had no idea that you were a Howard Academy graduate."

Peg shrugged. "Everyone has to go to school somewhere."

Except Jane, perhaps.

"Well yes, but . . ." I groped for words. "I'm just wondering why this never came up before. I've been working at Howard Academy for six months. I would think you'd have mentioned your connection to the school before this."

"Why?" asked Peg. "It's not as if it made any difference. I attended the school for grades one through eight, many, many years ago. I'm sure the school has changed dramatically since then."

"This is boring," Davey announced, sliding down off his chair. His plate was already empty. "Can I go outside and play with the dogs?"

"If you put on your jacket," I said automatically.

"And leave Faith in here with us," Aunt Peg added. "I'd hate to see anything happen to her coat, now that she's so close to finishing."

Faith ran to the door with the rest of the group and was deeply chagrined to discover that she wasn't going out with them. I cupped my hand around her nose, cradling her muzzle in my palm, and led her back to the table. Poodles "in hair" never wear collars, except when they're in the show ring; and that's the time-honored method of leading them from place to place. To cheer Faith up, I let her put her front legs in my lap and broke off a piece of angel food cake to hand-feed her.

"I hope you don't make a habit of that kind of behavior," Aunt Peg said as she piled the plates and dumped them in the sink. Obviously she takes her dogs' diets a good bit more seriously then she takes her own. "You'll have that bitch spoiled beyond redemption in no time."

I looked at Faith, her face only inches from mine, and grinned. "Are you beyond redemption?" I asked. The Poodle wagged her tail in happy agreement. Aunt Peg didn't look pleased.

To mollify her, I returned to our earlier topic. "The man who was murdered was the school caretaker, Eugene Krebbs. I'm told that he'd been at Howard Academy for decades, maybe even when you were there. Do you remember him?"

She thought for a moment. "The name doesn't sound familiar. Even if I knew who he was at the time, the memory's faded by now. The newspaper report hardly said a thing about his background. Who was he? Why would anyone have wanted to kill him?"

"Nobody knows. Detective Shertz speculated that robbery might have been the motive, but no one can think of anything that was stored in that old shed that would have been worth killing over."

"I hope you'll keep me posted," said Peg.

As if I'd have a choice.

"I don't know." I pretended to consider. "I'm not sure I've forgiven you yet for keeping Sam's first wife a secret."

"That news wasn't mine to tell," Peg said firmly. "Besides, for all I knew, the two of you might have already discussed it and decided it wasn't important."

"Not."

She ignored the interruption. "Since you've brought Sheila up, I should probably mention that I paid her a visit the other day."

"The other day when?" I sputtered. "We just found out she was here."

"You know how I hate to waste time. I stopped by Sunday afternoon with a housewarming present, and said how nice it was to have her in the neighborhood."

"She lives in North Salem. Her neighborhood is twenty miles from here."

"Semantics." Peg sniffed. "Do you want to hear what she had to say or not?"

She knew perfectly well that I did.

"Sheila seems like a nice woman, if you don't count the fact that she divorced Sam." In Peg's eyes, Sam can do no wrong. "We shared a pot of tea and had quite a pleasant conversation."

Translation: she'd pumped the woman for all she was worth. I wasn't complaining. "And?"

"At first we talked dogs, of course. But eventually I brought the subject around to Sam. Sheila said she was delighted to know he'd made such nice friends on the East Coast."

"Cut to the chase," I said. "Did you find out why they got divorced?"

"That was easy. Sheila admitted quite readily that it was all her fault. She was young, and at the time her career was very important to her. Sam wanted them to gear down a bit, perhaps think about having children. Sheila wasn't ready for that. She's very ambitious. She was on the fast track and she wasn't about to let him derail her."

"So she left him," I mused. "I wonder how Sam felt about it. Do you think he was devastated?"

"Sheila seems to think so. Apparently he told her if she ever got her priorities straight, she should look him up."

I felt a knot tighten in the pit of my stomach. Before Aunt Peg continued, I knew what she was going to say.

"So that's what she came here to do."

🐾 Eleven 🐾

Wednesday morning, I got to school early. It wasn't as if I had a choice. Michael Durant had scheduled the pageant committee meeting for eight o'clock.

Since that meant I had to leave home before the school bus came, I took Davey with me and dropped him off at Hunting Ridge Elementary. On the way, we stopped at a doughnut shop and picked up an assorted dozen. I like to think that my moral standards are pretty high, but times like this, I'm willing to resort to bribery if it will get the job done.

At the school, I let Davey out at the curb, then watched until he was safely inside. He'd been given strict instructions to take the box of doughnuts directly to the faculty lounge. That way, any teachers who'd already arrived would know he was in the building and I could be sure he was in good hands.

Ah, the joys of motherhood. If my son ever actually did grow up and leave home, I'd have so much free time on my hands I wouldn't know what to do with myself.

Though it was early, the teachers' parking lot at Howard Academy was already half-full. Not surprisingly, Russell Hanover's silver BMW was parked in its conspicuous spot next to the back door. He and I didn't always agree, but I had to admire the man's dedication to Howard Academy and all the school stood for. The headmaster was unrelenting in his quest to make the academy a showplace that any parent would be proud to be associated with.

Since the faculty lounge was bound to be busy first thing in the morning, Michael had asked us to meet in the library. Books had been important to Honoria, and the room she'd devoted to them was spacious and inviting. Volumes of poetry and literature filled the shelves; and a bevy of comfortable, overstuffed chairs enticed students to sit and read. Just entering the room always made me feel good.

Michael, seated at a long oak table near a window, saw my smile. "You're in a good mood this morning. I hope that bodes well for our meeting."

"Good mood be damned," growled Ed, coming in behind me. "Do you know how early I had to get out of bed to make it here in time?"

"No," said Rita, stepping out from behind one of the stacks. She was carrying a cup of hot coffee and looked as though she'd just as soon toss it at him as talk to him. "Why don't you tell us?"

"You think I'm joking," Ed groused. "The traffic on 95 is murder this time of day—"

"People!" Michael clapped his hands, cutting off the complaint. "Since we're all here, let's get down to business."

I pulled out a chair on the other side of the table. "What about Sally? Isn't she coming?"

"I haven't spoken to her," said Michael. "I left a note in her box, but I doubt she got it. She's been out of school since Monday, and as far as I know, she isn't back yet."

"She was here for our last meeting," Rita spoke up. "That was on Monday."

"Apparently she left right after we broke up and hasn't been seen since."

"Chicken," Ed muttered under his breath.

"Pardon me?" I said.

Ed chirped loudly and flapped his arms. Moron. "One small crisis and Sally Minor goes running home, leaving the rest of us to deal with it."

"I'd hardly call a murder a small crisis," Rita said quietly.

"Maybe she's sick," I said.

"We're all sick," said Ed. "Sick of running the media gauntlet. Sick of the police asking their interminable questions. It doesn't mean we aren't here, doing our duty by our students."

"That's enough," Michael said. "I'm sure there's a very good reason for Sally's absence, not that it's any of our business. We only have a limited amount of time this morning. Let's try to get something accomplished, shall we?"

It took him a minute to get everyone organized and concentrating on the job at hand, but Michael did manage to turn the meeting around. There wasn't much to discuss, however, as we still didn't have a topic for the pageant, much less a script.

"You'll continue looking through the archives, won't you?" Michael asked me, sounding almost desperate.

"Of course. I'm enjoying it."

"What about the Poodle?"

"What Poodle?" Rita looked back and forth between us.

"The one in the portrait," said Ed. "How could you miss it? It's sitting right next to Honoria. According to the plaque, its name is Poupee." Obviously French wasn't Ed's strong suit; he pronounced the name poopy.

"I think that's Poo-pay," Michael corrected smoothly. "It seems that Melanie has a dog at home that looks just like that one. I was hoping we might be able to make her part of our pageant."

Rita looked interested; predictably, Ed was frowning. "So now we're making this a pageant about *dogs?*"

"It was only an idea." Michael glanced around the table. "Something we've been sorely lacking in otherwise."

"Is she one of those fancy Poodles you see in

the Westminster dog show on TV?" asked Rita. "What fun! Do you ever bring her to school?"

"I haven't yet—"

"But you should! I'll bet the kids would love her. Old Mr. Bailey always used to bring Heidi to school, remember? It was like she was the school mascot."

Michael looked every bit as clueless as I felt, but Ed nodded grudgingly. "Bailey used to teach social studies. He retired at the end of last year. Had a Collie that looked just like Lassie. I don't know how it got started, but he always had Heidi here with him. She used to sleep in the corner of his classroom. Nobody seemed to mind." Ed shot me a look. "Of course, *his* dog was very well behaved."

"So is mine." The impulse to defend Faith was strong and automatic.

"You should ask Mr. Hanover if you can bring her to school," said Rita. "I'll bet he wouldn't mind, especially since she's going to have something to do in the pageant. The precedent's already been set, and I know the kids would be thrilled."

"I will," I said, delighted by the suggestion.

The only thing I'd ever regretted about taking on the responsibility of owning a dog was that Faith had to spend so much of each day alone. Poodles are naturally gregarious animals. Though she'd adapted to the situation, I knew Faith would be much happier if she could spend her days with me.

Out in the hall, the first bell rang. "Damn," said Michael, glancing at his watch. "At this rate, we'd be better off rescheduling the pageant for spring of next year."

"Don't worry," said Rita, gathering up her things. "It will come together. Things always do in the end."

I followed the others out the door and hurried to my classroom. I had three tutoring sessions scheduled back-to-back, followed by the appointment with Detective Shertz at eleven.

I hoped Jane was planning to show up. Especially after the preemptory way I'd summoned him to the school, Detective Shertz wasn't going to be pleased if she stood us up. Worse still, I wouldn't even have an address or phone number to offer in her stead.

Fortunately, I was too busy with my students to spend the next few hours worrying. What most of the kids I tutor have in common is parents who are wealthy enough to provide them with the best education money can buy. But money alone won't get you a Howard Academy diploma. Honoria Howard was a stern taskmaster, and her standards endure to this day. Any student who has hopes of making the grade at Howard Academy had better be prepared to work at the task.

Getting that point across isn't always easy, and that morning I had some of my biggest challenges. That's probably why it took me so long to notice that the carton of records I'd brought up from the basement on Monday had reappeared in my classroom. To my chagrin, I found the box by tripping over it.

"Ms. Travis, are you all right?" Willie Boyd, a tall eighth grader with long, dangling limbs and smooth brown skin, leapt out of his chair and rushed to help me up.

"I'm fine." I scrambled to my feet and dusted off my wool pants. "Where did that come from?"

"It was just sitting there," said Willie. He was a really bright kid, the kind who could keep up with the curriculum easily and would have if, as a scholarship student, he wasn't having some problems adjusting to the school's distinctive ambiance.

"But how did it get here?" I was thinking aloud and didn't really expect an answer, but Willie gave it a try.

"Maybe it's school supplies, and someone forgot to tell you they were coming."

"No, it isn't school supplies."

It was the archive box all right. Thank goodness the cleaning crew hadn't thrown it out. But why had it disappeared and how had it been returned? The box had no identifying marks on it. Once it had left my classroom, how would anyone have known this was where it belonged?

"It looks heavy," said Willie.

"It is," I said, rubbing my shin.

"Want me to run it down to the office for you? I bet they'll know what to do with it." His expression was suffused with sincerity, as if he truly hoped I wouldn't recognize his offer as a blatant attempt to get out of doing further schoolwork.

"No, it's okay here. I'll deal with it later."

Disappointed, Willie got back to his books. We'd already succeeded in pulling his C in English Literature up to a B. Now we were aiming higher.

By the time the session ended, it was almost eleven. I'd asked Detective Shertz to meet us in my classroom because I'd thought Jane might feel more comfortable there. So far, there was no sign of her.

As Willie packed up his books, the door to the classroom flew open and a teenage boy came swaggering in. He had spiky blond hair, broad shoulders, and well-muscled forearms. He gazed around the room with a derisive sneer. "Is this the place?"

"Which place is that?" I asked, moving forward to block his access. Clearly, he wasn't a student. Howard Academy only went through eighth grade; unless this boy had stayed back several years, he was much too old. "Who are you?"

"Brad." His gaze stopped roaming and settled on me. "I'm a friend of Jane's."

"Where is she?"

"She's coming. She sent me on ahead to scope out the place."

He walked around the room, peering in closets and out the windows. Checking for escape routes in case they needed to make a hasty exit? I almost laughed. It looked to me like Brad had been watching too many action/adventure movies.

"You okay, Ms. Travis?" Willie hesitated by the door, his expression troubled. "You want me to hang around for anything?"

"Everything's fine. Detective Shertz will be here any minute."

"I got a minute," Willie persisted, staring hard at Brad. The two hadn't exchanged a word, but the tension between them was palpable.

"No, go ahead to your next class. I wouldn't want you to be late."

Willie took his time leaving the room. I heard a thump in the hallway and realized he'd pushed the doorstop into position to hold the classroom door open. Interesting.

The gesture went for nothing when Detective Shertz appeared a moment later. He kicked the doorstop away and pulled the door shut behind him. Belatedly he seemed to realize that Jane wasn't in the room.

"Where's the girl?" he asked me. "I thought you said she'd be here. And what's with him?"

"Jane asked me to accompany her to this meeting for moral support." Brad's voice was stiff, his posture even more so. I wondered if he'd practiced the speech in front of a mirror.

"Her family ought to be here for moral support," Shertz said, frowning.

"Jane hasn't got any family that matters. She asked me to help out."

The doorknob turned, the door opened a sliver, and Jane slipped inside. She looked at Brad and smiled, nodded at me, then walked across the room to the policeman.

"You must be Detective Shertz. I heard you wanted to talk to me."

"And you're the girl who found the body." It was more a statement than a question.

Jane nodded.

"How old are you?"

"Twelve."

I gasped softly. I'd pegged her age as two years younger.

"Brad here says you don't have any family. What about a guardian? Who do you live with?"

"My grandmother. I guess she's my guardian. She thinks she's in charge, anyway."

"How about this?" said Shertz. "Let's call her

and get her over here. It'd be better if you had a grown-up here during questioning."

"No," Jane said firmly. "Ms. Travis is a grown-up. She can stay."

Patience didn't come easily to the detective. I could see him marshaling his. "Ms. Travis isn't a relative."

"It doesn't matter. She's the one I want. If you bring my grandmother over here, I won't say a word."

"What about him?" Shertz jerked a thumb in Brad's direction.

"He's my friend. When I told him I was going to be talking to the police, he said he'd better come along."

Shertz didn't look happy. "I guess that would be because he has experience in matters like this."

"Hey, man!" Brad jumped up from his perch on the edge of a table. "We don't have to be here. If you're not going to be civil, we'll walk."

"Oh Brad, calm down." Jane's voice sounded weary enough to make me wonder how often she had to soothe his moods. "It's no big deal. Let's just answer the man's questions and get it over with."

"Maybe you should have a lawyer," Brad said suddenly.

"That's certainly her option." Shertz's tone was mild.

"Don't be ridiculous," said Jane. "Brad, maybe it would be better if you waited for me outside, okay?"

"No, not okay." His face set in stubborn lines.

"I'll only be a few minutes."

"You need somebody here with you. Someone to be on your side."

"Ms. Travis will look out for me. Besides, I doubt Detective Shertz is planning to threaten me with his gun." She sounded amused. "Are you?"

"No, of course not." Shertz didn't find the question funny at all.

"There, you see? I'll be fine." Jane walked Brad to the door, pushed him through, and shut it behind him.

"Curious choice of friends you got there," Shertz mentioned as Jane walked back and sat down.

"We hang around together sometimes, that's all. I haven't lived here that long. Brad knows more about the town than I do. He looks out for me, acts as my protector."

"Down at the police station we know Brad pretty well," said Shertz. "To me he looks like the kind of guy who looks out for himself."

Jane remained composed. "I didn't come here to discuss my social life. Ms. Travis said you have some questions for me?"

Slowly, in great detail, Detective Shertz led

her through Monday's events. The story Jane told was much the same as the one she'd offered me. I doubt that the recital offered the detective many clues, but it probably filled in some gaps. When Jane came to the part about Krebbs's last word, Shertz made her repeat it twice.

"Jason," he said. "Like J-A-S-O-N?"

"That's what it sounded like."

He nodded and wrote the information down. In less than fifteen minutes, the interview was finished. Jane left immediately.

Detective Shertz remained in his seat. He didn't say anything for a minute.

"I'm surprised you didn't ask for her last name," I said. "We have to get in touch with her grandmother."

"I already have. We needed her permission to proceed today." Shertz glanced at me and smiled. "Don't look so surprised. It wasn't that hard. We had a first name. Jane's too young to drive, so we had a probable school district. Judging by what you said, we also had a history of truant behavior.

"The school doesn't know that, by the way. They think she has mono. Someone who says she's the grandmother calls in with periodic updates."

"Jane," I said.

"That girl's no dummy. On top of that, I gather she's used to looking out for herself. This arrangement with the grandmother only came

150

about in January. Before that she was in Boston with her mother."

"She told me her mother lived on the street."

"Sometimes she does. Sometimes Jane did, too. Bringing her down here was a last-resort option. I don't think anyone's welcomed her with open arms."

"Except maybe Brad," I said unhappily.

Shertz looked up. "He hang around here much?"

"Not that I know of. Today's the first time I've ever seen him. Why?"

"That kid's bad news. A high school dropout with no visible means of support. We've had him in a couple of times for vandalism and petty theft. He's a problem waiting to happen, and I can promise you this: he isn't doing Jane any good."

The detective got ready to leave. "There's something else. Didn't you tell me that Jane and Krebbs were at each other's throats? That kid thinks of Brad as her protector. Kind of makes you wonder who she needs protection from. By the way, I'd bet a bundle she doesn't know his last name."

"Does it matter?"

Shertz nodded slowly. "It sure as hell does. It's Jameson."

It took me a second to make the connection.

"Jason?" said Shertz. "Jameson? It just might be close enough."

🐾 Twelve 🐾

As soon as Detective Shertz left, I headed over to the dining room for lunch. The menu posted near the door promised spaghetti bolognese, garlic breadsticks, and Caesar salad. My mouth watered just reading about it.

The first course was being served when Sally Minor slid into an empty seat beside me. "Good, I'm not too late," she said, grabbing a napkin and smoothing it onto her lap. "Food always seems to disappear quickly on spaghetti day."

"That's because all the kids go for extra helpings." I passed the breadsticks her way. "Are you feeling okay?"

"Sure. Why?"

"We had a pageant committee meeting this morning before school and when you weren't there, Michael mentioned you'd gone home sick Monday afternoon."

"I'm okay." Sally's gaze dropped. "I guess I was just kind of in shock over what happened. I needed to get away."

We'd all been shocked, I thought. But with students who needed tending to, Sally was the last person I'd have expected to run.

"Anyway, I was here bright and early this morning. I just didn't know about the meeting in time to make it. Did I miss anything important?"

"Are you kidding?" A steaming bowl of pasta came my way and I took time out to serve myself a generous portion. "We're still wandering around in the dark, hoping for inspiration to strike."

"Are the archives turning out to be interesting?"

I nodded, my mouth too full to speak.

"Finding anything?"

"Lots of stuff. Letters, memos, but so far nothing to build the pageant around. I'm going back for another look this afternoon. You know what was odd though?"

Now it was Sally whose mouth was full. She lifted her brows.

"I'd brought one of the cartons up to my classroom on Monday, figuring I'd go through it when I had a chance. But when I looked for it on Tuesday, it was gone. This morning, it appeared again. It's really strange."

"I may be able to solve part of the mystery. Are you talking about an old cardboard box, frayed flaps, jumbled to the brim with papers?"

"That's it."

"I found it in my classroom when I got in this morning. All I could think was, great, I'm gone two days and people start using my room as a garbage dump. But then I looked inside and saw those old papers, and thought of you. I brought it down to your room and left it. You were probably at the committee meeting. Sorry, I guess I should have left a note."

"No, that's fine. Now at least I know half of what happened. Though that doesn't explain how the box got moved from my room to yours in the first place."

"Probably Krebbs," Sally said automatically, then paled.

During the semester and a half I'd been at Howard Academy, I'd heard people use that phrase numerous times, usually to assign responsibility for otherwise unexplainable events. Unlike the kitchen help who believed in ghosts, the faculty and administration tended, often with good reason, to blame the caretaker.

"Not this time," I said, attempting a small smile.

"God, I must be going nuts." Sally sat back and rubbed her eyes. "I can't believe I'm taking this whole thing so hard. It's not as if . . ."

"As if what?" I asked, curious.

"Nothing." Sally's answer was quick and sharp. "Forget I said anything. Pass me the salad, okay? Do you know that in Europe people eat the salad course after the meal? We Americans are the ones who are backwards. Eating the salad afterward is good for digestion."

I let her babble on and wondered what she'd been about to say. It's not as if . . . what? As if she liked Krebbs? As if they were friends?

I pondered that for a moment. Sally had been at Howard Academy longer than just about anyone else who was currently employed there. Maybe she and Krebbs shared some sort of past. The teacher and the caretaker? It seemed unlikely; but I supposed it wasn't impossible.

After lunch, I stopped in my classroom to retrieve the disappearing/reappearing carton and then headed, somewhat grudgingly, down to the basement. What had begun as a pleasant diversion was beginning to feel like a chore; and Michael's growing impatience for me to find a quick fix for the pageant didn't help matters any.

So far, I'd delved mainly through those cartons that were easily accessible, either piled near the table or in front of the stacks. Maybe it was time to try something different. With that in mind, I lifted off the top tier of boxes, set them aside, and dug into those beneath them.

The first I opened contained homework, mostly term papers written by Joshua's sons, James and Matthew, at their respective colleges. Skimming through several, I could see why Joshua hadn't been anxious to leave his considerable fortune in their hands. The next box I checked was devoted to clothing sketches and dress patterns, the papers interspersed with swatches of elegantly hued silks and satins.

Interesting, but still not the stuff of which spring pageants were made.

The contents of the bottom box had belonged to Joshua and Mabel's youngest daughter, Ruth. On top were several photographs, each carefully labeled and dated on the back. Ruth looked like a charming child, with auburn curls and dimpled cheeks. The snapshots showed her at varying ages: flying a kite, sailing a toy boat, picnicking in a garden. Judging by the pictures, Ruth had enjoyed a happy, carefree childhood.

Beneath the photos, I found a doll whose wispy blond hair and heavily soiled dress spoke of heavy use. Under that was a small, leather bound book. *My Diary.* The words were embossed in gold script across the front.

Eagerly I pulled the book out and turned to the first page. Ruth had written the date, March 1, 1934, and her full name, Ruth Winston Howard across the top. *Today I turn sixteen,* she'd written below. *Father says I'm nearly all grown up now. I've waited so long I'm sure this will be the best year of my life.*

Reading the hopeful, innocent words, I found myself wondering what had become of Joshua's youngest child. Or the rest of the siblings, for that matter. Having been born near the beginning of the century, any that were still alive would be quite old by now. There must have been descendants, though. Was the family still in Greenwich? I wondered. Did they maintain an interest in the school Joshua and Honoria had founded?

There was no time to look for more answers. The bell was ringing in the hallway above me, which meant I should have already been in my classroom. Hastily, I repiled the boxes out of the way against the wall. The diary, I took with me. It was small enough to be easily portable and offered the prospect of fascinating reading.

The remainder of the afternoon flew by. I had two more tutoring sessions, and spent forty-five minutes writing up a student evaluation. Paperwork. If anyone had told me before I became a teacher that there would be so much of it, I'd have been tempted to turn and run the other way.

Since I'd managed to catch Russell Hanover late in the day on Monday, I decided to give it another try. Harriet was once again guarding his outer office. I knew the headmaster had another life. I'd met his wife, Bitsy, and seen pictures of his kids. Harriet, I wasn't so sure about. Sometimes I suspected she simply curled up in a ball and slept beneath her desk at night.

The door to Russell's office was standing open. Though he was talking on the phone, he saw my approach and waved me in. Passing by Harriet's command post, I tried not to look too smug.

Russell quickly wrapped up his phone call.

"I'm glad you stopped by. I was wondering how things went this morning with Detective Shertz and that girl, Jane."

"It was fine," I said, wondering how he'd known about the interview. Perhaps Detective Shertz had mentioned it to him. I probably shouldn't have been surprised. Russell ran Howard Academy like his own private fiefdom. Nothing happened on his campus that he didn't know about. "I think the detective got all the information he needed."

"Good. That's good." Russell looked agitated. His fingers knotted together on his blotter, only to unclasp a moment later and begin to drum. "We want to do everything possible to aid the police in their investigation."

"Of course," I agreed, as the headmaster glanced toward the window. "Is something the matter?"

"No. Yes." He stopped and frowned. Russell was a master of control. I'd never seen him so distracted. "They're out there digging up the ground beneath the shed," he said.

"Digging? What for?"

"To see what they can find, obviously."

"Buried treasure?" One look at Russell's face told me this was no joking matter. I remembered that Shertz hadn't ruled out the possibility of a robbery. But what could have been hidden in the old caretaker's cottage?

158

"They're looking for drugs," said Russell.

Stunned, I sank down into a padded wing chair. *"Krebbs?"*

"Apparently so." He sighed. "You wouldn't have suspected it, would you? Certainly I never did. An old man like that, still collecting a salary here after all these years, his position secure for as long as he wanted it. I thought Krebbs kept coming to work every day because he had nothing else to do with his life. I guess I was very naive."

"No, you weren't," I said quickly.

Like any informed headmaster, Russell had taken a strong, proactive stance in the war against drugs. Howard Academy's no-tolerance policies were well-known and stringently enforced. Students as young as fourth grade took drug-awareness classes. Some private schools viewed this issue with complacency; not Howard Academy. What a blow it would have been for Russell to find out that a school employee was responsible for polluting his campus.

"Was Krebbs dealing?" I asked.

"I don't know, though I have to assume that's what the police suspect. Detective Shertz asked for permission to do everything but take the shed apart. Apparently he's been led to believe that something might have been stashed there."

"Not by Krebbs necessarily," I pointed out.

"I hate to say this, but it hardly matters. If the

police do find something, the fact that the drugs are on the campus at all is damning enough. Our reputation will be ruined. And to think, just yesterday I was worried sick when I only had a murder to contend with."

"Who tipped Shertz off?" I asked.

"I didn't think to ask," Russell replied thoughtfully. "I'm not sure he'd have told me in any case."

"If it helps, I've never seen evidence that anyone, student or employee, was doing drugs at this school."

"That's good to hear." He didn't look reassured. "Of course, anyone who's involved in that kind of behavior would hardly flaunt the fact."

"No, but they might be the kind of kids who got sent into my program because they needed extra help keeping up with their studies." I let that thought sink in for a moment. "I could be wrong, of course, but it's not what I'm seeing. These are good kids."

Russell brushed a hand back through his thinning hair. "Even good kids do drugs. It's everywhere these days. I just didn't expect to confront the problem in quite this way. Imagine how you'd feel right now if you were a Howard Academy parent. Enraged? Betrayed? I know I would."

That was easy enough to see. Just talking about the subject had Russell's face contorted in anger.

I could understand why. He'd devoted his life to enhancing Howard Academy's social standing and academic stature. Now, Krebbs's murder was threatening to tear down everything he'd accomplished.

How might Russell have reacted, I wondered, if he'd known about Krebbs's involvement with drugs before the older man's death? Would he have gone to the police and exposed the school to the sort of negative publicity it was experiencing now? Or would he have been tempted quietly to take matters into his own hands?

Krebbs had been killed with a pitchfork, a weapon that had been conveniently available to his assailant. Suppose Russell had gone out to the shed for some reason and happened unexpectedly upon evidence that the caretaker was engaged in illegal activity. The headmaster would have been shocked. He'd have probably lost his temper. Would he have been angry enough to pick up the nearest tool and impale Eugene Krebbs with it?

"Ms. Travis?"

I was miles away, and it took me a moment to realize Russell was speaking to me. Uptight, upright, Russell Hanover with his serious features and bespoke suits. He didn't make the most likely of murderers. "Yes?"

"You wanted to see me about something?"

"Right," I stalled, trying to push the other image out of my mind. "I wanted to talk to you about Faith."

"Religion? Really, Ms. Travis, I think we have enough to worry about right now. Perhaps we could table that discussion until after things have calmed down a bit."

"No, Faith the dog. My dog." I was still babbling. I took a deep breath and got my thoughts in order. "She's a Poodle, similar to a dog named Poupee, once owned by Honoria Howard. Since the spring pageant is going to be a celebration of the school's history, Mr. Durant mentioned that perhaps Faith might take part."

"I see." His tone encouraged me to continue. Now that we'd gotten past the drugs and murder part of our conversation, Russell seemed to be doing better.

"I was told that there used to be a teacher here, Mr. Bailey, who brought his dog to school?"

"Yes, Heidi. She was quite a favorite with the students."

"With that in mind, I was wondering if it might be possible for me to do the same with Faith? She's very well behaved. She won't bark, or be any sort of problem. She could spend the day in my classroom with me. Nobody would even know she was there . . ."

My voice trailed away as I waited for a

response. It took a minute. I hoped that was a good sign.

"One of the perks of working in the private sector is that one has some leeway when unusual situations arise," Russell said finally. "I always rather liked Heidi. Her presence here predated my arrival, so I was never consulted; nevertheless, she didn't detract from the school in any way. If anything, I might go so far as to say she enhanced the experience for some of the students. If your dog is as well behaved as you say—"

"She is!"

"I wouldn't be averse to offering her a trial period in your classroom. Say, a week?"

"Terrific. Thank you! Faith will be thrilled."

"And she will communicate that fact to you?" Russell asked dryly.

"Definitely."

I guessed he wasn't a dog man. Maybe Faith could change his mind.

"Quietly, I hope?"

"Very quietly," I assured him. "Can we start tomorrow?"

"Why not?" said Russell. "It's not as if things could get any worse."

❧ Thirteen ❧

I couldn't wait to get home and tell Faith the good news.

On the way, I stopped at Hunting Ridge Elementary to pick up Davey and his best friend, Joey Brickman. Joey lives down the block from us; and his mother, Alice, and I have been friends since we started making play dates when the kids were six months old.

Picking the boys up rather than waiting for the bus shaves half an hour off their ETA. Usually they spend that extra time playing, but today I had other plans. Davey and I dropped Joey off at home, swung by and picked up Faith, then headed north to Redding, a picturesque town in upper Fairfield County, that also happens to be where Sam Driver lives.

"Great," said Davey when I told him where we were going. "I like visiting Sam's house."

He should. Over the nearly two year span that Sam and I have known one another, Sam's house has changed a great deal, morphing from a well-appointed bachelor pad to a home that is definitely kid-friendly. Occasionally I complain that Sam is spoiling my son, but since I suspect he enjoys the indulgences as much as Davey, I try to keep the grumbling to a minimum.

Sam's house is a contemporary, perched high on a hill. In a month or two when the leaves have come back on the trees, it will be invisible from the road. Sam enjoys having his privacy. Aside from the mailbox next to the road, there's nothing to mark the steep, unpaved track as a driveway. Once you reach the house, however, the view is spectacular; and large windows in every room bring all of nature's beauty indoors.

"Does Sam know we're coming?" Davey asked, as I parked beside the garage.

"No. I thought we'd surprise him."

I climbed out and looked around. Sam's Blazer wasn't there. And though I could hear Sam's Poodles barking from inside the house, no one seemed to be responding to their announcement of our arrival.

"I don't think he's home." Davey's mouth drooped into a pout. "You should have called him like I did."

Just what I needed to make me feel worse, lessons in etiquette from a six-year-old.

"He works at home, so he's usually here when he's not traveling," I said. "Let's wait a few minutes and see if he comes back."

Faith jumped out of the car and began to chase around the front yard. After a day at home alone, she had plenty of surplus energy to run off. Hearing the dogs inside the house, she ran to the front door and jumped up to look inside.

"Let's go in," said Davey. "I know where there's a key."

I did, too, but all at once I wasn't sure I wanted to use it. A week earlier I wouldn't have hesitated to make myself at home; but suddenly everything felt different. Our relationship seemed to be shifting like sand beneath my feet. Things I'd taken for granted, I now found myself questioning. Things like whether or not I'd be welcome prowling around Sam's house when he wasn't there.

"Here it is!" Davey cried, turning over a rock at the edge of the yard. "I told you I could find it."

"Davey, we can't just invite ourselves into Sam's house."

"Sure we can." My son raced toward the door. "That's why Sam left us the key."

It was no use explaining that Sam hadn't left the key specifically for us. Davey was already using it to open the lock. A moment later, Faith's weight pushed the door inward and Sam's three adult Standard Poodles came spilling out into the yard.

Sam's breeding and showing operation is much smaller than Aunt Peg's, but he's been involved with Poodles for more than a decade. While he lacks her experience, he matches her in dedication; otherwise, Peg never would have trusted him with Tar. I could hear the puppy barking, still inside the house. No doubt Sam had left him crated while he was out.

Faith joined in the play with the three older Poodles. Two, Raven and Juniper, had finished their championships while Sam was still living in Michigan. The third, Casey, he'd had in the ring when we'd met two summers earlier. Fortunately, the three black Standards knew us well enough to obey when Davey and I called them back into the house.

"I'm going to find a snack," said Davey, heading toward the kitchen. The quartet of Poodles followed hopefully behind.

I went in the other direction to Sam's bedroom, where I knew I'd find Tar's crate. A Poodle show coat is a fragile thing. It takes years to grow and requires hours of maintenance on the part of the owner. One careless slip—a puppy left to play unattended with boisterous, older dogs— can cause holes and mats that will keep a Poodle out of the ring for months. Most Poodle owners leave their show dogs crated when they're not watching them, which includes when they're asleep. Hence the crate in the bedroom.

Though I could hear Tar whining eagerly at my approach, I still hesitated in the doorway to the room. I'd been in Sam's bedroom many times, but this was the first time I'd felt like an intruder. Worse, I was half-tempted to look around for telltale signs that Sheila might have been there.

No doubt about it, I thought irritably, my maturity level was hitting an all-time low.

Tar's scratching at the door to his crate got me moving. I crossed the room and flipped the latch. The puppy sprang out, an energetic ball of black hair and flying topknots. Tail whipping back and forth, he leapt over the bed and dashed into the hall. I heard him skid briefly on the hardwood floor, then he was gone. I hoped Davey would think to open the back door that led to Sam's big covered run when the puppy reached the kitchen.

There was, of course, no black negligee draped across the pillow. Nor were there any extra toiletries in the bathroom. Since I didn't touch anything, I figured I wasn't exactly snooping—more just having a friendly look around. I did notice, however, that the message light on Sam's answering machine was blinking.

Probably business calls, I told myself. Or maybe a puppy buyer checking to see if he'd had a litter recently.

Nothing that would interest me.

Nothing that Sam would mind if I heard.

We were planning to get married, weren't we? Didn't that mean we wouldn't keep any secrets from each other? I walked over to the night table beside the bed and hit the replay button.

"You have two messages," said the tinny voice, followed by a beep.

"Sam, it's me." Sheila's voice didn't sound tinny at all. Even on the machine, it was lush and sultry. And even after all this time, she clearly expected Sam to recognize it. "Call me, would you?"

A second beep brought Sheila back. "Sorry," she said. "Just checking in again. I have a little problem I'm hoping you can help me with. Whenever you get a chance. I'll be waiting . . ."

Angrily, I pushed the button and sent the tape spinning backward. I'll be waiting, my fanny!

I'd known women who made a career out of being helpless, who seemed to think that it flattered a man's ego to let him always be the one in charge. But from what both Sam and Aunt Peg had told me about Sheila, the driven career woman, she didn't seem like the type. So why was her life suddenly so full of little problems that nobody but Sam could solve?

I muttered under my breath all the way to the kitchen. Davey was there, munching on one of his favorite shortbread cookies and drinking a glass of milk. "I let Tar outside," he said. "Otherwise, he was going to pee on the floor."

There's nothing that warms a mother's heart like the knowledge she's raising a sensible child. "Good thinking."

"Do you think Sam will be back soon?"

"Probably."

I could afford to be confident. I knew Sam

wouldn't leave his Poodles unattended for too long. Indeed, barely five minutes had passed before the dogs all sat up and pricked their ears.

Davey pushed back his chair, grabbed two cookies, and ran to the door. I followed more slowly. Since I'd listened to Sam's messages, the light on his machine was no longer blinking. If I wanted, I could simply leave things at that. Sheila would certainly call back, and I wouldn't have to admit that I'd been checking up on him.

The idea had appeal, in a sneaky, underhanded, sort of way. But as anyone who's been raised by nuns can tell you, the specter of sin looms large in the psyche ever after. Instead of hiding my indiscretion, I found myself blurting it out the moment Sam walked through the door.

"What a nice surprise," he said.

He was wearing corduroy pants and a soft, faded, denim shirt, with a down vest thrown on top. His dark blond hair had been ruffled by the wind. In short, he looked terrific. I didn't have any difficulty at all understanding why Sheila kept calling.

"You should have let me know you were coming," he said. "I'd have been sure to be here."

"We've only been here a few minutes. Just long enough to let the dogs out, and um . . . listen to your messages."

Confession may be good for the soul, but Sam

didn't seem unduly impressed. "Was there any-thing interesting?"

"Sort of."

Maybe something in my tone alerted him. Sam turned to Davey. "I left a couple bags of groceries in the car. Do you think you could bring them in?"

"Sure!" My son's still at that wonderful age when being asked to do something confers a sense of responsibility. He hasn't yet come to think of helping out as work.

"Sheila called you," I said when he'd gone out-side. "Twice."

"And?"

"And what?"

Sam looked perplexed. "So what's the problem?"

"You don't find the fact that your ex-wife keeps calling you a problem?"

"No."

"Maybe you should." I heard my voice rise. One or two more decibels, and I'd be well on my way to shrill.

"What?" asked Sam. "What am I missing here?"

"Sheila is throwing herself at you, is that so hard to see?"

That made him grin. "That's crazy. Even if Sheila was still interested in me, *which she isn't,* this is hardly the way she'd try to get my attention."

Men can be so oblivious it's pathetic.

"She told Aunt Peg your divorce was a mistake, that she'd come here to tell you she'd changed her mind."

Sam shook his head. "In the first place, Sheila came to New York for a job. And in the second, even if she had changed her mind, don't you think I have any say in the matter? Do you really think so little of me as to believe that all another woman has to do is call and I'd go running?"

Put like that, I had to admit I was the one who sounded pretty pathetic. Still, stubbornness is one of my best traits. "Sheila's not just any other woman."

"Quite right," Sam agreed. "She's the source of the largest failure in my life. I can see why you'd assume I'd be in a hurry to try that again."

For once I was silent, letting his words sink in. The longer the notion rolled around in my head, the more sense it made. "I guess you've made your point," I said. "I've been acting like an idiot."

"It's not that bad." Sam closed the space between us and wrapped his arms around me.

"Yes, it is." The words were muffled, as I mumbled them into his shirt.

"You're determined to argue, aren't you?"

I tipped back my head. "Unless you can think of something better for us to do."

He could, and we did. At least until Davey reappeared.

172

"So that's why you sent me outside," my son said disgustedly. He was carrying one bag and dragging another behind him.

"No, it wasn't," said Sam, looking down over my shoulder. "We don't mind if you watch us kiss."

"I don't *think* so," Davey muttered, passing us by and heading for the kitchen.

Sam watched him go. "Isn't he a little young to be developing an attitude?"

Only a nonparent can afford to be that naive.

I stepped back out of his arms. "Kids grow up pretty quickly these days. Think you're up to the challenge?"

"I imagine I can handle it."

I imagined he could, too. Sam would be a great father. Already in the two years he'd known Davey, he'd been more of a positive influence in my son's life than Davey's real father had.

The more I thought about that, the more I realized how stupid of me it was to be jealous. Sam was right. What Sheila might or might not want was immaterial, so long as Sam was happy being part of our family. Taken in that light, it looked like I was the one who had some growing up to do.

When I reached the kitchen, Davey and Sam were putting the groceries away. Tar had been let back inside and was watching with thinly veiled annoyance as Faith chewed one of his bones. Sam's other Poodles were sacked on the floor. The scene was so homey it almost made my eyes tear up.

"Sorry I was fresh," said Davey.

"What?"

"Sam said I was fresh," Davey repeated. "He told me I had to apologize."

"He did, did he?"

My son nodded.

"Well, he would know. Sam's pretty smart. Thanks for the apology. By the way . . ." I glanced over at Sam, ready to demonstrate my new, mature attitude. "You probably should call Sheila back. She sounded pretty desperate."

"Sheila's good at that," he said. "It won't hurt her to wait. Besides, I've got more important things to tend to. Who's staying for dinner?"

"We are!" Davey cried happily.

It sounded like a plan to me.

☙ Fourteen ☙

Faith's first day at Howard Academy caused a minor sensation. It was not the way I'd have chosen to make a first impression.

Bearing in mind what Russell had said about a trial period, I'd been determined to keep a low profile until Faith became an accepted part of the school backdrop. Unfortunately, there's no way to make a Standard Poodle in full show coat inconspicuous.

I parked, as usual, in the back lot. Faith, who was thrilled not to have been left behind that morning, couldn't wait to get out of the car and explore her new surroundings. Even though she's very obedient, I'd slipped a nylon collar over her head and fastened a six-foot leather leash to it. It was a good thing I had.

Two teachers, arriving the same time as we did, merely stared. The kids we encountered inside the school weren't so restrained. They fell upon Faith with shouts that were equal parts glee and derision. It wasn't hard to understand why. Even though I'd been showing Poodles for two years, I didn't have any trouble remembering my own first impression of the continental trim.

In response to their rapid-fire questions, I

related the historic origins of Faith's clip, and explained why she was wearing so many banded topknots on her head and how the plastic wraps at the ends of her ear leathers protected the hair they held within. I also invited them to touch at will; assured them she was very friendly, and, on Faith's behalf, refused all offers of tidbits from their backpacks.

Finally we made it to our classroom. Faith spent the first five minutes casing the place. She sniffed in the corners, explored the supplies closet, and pressed her nose against the windows. Finally, satisfied with her new abode, she chose a spot beneath my desk and lay down, resting her head on top of her paws.

"Don't worry," I told her. "Things will get better once you stop being such a novelty."

Faith wagged her tail and rolled over on her side, in case I wanted to take the opportunity to scratch her stomach. Considering all the attention she'd had in the last fifteen minutes, I suspected she was pretty pleased with things the way they were. If I wasn't careful, I was going to end up with one very spoiled Standard Poodle.

I'd come in a little early to get Faith settled, so I had some time before my first session. Though I'd taken Ruth's diary with me the day before, I'd never had a chance to get back to it. Now I pulled it out and began to read.

Ruth wasn't a skilled diarist; she seemed to

make entries when she felt like it and let her writing lapse for days at a time when she had other things to do. Her grammar wasn't always perfect, and her prose tended toward teenage hyperbole, but despite all that, her story was compelling. Ruth's words made the era in which she'd lived come alive.

Skimming on ahead and checking the dates at the tops of the pages, I saw that the diary spanned not one year, but nearly two. Ruth was sixteen when it began and seventeen when it ended, rather abruptly, leaving a sheaf of empty pages at the back of the book.

By the time Ruth began keeping the journal, she, as baby of the family, was the only one of Joshua's children still living at home. After the hopeful beginning of the slender volume, Ruth's subsequent entries echoed with loneliness. Her mother had died two years earlier; her father was busy tending to his fortune. Honoria, who also lived in the Howard mansion in Deer Park, was concentrating all her efforts toward making Howard Academy a success. Reading between the lines, I surmised that Ruth's most consistent companion had been the Poodle, Poupee.

Ruth spent much of the early pages of the diary reminiscing about her younger childhood years, when her mother had been alive and the house had been filled with games and laughter. She'd particularly enjoyed playing treasure hunt, a game instigated by her mother to entertain the six siblings on rainy afternoons. Play consisted of Mabel Howard hiding valuable objects in unlikely places, then issuing subtle clues to their whereabouts. The children had competed fiercely to solve their mother's puzzles

Ruth did such a good job of taking me back in time that I was still immersed in her prose when the door to my classroom opened and Willie Boyd came sauntering in. Immediately, Faith leapt to her feet. Having accepted the classroom as my space, she now felt honor-bound to defend it.

"Whoa!" Willie stopped where he stood. "What is that thing? A bear?"

"No, it's a Standard Poodle named Faith. She's going to be coming to school with me from now on."

Willie snorted his disbelief. "That ain't no dog."

His grammar earned him a hard stare.

"Sorry." The boy grinned. He had a great smile and he knew it. "Are you sure that's a Poodle? My aunt had a Poodle, and it didn't look like that. That's Fifi on steroids."

"Poodles come in three different sizes," I explained. "Your aunt's was probably one of the smaller ones. Faith is the biggest size."

"You got that right." Willie set his books down on the table and extended a hand to Faith. She reached out and sniffed his fingers politely.

"What's she here for, anyway? Some sort of guard dog?"

"Guard dog?"

"You know, because of what happened to Krebbs."

His response took me by surprise, and I quickly moved to correct him. "No, she's actually here to try out for a part in the spring pageant."

"Go on."

"It's true. But since we're speaking of Krebbs, there's something I wanted to ask you about. There's a rumor going around that he might have been involved with drugs."

Immediately, Willie's smile faded. "You asking me that because I'm black?"

"No." I held his stare. "I'm asking you that because your background is a little different than some of the other kids who go to school here. Your exposure to real life has been broader. For starters, I got the impression you knew Brad Jameson the other day."

"Yeah," said Willie. "I know him. At least I know who he is. Brad's no friend of mine."

"I should hope not. Detective Shertz says he's trouble."

"He's mean. I don't have any reason to get in his way, and I don't."

"Does he sell drugs?"

Willie only shrugged, and I decided not to press him on it.

"What about Krebbs?"

"He was old." Willie's tone was definite. As if that explained everything.

"Was he dealing on this campus?"

"Not that I knew of." He shrugged again, clearly uncomfortable with the topic. "It's not the kind of thing I would have needed to know, you understand?"

I understood. Willie was a good kid, and he had two strong, smart parents who were determined he was going to grow up to be somebody. I wished all my students were so lucky.

"Okay," I said. "Enough questions. Take a seat and let's get to work."

Last period before lunch, Sally Minor dropped by to see Faith. Her face lit up at the sight of the Poodle. She dropped to her knees and called Faith to her. "Hello, gorgeous. Aren't you a pretty girl?"

"That's just what she needs, more spoiling."

Sally rocked back on her heels. "Dogs are like kids. You can never give them too much attention."

"You'll have to meet my Aunt Peg sometime. The two of you would get along famously. I was just about to take Faith outside for a walk. Do you want to come?"

"I'd love to. Anything beats being cooped up inside all day. Let me just get a jacket." Sally ran back to her classroom and reappeared a minute later. The hall was relatively empty, and we were able to slip out without causing a fuss.

"Listen," Sally said when we were outside. "I want to apologize for the way I behaved yesterday at lunch."

Taking Faith to the edge of the parking lot, I paused as she sniffed a likely spot. "You don't have anything to apologize for."

"Yes, I do. I was pretty rude. I just didn't feel up to talking about Krebbs."

"There's no reason you should have to."

"No, but I can't seem to get it out of my mind. I know you've been talking to the police. What do they think happened?"

"I'm not really sure. Right now, they're investigating the possibility that Krebbs might have been selling drugs on campus."

"Drugs?" Sally scowled. "That's absurd. Why on earth would he have wanted to do something like that?"

"Probably for the same reason anyone does, to make money."

"Krebbs didn't need money. He was an old man who had a place to live and a guaranteed source of income for as long as he wanted it."

"Maybe he didn't want to work anymore," I said, playing devil's advocate. "You're right, he was an old man. Maybe he wanted to retire but he couldn't afford to—"

181

"No." Sally was shaking her head vehemently. "That's not the way it was at all."

I looked away, pretending to be distracted by Faith's wanderings. "You sound pretty sure of yourself."

"I am. There's no way Krebbs would have gotten involved in anything as sordid as drug dealing. Besides, he loved this place. He'd made it his whole life. He would never have done anything to harm the school. Somebody's trying to set him up."

"Set him up for what?" I asked. "He's dead."

Angrily, Sally strode on ahead. I waited a minute, then followed, with Faith trotting obligingly alongside. "I guess you knew Krebbs better than most people," I said when we'd caught up.

Though the sun was shining, the wind was still cool. Sally had her head down and her arms wrapped tightly around herself. She didn't look cold, though; she looked upset.

"What's that supposed to mean?" she demanded.

"You're the first person I've heard stick up for him. And the only one who seems to know how he felt. I guess maybe since you've been here longer than the rest of us . . ."

"That had nothing to do with it," Sally said flatly. She was walking quickly now and Faith and I had to hurry to keep up. "I knew Eugene

182

Krebbs before I ever came to Howard Academy. At least I knew who he was. Krebbs was my father's cousin."

Abruptly I stopped walking. Faith hit the end of the six-foot lead and turned to look at me reproachfully. The dog was leash-broken; it was the owner who needed to mind her footwork.

"You were related to Krebbs?" I asked. "I had no idea."

Frowning, Sally circled back. "Nobody does. It's not as if I wanted to advertise the fact that I was related to the school's caretaker. My father came from what you might call humble beginnings, but he worked hard to ensure that his children could make something of themselves, and we did.

"I got my master's at Columbia. I doubt that Krebbs even finished high school. I'll never understand why anyone would be content to push a broom for a living, but apparently he was."

"Did the fact that he was working at Howard Academy have anything to do with your getting a position here?"

"Only peripherally. It's not as if he pulled strings or anything." Her tone was contemptuous. "It's not as if he had any strings to pull. And you'd better believe that once I was here I made it perfectly clear that nobody needed to know a thing about our connection."

"Did Krebbs mind that?"

"It wasn't up to him to mind or not mind. It was the way things were going to be. I had no desire to have the rest of the faculty snickering behind my back."

How close to the truth was Sally's assessment? I wondered. Howard Academy certainly had its share of snobs among the faculty and the student body alike. I could see how she might feel that having the relationship come to light might diminish her stature.

"Nevertheless," said Sally, "this whole drug idea is nuts. Krebbs was complacent and not too bright. He was satisfied with his station; he would never have done anything to jeopardize it."

"Have you told any of this to Detective Shertz?"

"Of course not. There wasn't any point in it. Besides, as soon as the police realize there's nothing to this drug theory of theirs, they'll move on. There's no need for me to get involved."

As we talked, we'd started walking again, and now we'd circled the entire parking lot and come to the back door. Faith tugged on the leash, ready to go around again, but Sally reached for the handle and pulled the door open.

"I'd appreciate it if you didn't repeat what I told you," she said, pausing on the step. "Now, more than ever, there's no way I want my name and reputation to be linked to Krebbs."

Before I could answer, she hurried through the door and let it shut between us.

❧ Fifteen ❧

By midafternoon, my classroom had begun to feel like Grand Central Station. Every teacher or student who could come up with an excuse to stop by and check out Faith, had done so. Even Ed Weinstein, whom I'd judged to be devoid of any kindness whatsoever, managed to smuggle her a small piece of steak from lunch.

"Will she bite me if I feed it to her?" he asked.

I almost laughed, but caught myself in time. I'd turned down all other offers of goodies because I didn't want my dog to think such treatment was the norm, but Ed's largesse was so unexpected I decided to let Faith go ahead and enjoy.

"Don't worry, your fingers are perfectly safe," I assured him.

He watched as she chewed daintily on the morsel. "I hate to say it but Michael was right. She does look like the dog in the painting. Is that guy Mr. Lucky, or what?"

Actually, I was the one who was feeling pretty lucky about the way things had turned out. Michael might have instigated the process, but I couldn't see how he benefited from it. That fact hadn't registered with Ed, however.

"You and Michael don't get along very well, do you?"

"We get along fine, if you don't count the fact a guy with no seniority and iffy credentials, comes waltzing in here to teach drama, of all things, and ends up pulling down almost the same salary as I'm making. Other than that, we probably don't have much to disagree about at all."

"I thought the remuneration packages were private."

"That's what they want you to think. But after you've been here a while, you'll see. There's a way to get around everything at Howard Academy. You just have to know the ropes."

"And you do?"

"Do I ever." Ed's face creased in an oily grin. "Anytime you want me to clue you in, just let me know. We could work on it after hours, if you know what I mean."

I knew all right. Obviously I'd moved too fast in crediting him with kindness, or any appealing qualities at all. I walked over and opened my door. Looking not the slightest bit offended, Ed took the hint and left.

I'd barely gone back to my desk and sat down before my next visitor arrived.

"That guy looked like a creep," said Jane.

"He is, but don't let it worry you. He's a teacher, and since you don't do things like school, it's unlikely you'll run into him."

Jane pursed her lips. "If you're going to be rude, I'll leave."

"That's up to you."

I was growing tired of this game we were playing, where she held all the cards and I had no control over the outcome. I wasn't going to chase Jane anymore. Now it was her turn to make some concessions.

"Don't you even care why I'm here?"

"If you want to tell me, I'm sure you will." As I scooted my chair forward, I accidently knocked into Faith, who leapt to her feet. The Poodle had long since passed the point of needing to check out each new visitor. Now, after the long and busy day she'd had, Faith was simply hoping to catch a nap beneath my desk.

Jane's eyes immediately lit up. "Hey, cool!" she cried. "Where did he come from?"

"Faith's a she, not a he, and she's mine."

"Can I pet her?" Jane hung back a step, the first moment of shyness I'd ever seen her exhibit. It was almost as if the prospect was so enticing, she was half-afraid I'd snatch it away.

"Sure, go ahead. I think she'd like that."

Tentatively, Jane extended her hand. Faith stood perfectly still as the girl patted her head, then her neck. Dogs prefer a firm touch, even when the intent is friendly, but seeming to sense Jane's hesitation, Faith held her ground.

"I always wanted a dog," she said softly.

"Me too. My mother wouldn't let us get one when I was little."

"Mine wouldn't either. She said we had no place to keep it."

I remembered what Detective Shertz had said about Jane and her mother living on the street and felt a pang. No wonder Jane kept running away. There'd been so little stability in her life, she probably had no idea how to respond to someone who was trying to help.

"My aunt has a whole bunch of dogs," I said impulsively. "They're all Faith's relatives. Maybe you'd like to come with me sometime and see them?"

Jane's eyes widened, and her mouth formed a small circle. "Could I?"

"Sure, as long as it's okay with your grand-mother."

In the space of an instant, her expression changed. The joy drained away, and resignation took its place. "Gran won't let me. She never lets me do anything."

"We could ask her."

"Yeah, sure." Jane didn't sound hopeful.

"Detective Shertz talked to her, you know. He's concerned about you, too. He thinks Brad isn't the greatest person for you to be hanging around with."

"Brad's all right. Everybody thinks he's bad news just because he's been in some trouble, but most of it wasn't his fault."

"No?" I said skeptically. "Just like I suppose

it's not your fault you've been cutting school?"

Abruptly Jane stood. "I thought you understood. I thought you wanted to be my friend."

"I *do* want to be your friend. That's why I'm worried about you. I know you've gone through some tough times—"

"You don't know anything about it!"

"You're right, I don't. But I'd like for you to tell me. I also think you should talk to a friend of mine about what happened on Monday. Her name is Mary Ellen and she's the school's counselor. She's also a licensed therapist—"

Jane started backing toward the door. "A therapist? So now you think I'm crazy?"

"Not at all," I said, giving myself a mental kick. I was losing her again. "But I know that you went through a terrible experience. Trust me, talking to someone about it will make you feel much better."

"I did talk to someone. I talked to you and Brad and Detective Shertz. And all it did was land me in a big, fat mess."

She slammed the door behind her on the way out. Faith's ears flattened to her head at the noise. Belatedly, I realized Jane never had told me the reason for her visit. I hoped it wasn't something important.

When the last bell finally rang, Faith and I were more than ready to make our escape. Being the center of so much attention had been tiring for both of us. Hopefully the excitement would die down soon and people would start to take her presence for granted.

I waited a few minutes until the halls were mostly empty and the congestion in the parking lot had cleared. That way I could take Faith outside unleashed and let her enjoy a few minutes of freedom before putting her in the car. I'd just thrown my stuff in the Volvo and was turning to call her when Russell Hanover came walking out the back door to the school.

"I'm glad I caught you," he said.

Faith was in the field beside the parking lot chasing a squirrel. She treed the animal, then circled around the trunk and doubled back, checking to see if I'd noticed her accomplishment. Russell certainly had. Though he'd seen the portrait of Honoria's Poodle, Poupee, he seemed startled by the sight of her. To his credit, he recovered quickly.

"That must be Faith," he said. "She's quite large, isn't she?"

This wasn't the way I'd pictured their first meeting taking place. Arm down, hand dangling next to my thigh, I snapped my fingers insistently. Faith caught my cue and came running. She slid to a stop beside me, tail wagging.

"She's a little bigger than Poupee," I admitted. Was it my fault he'd gone for the stereotype and assumed that a Poodle would be small? "Poodles come in three sizes. Faith is a Standard Poodle."

"So I see. She seems quite obedient. You must spend a lot of time training her."

Because of the dictates of her show coat, I probably spent more time brushing her, but I didn't see any need to admit that. "I do. Faith is a show dog. She's well on her way to completing her championship, and she won her first major last week."

"Congratulations, she sounds very accomplished." Like most people, Russell looked like he hadn't a clue when it came to dog shows. "And did she enjoy her first day of school?"

"Very much so." I reached down and ruffled the hair behind Faith's ears. She leaned into the caress. "It's really a treat for her not to have to stay home by herself."

"Hopefully it will be a treat for us to have her here as well. So far, I've heard nothing but good things. As long as that continues, we'll be delighted to have her as part of our family."

"Great." Apparently we'd cleared the first hurdle. "You said you were looking for me?"

Russell nodded. "I believe I mentioned we'd be holding a small memorial service for Eugene Krebbs in the chapel this weekend? It will be Saturday morning at eleven o'clock. Attendance isn't mandatory by any means, but I'd like everyone to know that they're welcome if they wish to come.

"Krebbs was an institution at Howard Academy for many years and as he has no other family, I think it only fitting that we organize a tribute to his long life and dedicated service. If you will let Harriet know of your plans by tomorrow afternoon, we'd like to get an idea of the numbers."

"I'll do that," I said. "Have you spoken to Detective Shertz? How is the investigation coming?"

"Well enough, I suppose." Russell looked pained. "Unfortunately, the police don't feel any compunction to keep me informed."

"Did they find what they were looking for in the cottage?"

"You mean drugs? Yes, I'm afraid so. I'm told there was nearly half a pound of marijuana tucked away in a hiding place behind the tractor."

"So Krebbs was dealing?"

"That's one possibility. It's equally possible that the drugs could have belonged to a member of the work crew, all of whom have access to the cottage. There's no way of knowing whether the stash was the cause of Krebbs's murder, or whether its presence there was entirely unrelated. The detective is of the opinion that Krebbs may have interrupted a burglary and suffered the consequences."

"But the drugs were still there," I said. "If

that's what the murderer was after, why did he leave them behind?"

"Maybe he couldn't find them," Russell speculated. "Maybe he heard someone coming and ran out of time."

I glanced in the direction of the dilapidated building. "There's something else the police should consider. The work crew aren't the only ones with access to that shed. Just about anyone could stop in there during the day without someone noticing. Until Krebbs was killed there, it probably made a dandy hiding place."

"You're probably right." Russell sighed. His gaze drifted upward into the trees above us. "I was a teenager in the sixties so I'm not what you would call uninformed on the subject. And yet this is something I would never have suspected. That a member of our own staff, much less a man who's been with the school for nearly half a century, would be a party to this base sort of behavior. Is it possible that I'm that out of touch? And if so, am I truly fit to serve as headmaster of this school?"

I sincerely hoped the question was rhetorical as I had no intention of answering it. Instead, I waited a minute, then changed the subject. "Do you know if Krebbs left a will?"

"He certainly did. The police found one among his papers, and it matched a copy that was on file at a law office downtown. When it came to money, Krebbs was surprisingly organized. And rather well invested, as it turns out. According to his attorney, the estate is worth in excess of a quarter of a million dollars."

"You're joking!"

Russell gave me a disapproving look. I deserved it. He wasn't the type of man to joke around, and I should have known it.

"It's possible he saved that much through a lifetime of diligence," Russell continued. "Unfortunately, it's equally possible that the money is the result of ill-gotten gains. At the moment, nobody seems to know which is the case."

He seemed pretty well informed for a man who claimed not to be getting updates from the police, I thought. As we spoke, Faith had begun to fidget at my side. Since Russell didn't seem to be paying any attention to her, I lifted my hand and let her run back into the field.

"How did you find out about it?" I asked.

"The school was contacted yesterday. Apparently our former caretaker has left us a sizable bequest. Half his assets are to come to Howard Academy, earmarked for the refurbishment of the computer lab."

"That's wonderful," I said, knowing how badly the job needed to be done. The school's computers, state-of-the-art a dozen years earlier, were now woefully out of date. Our students, many of whom carried far superior laptops in their backpacks, had been heard to refer to the school machines as prehistoric.

I knew Russell had plans to mount a fund-raising campaign with that end in mind. He should have been thrilled. Instead, he looked anything but.

"What's the matter?"

"I should think that would be obvious. It will be damaging enough if it turns out that Krebbs was promoting the use of drugs on our campus. How much worse is it going to look if we appear to be profiting from his illegal activities? That money would be a godsend, and I'd be the first to admit how much we need it. But under the circumstances, I'm not sure there's any way we can accept it."

He had a point. Big time.

"You said half the estate comes to the school. What about the rest of the money? Who does that go to?"

Russell waved a hand dismissively. "Some woman who's a distant relation. Sarah Fingerhut, I think the name was. She must be very distant because I'd never heard Krebbs speak of her. There was a catch with that bequest though. The woman has to come forward and claim the money publicly. If she doesn't do so, she loses the inheritance and those assets come to the school as well."

Sarah? I thought. Sally? It wasn't impossible.

Sally had refused to acknowledge Krebbs when he was alive, and he'd abided by her wishes. Now, maybe, he was having the last laugh.

I wondered if she knew about the terms of Krebbs's will. Or the size of his estate. If there's one thing I've learned, it's that money, especially that kind of money, can act as a great motivator.

"Has the lawyer gotten in touch with the woman yet?" I asked.

"I have no idea. I'm afraid I have enough problems of my own right at the moment without worrying about something like that."

Faith circled back and I opened the door to the Volvo. Without breaking stride, she leapt onto the backseat and sat down. Her long pink tongue lolled out of her mouth as she panted happily and waited for me to join her.

"It's nice having a dog around the place again," Russell said absently. "It will be nicer still when things finally start getting back to normal." With a nod in my direction, he turned and headed back into the school.

As I drove home, I thought about our conversation. I'd heard it said that the first rule of a murder investigation was to follow the money. In this case, I wasn't sure where that path led.

The murder victim had left each of two beneficiaries a sizable bequest; and in each case, the money seemed likely to cause more problems than it solved. Kind of like the job Krebbs had done as caretaker.

But luckily, I decided, none of that was my problem. All I had to do was stand by and watch Detective Shertz do his job.

It was a nice thought while it lasted.

🐾 Sixteen 🐾

That night, after Davey went to bed, I pulled out Ruth's diary. Outside, rain was pouring down in sheets; but inside, my house felt warm and cozy. It was the perfect night to heat some hot chocolate and settle in with a good book. I curled up on the couch with Faith draped across the cushion beside me, her head resting on my lap, and began to read.

When I'd first found the leather-bound book, I'd had high hopes that it might provide insights around which we could construct a plot for the spring pageant. But now, as I delved further into the diary's pages, it became clear that I was going to have to lower my expectations. Entertaining as Ruth's writing was, the entries were obviously the musings of a sheltered, sixteen-year-old girl.

For every glimpse she provided of her family's life, or the happenings in Depression-era Greenwich, there were pages of fanciful, romantic daydreams, most of them centering around a darkly handsome, eighteen-year-old boy from Byram. His name was Jay Silverman; and he'd appeared at her house one summer afternoon as part of a masonry crew hired to replace a crumbling length of stone wall.

For the first two days, Ruth had merely watched him from her bedroom window. By the third, she'd grown bold enough to mix a pitcher of lemonade and take it outside to the sweaty workers. *He hardly even noticed me,* she wrote in a tone of semidespair. *But he did seem to enjoy the lemonade. He drank the whole glass (which I have brought back to my room, unwashed!) Oooh but he has the sweetest smile . . .*

Oooh to be sixteen and that innocent, I thought, smiling myself. I pictured Ruth pining from her second-story window while Jay toiled, oblivious, below. Maybe we could work the pageant into a variation of "Rapunzel." Or perhaps *Romeo and Juliet.* I wondered if this romance had a happier ending.

Skimming quickly ahead, I found that things seemed to be heading in that direction. Before the wall was completed, Ruth had succeeded in catching Jay's eye. After his crew moved on to other jobs in the neighborhood, they continued to see each other. Certain of their disapproval, Ruth hid their meetings from her father and aunt. Rather than detracting from the relationship, however, the subterfuge only seemed to add to her enjoyment.

Ruth was in the midst of describing their date at a boisterous holiday parade; she and Jay holding hands to race the block between Mason

Street and Greenwich Avenue so they could view the marchers twice, when the phone rang. Reluctantly, I pushed Faith aside and went to answer it.

"It's high time you did something," said Aunt Peg.

Wrenching my thoughts back to the present was hard enough. Figuring out what she was referring to, was impossible. "About what?"

"Sheila Vaughn, that's what. Or more correctly, who."

I sighed. "What's the matter now?"

"The same thing that was the matter the last time we spoke," Peg said crisply. "Honestly, Melanie, I can't believe you're not taking this more seriously. That woman is after your fiancé. She as much as told me so, straight out."

"What would you like me to do?" I asked. "Stop by Sheila's house and threaten to run her out of town?"

"It would be better than doing nothing, which seems to be the alternative you've chosen."

Aunt Peg likes grand gestures and big drama. Since she'd ferreted out Sheila's motives earlier in the week, she'd probably been waiting to hear explosions coming from the direction of North Salem. Clearly she'd been disappointed.

"Sam and I talked that all out," I said. "Sheila may be interested in rekindling old flames, but he isn't. End of story."

"Fine time you picked to turn into an optimist. Sheila struck me as a rather determined woman. I hope you're not underestimating her."

So did I, but I kept the thought to myself. Trust me, it just made life easier.

"You worry too much," I said instead.

"And you don't worry enough." She paused for a moment, then added, "I guess that murder at your school must be keeping you pretty busy."

"Not at all." I carried the phone over to a kitchen chair and sat down. It was beginning to look as though I might be there a while. "It has nothing to do with me."

"Don't be silly. It happened practically right in front of you. And now you have a ringside seat. Go ahead and tell me everything."

Aunt Peg could argue the spots off a Dalmatian. When she makes a request, it's usually easier just to acquiesce. I spent the next ten minutes telling her all about Jane and her protector, Brad; Krebbs and his alleged involvement with drugs; and Sally, the long-lost relative who might or might not claim her inheritance.

"So who did it?" she asked at the end.

"I have no idea."

"What kind of answer is that?" Peg sniffed. "I'm surprised Detective Shertz hasn't been coming to you for insights. After all, you've done a fair amount of detecting yourself."

"Why should he? He seems to be handling things just fine. I'm sure he'll have Krebbs's killer locked up in no time." I didn't actually believe that, but it seemed like a wise idea to project all the confidence I could muster before Peg got the notion to call the police station and volunteer my services. "Right now the only problem I have to worry about is the spring pageant—"

"Oh please. If you want me to hang up, Melanie, kindly just say so. Don't try to bore me to death."

"I wasn't—"

"Yes, I know dear. Listen, there's something else I need you to do. It's the reason I called, actually."

Uh-oh. Usually Aunt Peg blurts out her requests up front. The fact that she'd hesitated before presenting this one couldn't possibly be a good sign.

"I've invited Sheila over for lunch on Saturday at one o'clock. You'll come, too, won't you?"

"Aunt Peg, what are you up to?"

"Me? Nothing. I'm just trying to be neighborly. Besides, it seems only prudent that you should meet the woman who's trying to make off with your fiancé."

I told her I'd be there. Put like that, how could I refuse?

• • •

The conversation I'd had with Aunt Peg left me so distracted that I never did go back to Ruth's diary. Instead, I spent the rest of the night worrying about my impending meeting with Sam's ex-wife. Sam's and Aunt Peg's reactions to Sheila Vaughn's appearance on the East Coast lay at opposite ends of the emotional spectrum. Trying my best to view the situation impartially, I suspected the truth lay somewhere in the middle.

Sam was a great catch. I wouldn't have been at all surprised to discover that Sheila regretted letting him go. Perhaps she had come to New York to find out if he'd be interested in renewing their relationship. That still didn't mean I was ready to label the woman a predator.

Presumably, Sam had told Sheila he wasn't interested. Presumably she'd taken him at his word. But none of that explained how the woman had suddenly become such a pervasive presence in our lives. Every time I turned around, her name came up again.

Aunt Peg was probably right, I decided. It was time to face the problem head on.

With thoughts like that turning cartwheels in my brain it was no wonder I left Ruth's diary sitting in the living room when Faith and I went dashing off to school the next morning. Though we'd been up and ready to go in plenty of time, Davey's school bus was late, leaving the three of us waiting at the curb for ten toe-tapping minutes. Sometimes it's the little things that make you want to tear your hair out.

For the first several hours, it looked as though Faith's second day at Howard Academy was going to mirror her first. Everyone who hadn't already stopped by managed to fit a visit into his or her schedule. The fact that all the interruptions played havoc with my schedule didn't seem to occur to any of them.

When third period ended at ten-forty-five, I sent Wendy on her way and whistled Faith to her feet. My next student wasn't due until eleven-thirty, and both Faith and I could use a break. The rain had ended overnight, and the weather outside was crisp. I grabbed my coat, and we headed outside.

Early spring in Connecticut is nothing to cheer about. It's a season that offers unpredictable temperatures and a preponderance of mud. On the plus side, however, winter's almost over. For a nonskier like me, that's cause enough for celebration.

Faith and I cut across the parking lot and headed down the hill toward the playing fields. As it happened, our route took us past the care-taker's cottage. All right, so we made a small detour. Under the circumstances, it was hard not to be curious.

As Faith ran on ahead, I paused beside the

tumbledown shed. A stream of yellow crime-scene tape had been strung across the doorway and a sturdy padlock held the door shut.

Though Russell had made it clear at morning assemblies that any sight-seeing was to be discouraged, I nevertheless found myself sidling over to one of the grimy windows to take a peek inside. Unfortunately, though I shaded my eyes and pressed my nose against the glass, it was too dark to make out anything more than an assorted jumble of shapes.

"See anything interesting?"

I let out a small shriek, jumped straight up in the air, and bumped my head on the window's upper ledge. Ed Weinstein seemed to enjoy the show because he was grinning when I whirled around to face him.

"Was that really necessary?" I demanded, rubbing my forehead.

"What? All I did was ask a question."

"And sneak up on me."

Ed held up a sneaker-clad foot. "It's not my fault that cross-trainers are quiet. So what's the school's most famous snoop up to? Sniffing out a killer?"

Subtle, Ed wasn't. He made an exaggerated sniffing sound to bludgeon home his point. Without thinking, I took a sniff, too. A sweetish, faintly familiar, smell hung in the air. Pipe tobacco?

"I brought Faith outside for a walk," I said, stepping away from the shed. "It's easier for her if I break the day up a bit. What about you? What are you doing out here?"

"What else? I came out for a smoke."

Ed didn't smoke a pipe. And according to Sally, he was just as likely to sneak his cigarettes in the boys' bathroom. If Russell and I hadn't just been discussing the subject, I probably wouldn't even have noticed. As it was, it still took a moment before memory clicked in.

When it did, I could scarcely believe it. Marijuana, that's what I smelled. Ed had ducked outside to smoke a joint.

"Rolling your own these days?" I asked.

"Hardly." His voice was firm, but his Adam's apple bobbed in his neck. Ed pulled a pack of Camels from his pocket and showed them to me. "I stick with store-bought, just like everyone else."

"It's a nasty habit."

"So the whole world tells me."

"Why don't you stop?"

Ed stared at me, clearly annoyed. "Did you ever smoke?"

"No."

"Then there's no way you can understand. I started when I was twelve. By the time I was old enough to know better, I was hooked."

"Lots of people have gotten unhooked."

"I will, too, eventually. In the meantime, you and everyone else can just butt out."

Ed seemed pleased with the cleverness of his pun. I left him to his self-satisfaction, called Faith to me, and headed inside.

Interesting, I thought, that I'd run into Ed by the cottage. Had he been snooping around, too? I wondered if he knew about the stash of marijuana that had been found there. More to the point, had he known it was there before Krebbs was murdered? Maybe he was a customer. Maybe he had an idea about who Krebbs might have angered enough to want to kill him . . .

"Excuse me!"

I heard the shout, but I was so deep in thought that the warning didn't penetrate quickly enough. By the time I looked up, it was too late. I'd already gone barreling straight into what looked like a moving mountain of velvet curtains.

"Oomph." The curtains cushioned the impact, then slowly slid to the floor. Behind them stood Michael, now empty-handed.

"Sorry," I said weakly. "I wasn't looking where I was going."

"No harm done." He stooped down and began to gather the bundle which had separated and slithered in several directions. "They were on their way to the cleaner anyway."

When I'd stopped, Faith sat. Because animation is highly prized in the conformation ring, she hasn't been taught to heel. Even so, when we're walking together, she understands the idea of keeping her handler within easy reach at all times. One of the curtains had rolled into a puddle at her feet. She sniffed the musty material curiously, then quickly withdrew, wrinkling her nose.

"That must be Faith," Michael said admiringly. "She's a beauty, much nicer looking than Poupee."

"Thank you." Faith and I preened together. "And thank you for suggesting that she take part in the pageant. I love being able to bring her to school with me. It's working out really well."

"I'm glad to hear that." Michael's brown eyes found mine and held them. The intensity he projected was more than a little unnerving.

I shifted my gaze away. Sometimes I babble when I'm uncomfortable. Now, next thing I knew, I was chattering like a demented parrot. "I'm still sorting through the archives. As a matter of fact, I'm on my way down there now. I've found something really interesting, actually. Do you know who Ruth Howard was, Joshua's youngest daughter?"

Michael nodded encouragingly.

"She kept a diary for about a year and a half starting when she was sixteen. I found it in one of the boxes, day before yesterday. It's fascinating reading. I'm hoping it will contain something we can use."

"Terrific." Michael's enthusiasm sounded a little forced. Now he was staring at my legs. As he reached out to pull a piece of heavy curtain toward him, the tips of his fingers grazed my calf. "I'd love to have a look at that myself."

A tiny shiver shot up my leg, surprising me, tantalizing me, filling me with chagrin. The only touch I was supposed to be tingling to was Sam's.

Hastily I stepped back, nearly tripping over Faith. Somehow I'd forgotten she was there.

"I'll get the diary to you as soon as I'm finished." It seemed like a good idea not to mention that I'd taken school property home and accidentally left it there. "As I said, I'm on my way down to the basement to do some more reading now."

Michael's eyes were dancing with amusement. His tone was smooth as the velvet he held in his hands. "Enjoy yourself."

"I will," I said primly, and hurried on my way.

This was Faith's first excursion to the Howard Academy basement. She bounded down the stairs ahead of me, as excited as a child on her way to an amusement park. She raced around the large room, darting behind pillars and snuffling into corners, her pom-ponned tail wagging in a wide arc over her back.

Two days earlier when I'd last visited the storeroom, I'd locked the door behind me on the way out. Now, though the room within was dark, the door was standing slightly ajar. "Hello?" I called, hesitating as I drew near.

No one answered.

I reached the doorway and angled my hand around inside, flipping the light switch before entering. My heart sank at the sight that greeted me.

The archive storeroom had never been neat; now it was totally trashed. Boxes were strewn around the room. Several had been dumped out on the table. Papers were piled on the wooden surface; more had spilled down onto the floor.

"Just great," I muttered. Obviously mine wasn't the only key Russell had handed out. Too bad he hadn't chosen the other recipients with more care.

Faith pricked her ears. Even when I'm talking to myself, she likes to listen in. I reached down and gave her an absent pat.

So much for my plans to do more reading. I'd hoped to be able to discover what had become of Ruth and her siblings. Instead it looked as though I'd be spending the time neatening up.

Even worse, as I quickly found out, the boxes I'd already gone through were now mixed in with the ones I had yet to open. And since they all looked alike from the outside, there was no way to tell which were which except by opening each one and rifling through it, before putting it back in the stack along the wall.

It was hot, dusty work, and the fact that Faith kept pacing back and forth across the small room did nothing to improve my mood. The first time she ran out into the larger area of the basement, I called her back. The second, I closed the door. Despite Russell's optimistic words the day before, we were still undergoing a trial period. I had no intention of letting the Poodle out of my sight.

"Lie down," I said firmly.

Faith whined under her breath.

"I know you're bored. We'll only be here a few more minutes. Go to sleep."

My Poodle didn't look sleepy in the slightest. Nor did she lie down. In deference to my wishes, she did deign to sit, but her gaze was still focused intently on the door.

"What'd you see out there?" I asked, as I struggled to lift a heavy carton back on top of the stack. "A mouse? I hope it wasn't a bat."

Faith got up and trotted back to the door. Her whine was louder this time, and she scratched at the wooden panel with a front paw.

"Oh, all right." I nudged the box into place. The room wasn't in great shape, but at least I'd managed to create a semblance of order.

"You win; we'll go back upstairs. I've got to get cleaned up before next period anyway."

I dusted off my hands and walked over to the door. As I drew near, Faith's agitation increased. She gave a sharp bark to urge me on.

"What?" I said. "I'm coming."

Too bad Faith couldn't answer that question, because if I'd paid attention to her sooner we'd have been a lot better off.

As it was, the first inkling I had that something was wrong came when I opened the door and a searing wall of heat slammed into the room. Thick, dark smoke billowed after it. Orange spears of flame danced on the wall outside.

The basement was on fire.

❦ Seventeen ❦

"Oh, God."

Opening my mouth, even to pray, was a big mistake. I took in a lungful of smoke and fell back, gasping. Luckily, instinct kicked in. I grabbed my dog and pulled her back, then slammed the door shut.

Faith's barking was loud and insistent, and the sound seemed to bounce off the walls in the small enclosed space. A moment later, that noise was joined by another, more welcome one. The fire alarm went off, its siren wailing a warning in the hallway above us.

Any minute now, students and teachers would begin filing out of the building. The faculty would know this wasn't a drill, but I doubted anyone would miss me. I could only hope the firefighters would arrive quickly and that the smoke would be copious enough to lead them to the site of the blaze.

What little air the room held was quickly becoming stifling. Since most of the space was underground, there was only one small window, tucked in just below the ceiling. The glass was grimy from years of neglect, and the hinges were old and rusted. Quickly, I dragged the chair over to the wall and climbed up to have a closer look.

Originally the casement window had been meant to open from the top. I grasped the handle and tried to turn it. It wouldn't budge. I gritted my teeth and tried again. Still nothing.

I glanced back at the door. Smoke was seeping in around all four sides. No matter how quickly the firemen arrived, it might not be soon enough. Our only chance was to break the window and hope that we could wriggle out.

I hopped down off the chair and led Faith to the other side of the room. "Stay!"

My Poodle understands about a dozen basic commands. In a normal situation, she'd have done what I asked. Now, however, Faith knew that something was terribly wrong. Her first impulse was to keep as close to me as possible.

She pushed her nose into my hand and followed me back across the room, her shoulder crowding against my leg. What she didn't understand was that when I broke the window, glass was going to go flying. It was bad enough I had to stand within range, but there was no point in both of us getting hurt.

I hurried back to the table and swept my arm across the surface, sending papers flying. Like all show Poodles, Faith has been table-trained for her own safety and security. Even though it's only a short hop to the ground, she knows it's an unbreakable rule not to budge once she's been left. This wasn't the rubber-matted grooming table she was used to, but I hoped she would make the connection.

"Up," I said, patting the wooden top.

Faith hesitated, then jumped up and placed her front paws on the table's edge. I reached around behind and lifted her hindquarter. "Down!"

She gave me a reproachful look, and I could read the concern in her eyes. Faith thought I was going to leave her behind. My heart wrenched, but I didn't have time to argue.

"Down!" I repeated, pulling her front paws toward me. Though I could feel her resistance, she sank down slowly onto the table. "Stay!"

Faith whined under her breath, but she didn't move when I walked back to the wall. Quickly I yanked my sweater off over my head and wrapped it around my fisted hand. It didn't look like it would offer much protection.

Ignoring that thought, I climbed back up on the chair's smooth seat. The legs were uneven and it wobbled beneath me as I took aim at the window. Turning my face away, I shielded my eyes with my left hand and let fly with my right.

A hot knife of pain shot up through my elbow and into my shoulder. My fist felt like it had connected with a brick wall. Opening my eyes, I saw that the window was still in one piece.

I'd managed to crack it, though. A network of tiny lines emanated out from the site where my fist had landed. Faith was on her feet now, barking again. The smoke in the room was growing thicker. I drew back my arm, gritted my teeth, and punched at the window again.

This time, my battered knuckles met only brief resistance, then plowed on through. It still hurt like hell. I heard a ripping sound as the sweater shredded on a jagged edge and felt the same sharp shard dig into my wrist.

Most of the glass scattered outward but some came raining back into the room. I felt the pieces bounce off my shoulders and sprinkle through my hair. A welcome rush of cool air accompanied them.

Hurriedly I pulled the sweater off my hand, then rewound it. Blood was flowing freely underneath, and the scratchy wool stuck to the site of the cut. Worrying about that was a luxury I didn't have time for.

I turned my face away again and used my repadded hand to beat around the edges of the hole, enlarging it out to the frame. As the glass gave way, I heard the glorious sound of sirens, growing steadily nearer.

Standing on the chair, I could just barely see out the window. I knew the fire drill procedure. It would have sent the majority of the building's inhabitants out the back toward the parking lot.

By my estimation, this small window was on

the side of the mansion, nearer to the administrative offices than the classrooms. A row of bushes ran along this wall, so the window was at least partially hidden. The lawn beyond was probably empty as faculty and students gathered in the designated areas to count noses.

No doubt about it, this wasn't my lucky day. I could only hope that someone would hear my shouts before the approaching sirens drowned them out. I stood up on my toes, lifted my mouth toward the opening, and screamed as loudly as I could.

"What the hell!"

The voice came from just outside and sounded just as startled as I was. "I need help. Who's there?"

"Yo! Where the hell are you? I don't see nobody."

I tried to place the voice, but couldn't. It didn't matter. Whoever he was, he sounded like an angel to me.

"Look behind the bushes, there's a window. The basement is on fire, and I'm trapped down here."

"Hot damn," he said, and I heard the bushes rustle. "Where are you?"

"The window with all the broken glass around it. Watch your step." Once a mother, always a mother. "The fire's right outside this room. I've got to get out of here."

"Lady, you aren't going to fit through that window." There was a pause, then the face of the speaker loomed in the opening above me. It was Jane's friend, Brad.

"Do I look like I have a choice?" I demanded. "If you can't pull me out, then go get someone who can."

"I'm going." The face pulled back. "Stay right there."

Not a deep thinker, that boy.

He was only gone for a minute or two, but it felt like an eternity. The temperature in the room was rising. I felt it even more keenly when I hopped down off the chair and went to get Faith. With the draw from the window, the room was filling even faster with thick, dark smoke. My lungs burned as I drew it in.

The Poodle's frantic barks had quieted. Her tail was down and her ears pressed tight against her head. Her eyes were watering; so were mine. I scratched beneath her chin for reassurance, but she didn't look convinced.

Adrenaline pumping through me, I managed to drag the heavy table over beside the wall. It was taller than the chair. When I climbed up to stand on top, the window was at shoulder height. The clear blue sky looked wonderful, the earth below it, empty. Where was everyone?

I got Faith up beside me then started yelling again. I prayed Brad had gone for help, but the fact that he'd run away wasn't entirely reassuring. For all I knew, he could be halfway to downtown Greenwich.

After a moment, I heard voices. One was raised in anger. "I'm telling you there's someone down there," Brad was saying. "She says she's stuck."

"Hello?" I rasped. My voice was growing hoarse. "We need help."

"I told you so!" The teenage anthem, delivered at full decibel.

"Ms. Travis? Is that you? Where are you?"

Thank you, God. It was Russell Hanover. The troops had arrived. And none too soon either.

"I'm in the basement. There's a window in the foundation wall behind the bushes. Faith and I are trapped in the storeroom. The fire's right outside the door. I think this is where it started. You've got to get the firemen down here."

"Yes, yes. I'll do that." The bushes shoved aside as he spoke. Russell squatted down and peered in the window.

Ed Weinstein loomed just behind him. His hand was clasped around Brad's arm, and there was nothing friendly in the gesture. Off to the rear, Harriet was hurrying away, presumably to alert the firemen.

"My God!" Russell cried, seeing the smoke. It was as close to profanity as I'd ever heard him come. "We've got to get you out of there."

"Good idea," I agreed. "Faith's here, too. She has to go first. If I can lift her up, will you pull her through the window?"

Russell looked at the opening dubiously. "Will she fit?"

"She's a dog, for Pete's sake." Ed elbowed some branches aside and knelt down on the soft turf outside the window. "Don't worry about her. Melanie, give me your hands and I'll pull you out."

"Not a chance." I drew back from the opening. "Faith comes first. Without me here there's no way she can reach the window."

Ed scowled. Russell frowned. "Now, Melanie," he said in the soothing tone one might use to address an idiot, "this may not be the time—"

"Damn it, it's the only time! This room is filling up with smoke, and there's a fire burning just on the other side of a very flimsy door. If you can't help me, clear out of the way and let me call for someone who will."

Later it would occur to me that yelling at my boss was no way to foster job security. Now, however, my fit of temper had the desired effect.

"Of course Ed and I will help you," Russell said, moving into position. "Tell us what you want us to do."

"Not me." Ed backed away. "I'm not getting myself bitten by some stupid dog."

"Men!" The epithet was heartfelt. A pump-clad foot applied itself to Ed's butt, and abruptly he went tumbling away. "Melanie? It's Rita Kinney. What do you need?"

Her face appeared in the opening, looking pale, but determined. Ed might be stronger, but I'd take Rita's conviction any day.

"Help Russell pull Faith out through the window."

"You got it."

Faith came up into my arms compliantly, but when I lifted her toward the opening she began to struggle. It would have been hard enough raising forty-five pounds of deadweight to shoulder height; her wiggling made the task almost impossible.

"Shhh," I crooned. "It's all right. You're a good girl. You go first, and I'll be right behind you."

Faith didn't look happy, but she seemed to understand what I needed her to do. Thank God she was a Poodle and could reason things through. Her paws scrambled for purchase on the sill. Her head ducked down and through the opening. Her neck and shoulders followed.

Despite Russell's doubts, Faith's body wasn't too big to fit through the window. It was her luxurious coat of mane hair that made her appear so much larger than she was. As I braced against her hindquarter to push with my shoulder, Faith cried out sharply.

She was stuck. A piece of glass, caught in the sash, had snagged in her neck hair and held her fast. By that time, Russell had grasped Faith's front legs. Rita moved in to loop an arm around the Poodle's neck.

"Just pull it free," I said tersely. A mane coat that had taken nearly two years to grow was about to be ruined. "We don't have time to worry about it."

Faith whimpered softly as Rita went to work, but she didn't show her teeth. Seconds later, a hank of long black hair fell away. Realizing she was loose, the Poodle began to struggle toward the outside. I gave her hindquarter one last shove. Faith stumbled slightly, then sprang free.

"Somebody grab her!" I yelled. Faith had never run away before, but I didn't want to take any chances.

"I've got her," said Rita. "Don't worry, she's fine."

"Now you," Russell said quickly. "Ed, get over here."

Looking somewhat sheepish, Ed Weinstein complied. "Look," he said, "it's not like I was afraid of the dog or anything."

"Nobody cares." I couldn't be bothered to deal with his attempts to save face. "Just get me out of here."

While Faith's body had fit through the window

easily, however, mine did not. Russell used his foot to kick away the last of the glass so the sash was clear. Even so, my shoulders were almost as wide as the opening.

Each man grasping an arm, they began to pull. I twisted and turned, feeling like a piece of laundry being put through an old-fashioned wringer.

"Too bad I'm not double jointed," I muttered.

Ed snickered like a dirty old man. If I hadn't needed him so badly, I might have been tempted to tell him how repulsive I found him.

"There," Russell said triumphantly, as my bruised shoulders finally pulled free. "Now just keep her straight, and we've got it."

Moments later, I was lying on the cool ground, my cheek pressed against the sparse winter grass. I inhaled the clear air deeply and smelled the earth beneath me. Nothing had ever smelled so good.

Out of the corner of one eye, I saw Faith leap free from Rita's grasp. The Poodle bounded to me joyously and began to lick my face. Usually I try to project a more dignified image at work, but I had neither the energy nor the desire to push her away.

"Thank you," I said to Russell, who was looking like he was trying not to smile.

"Don't mention it." He waved a hand dismissively, then realized it was covered with blood. His gaze quickly went from his hand to mine. "Ms. Travis, you're bleeding."

I'd forgotten all about that. "I cut my wrist when I broke the window."

"You may need stitches. We'd better have the paramedics have a look at that."

There was the sound of a splintering crash behind me. Faith peered down into the storeroom. I turned and did the same. The door was open and the smoke was clearing as a wide arc of water sprayed into the room.

Two firefighters followed it and a face appeared in the window below us. "I was told there was somebody down here."

"That was me," I said.

"How's the fire?" Russell asked anxiously.

"Just about out. Getting right to the source helped a lot. You had more smoke here than flames. We've managed to contain it to this area of the basement, but you're going to have considerable smoke and water damage."

"Thank goodness it wasn't worse," said Russell. "Any sign of what started it?"

"I'd say so." The fireman frowned. "Somebody set this blaze."

❧ Eighteen ❧

"No doubt about it," said Detective Shertz. "It was arson. Whoever set the fire used a bundle of rags soaked with paint thinner as an accelerant. Left them right outside the door. Lucky for you, there wasn't much in the vicinity that would burn."

I slumped back in the wing chair in Russell's office, feeling numb. Maybe I was going into shock, I thought. It was bad enough knowing that the fire had been set deliberately. Now I had to contemplate who, or what, had been the target.

More than two hours had passed since Faith and I had been rescued from the basement. In that time, the firefighters had secured the area and made sure that the blaze was totally out. The arson investigator had arrived to have a look; Detective Shertz had shown up as well. School had been dismissed for the day, and the media was once again camped at the end of the driveway.

On a personal front, I'd just arrived back at Howard Academy after a trip to Greenwich Hospital to have my wrist attended to. Rita had driven while I'd held my arm upright and wrapped in a towel, so the blood wouldn't ruin her upholstery. She'd been kind enough to let Faith ride in the backseat.

One tetanus shot and six stitches later, I had failed to see the humor when the ER doctor joked that, for a suicide, I had lousy aim I almost told him I'd do better next time. But hey, why drag his day down to the level of mine?

As soon as we got back to school, Harriet had hunted me down. The detective and Mr. Hanover were in his office. They requested the pleasure of my company. Immediately. That's the way things are done in private school—an iron fist inside the velvet glove.

I didn't hurry. Instead, I walked Faith around outside and let her sniff a few spots in case there was anything she needed to do. I figured I could blame my tardiness on blood loss.

My dog seemed to have come through our adventure in fine shape. If you didn't count the section of hair that was missing on the back of her neck, that is. Six inches or more gone, sliced off in an irregular line. I could trim the hair around it, but I was never going to be able to hide a hole like that.

Any Poodle person will tell you that in the show ring, neck hair makes the trim. Aunt Peg was going to have a fit when she saw what had happened.

It probably says something about my state of mind that I was thinking about Poodle hair when I should have been worrying about the larger picture. Things like life and death, and how slender the line between them sometimes seems. By the time I went inside, I'd almost convinced myself that the fireman had been wrong, that the fire had been a fluke, caused by old wiring or a faulty electrical system.

Detective Shertz managed to destroy my illusions with his first sentence. To his credit, he didn't look too pleased about the situation either.

"Did you hear what I said, Ms. Travis?" he was asking now. "That fire was set deliberately, right outside a room where you were the only occupant. I'm wondering what you think about that."

I let my arm dangle over the side of the chair, fingers scratching Faith's ear. Usually, she'd have been content to stay somewhere in my vicinity; now she was lying on top of my feet, her body pressed hard against my legs. I knew just how she felt.

"I don't know what to think," I replied honestly. It was true I'd placed myself in jeopardy once or twice before, in the course of other murder investigations. But Krebbs's death had nothing to do with me. Hadn't I made that clear to everyone? "Maybe it was a prank."

"Could be, although that wouldn't be my first guess." Shertz turned to Russell. "In your time at Howard Academy, how many other fires have there been?"

"None," the headmaster said quickly. "As far as I know, this is the first such incident in the history of the school."

"Following hard on the heels of the first murder," Shertz said. "You see what I'm getting at? I'm not a big believer in coincidence."

"I don't understand what you want me to tell you," I said. "Do you think I had something to do with the fire?"

"I know you have a tendency to get involved in murder investigations . . ."

Only one in Greenwich, I thought. Well, two, if you counted Uncle Max. The problem I'd dealt with in the fall had been in Stamford. And the one the year before that had been in Ridgefield, so there was really no reason Shertz needed to feel that his toes were being stepped on.

". . . and I'm thinking maybe someone doesn't want you involved in this one."

"But that's just it. I'm *not* involved. Aside from the fact that I teach at Howard Academy and knew the man slightly, I have no connection to Krebbs at all."

"Would you mind explaining what you were doing down in the basement, where the fire just happened to take place?"

As Shertz's tone had grown increasingly strident, Russell's frown had deepened. Now he cleared his throat and stepped in. "That was my doing. Ms. Travis is a member of the committee that's putting together our spring pageant. We're planning a play to celebrate the lives of the school's founding family. Many of the old Howard family records are stored in the basement, and I recommended she have a look at them, in case there was something we could use."

"So the only thing in the room were boxes of old papers?"

"That's right."

"Were these papers valuable?"

"Not that I'm aware of. Perhaps a collector might have a small amount of interest in what's housed there, but the chances of there being something of real value . . ." Russell's voice trailed off as he shook his head. "I'm afraid I would find that hard to believe."

"How about you?" Shertz turned back to me. "You're the one who was reading the stuff. What did you find?"

"Old receipts and bills of sale, correspondence between Joshua Howard and his sister, Honoria. Pictures and mementos of the children's early years. From what I'd been able to tell so far, it was all just mundane, day-to-day stuff. Nothing that would be worth committing murder over, if that's what you're asking."

"So we're back to where we started," said the

detective. "If the fire wasn't set to destroy the records, what was the arsonist after?"

"I'm telling you, *I don't know.*"

"Been doing a little digging around on your own?"

Russell glanced my way. His lips pursed as though he was considering the notion. I was pleased it hadn't occurred to him earlier.

"No," I said emphatically.

"What about that girl, Jane?"

"What about her?"

"Seen her hanging around anymore?"

"Once. Briefly. But her friend, Brad . . ." I stopped, remembering. "He was here."

"When?"

"Right after the fire started. He was the one who heard me yelling for help."

"Is that the boy who came to get me?" asked Russell. "I wondered who he was. Then, in all the excitement, I forgot all about him."

"By the time I was out, he was gone. I was going to thank him, but I didn't see him anywhere."

"That gives us something to start with." The detective pulled out a pad and made a note. "We'll hunt Jameson down and have a chat."

"Do you think he might have been the person responsible for the fire?" asked Russell.

"Hard to know just yet, but it's certainly worth looking into. The kid's a troublemaker, though arson would be a new string in his bow. If he wasn't involved, I guess he's going to have to come up with a good reason to explain why he was out here hanging around."

Shertz flipped the pad shut. "I guess that's all for now. If either of you think of anything else I ought to know, you know where to reach me."

"Thank you," said Russell, coming out from behind his desk to walk the detective to the door. "We greatly appreciate the efforts you've made on our behalf and we look forward to the speedy resolution of our problems."

Jeez, I thought. With rhetoric like that at his disposal, the guy ought to run for political office.

"There's something I've been curious about," I said. Both men paused. "Who tipped you off that there might be something hidden in the caretaker's cottage?"

"Funny you should ask a question like that," Shertz said slowly. "Seeing as you don't have any interest in Krebbs's murder and all."

I might not be involved, but I wasn't brain-dead either. Russell was looking interested as well.

"As it happens, we got an anonymous call down at the station. It came in through the switchboard."

"Do you guys have caller ID?"

The only sign of Shertz's annoyance was a slight narrowing of his eyes. "The call came from this school. The pay phone out by the front hall. Somebody here tipped us off. And whoever it was, he knew what he was talking about."

As soon as Detective Shertz left, Russell told me to go home. The students had already been dismissed for the weekend and most of the faculty had left as well. There was concern in his expression when he asked if Faith and I needed any help. I'm sure I looked a little ragged around the edges. I know I felt that way.

"No, we'll be fine," I said, though I was grateful for his interest.

My shoulders were throbbing; and now that the painkillers I'd had at the emergency room were beginning to wear off, my wrist hurt like hell. Still, if there's one thing a single mother learns how to do, it's cope with adversity. I was sure we'd be able to manage.

"I imagine the pageant committee will need to have another brainstorming session on Monday," Russell said absently. "The archives in the storeroom were nearly a total loss."

I glanced up, surprised. "I thought the fire never reached them."

"It didn't, but the water damage was extensive. Even if anyone wanted to go through the task of separating the papers and drying them out, I'm not sure it would be possible to salvage most of what was there."

"I'm sorry to hear that," I said quietly. "I know those records were an important part of the school's history."

Russell shrugged slightly. "A week ago, I imagine I'd have found the loss devastating. Now I find myself putting things in perspective. At least this time nobody was seriously injured."

He looked so forlorn that I found myself blurting out a small confession. "Not everything was destroyed. Joshua's youngest daughter, Ruth, kept a diary when she was a teenager. It talks quite a bit about the family life in Deer Park. I took the book home with me last night and forgot to bring it back. It wasn't in the room when the fire started."

"I guess that's something," said Russell. He thought for a moment. "Does anyone else know about this?"

"I mentioned the book to Michael Durant, and maybe a couple other people. But nobody else knows that it wasn't ruined with the rest of the stuff. Do you think it matters?"

"It's hard to know what to think, isn't it?" Russell closed his eyes and pinched his fingers against the bridge of his nose. "The fire might have been somebody's idea of a sick joke, but like Detective Shertz, I'm not inclined to think so.

"That leaves us with two options, neither of which is very appealing. All I can say is, if we do have a monster in our midst, the sooner we discover his or her identity, the better. I want your assurance on something."

"Of course," I said.

"Detective Shertz seemed concerned that you might feel the need to take part in the murder investigation. I must say, for a number of reasons, that I think that would be a very bad idea."

"You're right," I agreed quickly. Though I'd only been at Howard Academy six months, I already knew this was where I wanted to spend the rest of my teaching career. I had no intention of jeopardizing my position at the school. "I promise you, I haven't done anything but try to stay out of the way."

"I wouldn't say your efforts have been entirely successful."

"I'll try harder."

"Do that. And one more thing. I'd appreciate it if you'd bring Ruth's diary back to school. Perhaps you could deliver it to me first thing Monday morning?"

"Certainly." I stood up. Faith, ever the trusty companion, did the same. Together, we headed for the door. "I wonder if you'd answer one more question."

"Perhaps."

"Reading through the Howard family records has made me curious. Whatever happened to

Joshua and Mabel's children? There were six of them. Are any still alive? Do their descendants take an interest in the school?"

Russell shook his head sharply. He didn't look pleased by the topic I'd chosen. "The Howard family has all but divorced itself from this institution. Their interests and ours ceased to coincide many decades ago."

"Why?"

His frown grew. For a moment, I thought he wasn't going to answer.

"I gather there was a good deal of acrimony about the financial decisions Joshua made at the time. Some, if not all, of the children seemed to feel that the school received money that by rights should have been their inheritance."

"That was their father's decision."

"Quite so, but that didn't alleviate the bitter feelings that arose. While Joshua was still alive, there were plenty of resources to go around. The children, who were of course quite grown up by the time the school was established, felt they had nothing to lose by indulging their father's 'hobby.' It wasn't until later, when his will was read, that they realized how total his commitment to Howard Academy had been."

"It seems a shame," I mused.

"Yes, it does," Russell said brusquely. "But it all happened a long time ago. It's nothing you need concern yourself with now."

He was right. It wasn't as if I didn't have plenty of bigger, and more immediate, problems.

A phone call when I got home arranged for Davey to spend the night with Joey Brickman. Joey's mother, Alice, stopped by to pick up some of his things. She saw the bandage on my arm, heard a much-abbreviated version of what I'd been up to, and promised to keep my son until late afternoon Saturday.

Alice is an angel of mercy. I took her up on her offer before the words were even out of her mouth.

Though it was barely dusk, I fed Faith her dinner and fell into bed, exhausted. Sleep claimed me like a black void. I was half-afraid I'd dream of smoke and fire and pools of blood, but I was wrong.

I slept like the dead and dreamed of nothing at all.

🐾 Nineteen 🐾

I woke up Saturday morning with an aching wrist, a groggy head, and a dog who needed desperately to pee. At least one of the three was easy to fix.

Eugene Krebbs's memorial service was scheduled for eleven o'clock. By ten-thirty, after several cups of strong, black coffee, a long walk around the neighborhood with Faith, and a cold, bracing shower, I found myself struggling to pull on panty hose one-handed.

Until that moment, I hadn't been sure I was going to attend. Krebbs had been, at most, an acquaintance. To be honest, his death wouldn't have made much of an impression on me if the fact that he'd been murdered didn't keep intruding on my otherwise peaceful life.

Now, however, I was curious to see who else would put in an appearance. It also wouldn't hurt to show myself, bandage and all, and see if that elicited any shifty looks among the assemblage. Besides, if I stayed home that would only give me more time to worry about the upcoming luncheon with Peg and Sheila Vaughn.

All in all, I was better off keeping busy.

Since I planned to go straight from the service

to Aunt Peg's, I took Faith with me. The March weather was suitably cool, and I cracked the windows in the Volvo and left her lying on the backseat, chewing on a new pig's ear. Earlier, I'd brushed through her mane coat and tried some artful draping to hide the hole near her neck. It didn't do any good. Barring an unexpected miracle, Faith was going to be out of the show ring for at least several months.

The chapel was a small building, seldom used, and joined by a covered walkway to the far end of the original stone mansion. Neither Joshua nor Honoria had been deeply religious, and Howard Academy was nondenominational. I imagined that the chapel's original purpose must have been to serve as a refuge, or place of solace, rather than a house of prayer.

The one room was octagonal in shape. Stained-glass windows, depicting patterns of color rather than religious figures, adorned three walls. The pews were few in number, and when I walked through the door, most everyone I saw was standing. It looked as though the majority of the Howard Academy faculty had decided to attend. Since I doubted most of then had known Krebbs any better than I had, I could only assume that they'd all taken Russell's speech about family to heart.

The headmaster stood up at the lectern first. He thanked everyone for coming, then spoke about

Eugene Krebbs's tenure at Howard Academy and the contribution the caretaker had made to the school. His eulogy was short on substance and heavy on hyperbole. After the first minute or two, I let my gaze drift around the room.

Michael Durant was there, looking bored. Obviously only his sense of obligation had brought him back to school on a Saturday morning. Ed Weinstein and Rita Kinney were seated in one of the pews with several other middle-school teachers.

Sally was standing off by herself. Her eyes were dry, and her expression, stony. I wondered if she'd heard about Krebbs's will yet, and resolved to ask her about it when the service was over.

Detective Shertz arrived late and stood in the back of the room. He, too, let his gaze wander around the assembly of mourners. When our eyes met, I deliberately shifted mine away.

When Russell was finished, several of the older teachers stood up and talked about Krebbs as well. Though Sally had been at Howard Academy as long as any of them, she didn't make a contribution. As soon as the last speaker finished, she bolted for the door.

Quickly, I jumped up and followed. Toward the back of the room, I glimpsed a flash of unexpected color: Jane, dressed in her customary blue jeans and sweatshirt. She glared at me defiantly, as if daring me to contest her right to be there. First things, first.

"Sally, wait!"

Her steps slowed, then stopped. Refreshments were going to be served in the dining room, but Sally was headed in the other direction. Her eyes flickered down to the bandage on my wrist, then quickly away.

"I heard you had some excitement yesterday," she said. "How are you feeling?"

"Not great," I admitted. "Faith and I were lucky to get out in time."

"So I heard. Everyone's talking about it. Is it true somebody set the fire on purpose?"

"Apparently so."

Sally shook her head. "Is that crazy, or what? Two weeks ago, I'd have told you this school was just about the safest place on earth. The older I get, the more I realize the world is a strange and scary place."

Just another cheery thought with which to face the day.

"I wanted to ask you about something," I said. "Two things, actually."

Sally looked at her watch. I wondered where she was in such a hurry to get to.

"Last time we spoke, you seemed pretty sure Krebbs wouldn't have anything to do with bringing drugs on campus."

"Yeah, so?"

"Nothing stays quiet around here for long. I assume you've heard that the police found half a pound of marijuana in the cottage."

"That doesn't prove anything."

"No, but it sure doesn't lay any suspicions to rest, either. And there's something else."

She rolled her eyes heavenward. "Why wouldn't there be? Ever since this whole mess got started, it's been one damn thing after another. Now what?"

"Have you heard about Krebbs's will?"

"No." Sally's tone was cautious. "What about it?"

"He left behind a pretty sizable estate. Half is supposed to come to the school. The other half goes to a distant cousin by the name of Sarah Fingerhut, on the condition that she come forward to claim the money and acknowledge their relationship."

Sally was frowning. She didn't say a word.

"Does the name ring a bell?"

"Of course," she snapped. "Fingerhut is my maiden name. I imagine that doesn't surprise you."

No, it didn't. But what did surprise me was the way Sally seemed to be taking the news in stride. Though she'd professed not to have heard about Krebbs's bequests, I had the distinct impression that she not only already knew about her cousin's will, but she'd also decided what her response was going to be.

"So now what?" I asked.

"As if I have a choice," Sally muttered.

"Don't you?"

"Not anymore. I'm fifty-three years old, and I've spent my entire life working in a profession I love that pays me a fraction of what I'm worth. I'm not stupid. I've lived frugally and put money aside. I was the kind of person who thought she was never going to have to depend on anybody for anything, you know what I mean?"

I nodded.

"Six years ago my mother developed Alzheimer's. Three years ago I had to put her in a nursing home. Her health insurance doesn't begin to cover the costs. I'm her only child. If I don't take care of her, no one will. So I do."

Sally sighed. "Don't get me wrong. The only sense in which this is a burden is financially. I'm to the point now where if I found a wallet on the street, I'd probably keep it. Of course, I'll take Krebbs's money. I'd take the devil's money if he offered it to me."

"I'm sorry," I said softly.

"It's not your fault. It's just the way things are." Sally spun around and walked away.

In a week when both a stash of drugs and a dead body had been found at the school, you had to wonder about a woman who'd said she deal with the devil if the price was right.

• • •

When I got to the Howard Academy dining room, the first person I saw was Jane. Standing near the buffet table, she was holding a glass of milk in one hand and a plate of finger sandwiches in the other. She was hesitating at the end of the table, gazing with naked longing at a tray filled with pastries and wishing, no doubt, for a third hand.

"Need some help?" I asked, walking over.

"No." Her tone was sullen. "Why would I need any help?"

"I was thinking maybe you'd like an eclair or two to go with your sandwiches."

"I figured I'd come back later. But you never know, they might be gone, so as long as you're offering . . ."

I picked up an empty plate and selected several pastries from the tray. As I walked back to Jane, I noticed several people staring at the girl. For one thing, she was the only child in the room. For another, her attire was entirely inappropriate for the occasion.

But if Jane was aware of the attention she was receiving, she didn't seem to care. By the time I got back to her, she'd already found a seat and polished off several sandwiches. She was licking her fingers when I sat down beside her.

"You're not supposed to inhale those," I said, handing her a napkin.

She placed the linen square on her lap, but didn't look as though she planned to find much use for it. "They're too small. Barely more than a bite apiece."

"They're delicate. You're supposed to nibble at them delicately."

"Nibbling is for gerbils." Jane wolfed down another sandwich.

"And proper ladies."

"No wonder it didn't occur to me."

"I didn't expect to see you here," I said.

"Why not? I heard Mr. Hanover say that everyone was welcome to come. So I came."

The girl certainly got around. I wondered how many other tidbits of information she'd over-heard while skulking around the school. "It's just that I didn't get the impression that you and Krebbs were friends."

"So what? Nobody said that was a require-ment. And the food around here is pretty good."

"Mind if I join you?"

I looked up and saw Michael hovering above us, plate in hand.

"Not at all." I pushed back the chair beside me, and made the introductions.

"I know who you are," Michael said, eyeing Jane curiously. "You're the girl who found . . ." Abruptly his voice died.

"Krebbs, yeah." Jane finished for him. "That was me."

"That must have been awful for you."

"Must have been." Jane's snotty tone was back. I wondered if that was a response to adults in general, or to Michael in particular. As far as I knew, the two of them had never met.

"I'm sorry you had to go through that." Michael leaned toward Jane, trying valiantly to connect with the girl. I knew where he was coming from; it's a teacher thing. "Finding a dead body would be a traumatic experience for anyone, let alone someone your age—"

"Here's something really traumatic," Jane said, shoving back her chair. "Krebbs wasn't dead when I got there, so I got to see him die. I'm going to go get some more food." She picked up her plate and left.

I glanced over at Michael. He looked pale. "Sorry about that," I said.

"She's a tough little cookie, isn't she?"

"She thinks she is, anyway. Jane's had a rough life, spent part of it living on the streets with her mother. Now her grandmother's supposed to be taking care of her, but she seems to come and go as she pleases."

"It's a real shame." Michael sighed. His plate was empty, and he pushed it aside. "I need a cup of coffee. You want some?"

"No, I'm fine."

After he left, Jane returned. She'd filled a plate with a second helping of dessert and looked as though she could probably handle a third. "How come you're not eating anything?" she asked as she sat back down.

"I'm going from here to a luncheon."

"Well la-di-da." Jane grinned. "That sounds pretty fancy. You'd better stock up here. They're probably serving these stupid little sandwiches."

"Not this luncheon. My Aunt Peg's the hostess, and she can put away food like a longshore-man. That's why I'm saving my appetite."

"Is she the one with all the dogs?"

"The very same."

"Wow. Can I come with you? You said I could meet her sometime."

I thought for a moment. Ever since Aunt Peg had announced her intention to get me and Sheila together, I'd been dreading this meeting. Having Jane along might provide just the sort of distraction I needed.

"Two conditions," I said.

"Let's hear them."

"You'll have to ride in the backseat with Faith, and she'll probably climb into your lap."

"Okay." Jane said eagerly. "What else?"

"We stop by your house first and make sure this is okay with your grandmother."

Her face fell. "She won't care, honest. She won't even miss me. As long as I show up at home later, she'll never even know I was gone."

"Sorry," I said. "That's the deal. Take it or leave it."

"I guess I'll take it." Jane didn't look happy.

"Great. I'm ready to go, how about you?"

"Just give me a sec." She leapt up and headed back toward the buffet table. "I need one more eclair for the road."

As I'd predicted, Faith immediately decided that Jane's lap made the perfect pillow on which to drape the front half of her body. For her part, Jane didn't look as though she minded a bit. As we turned out the gate at the foot of the driveway, she gave me directions to her grandmother's house.

Two turns took us into a quiet residential neighborhood within walking distance of downtown Greenwich. The houses were post-World War II vintage, and the plots of land they sat upon were tiny. New, they'd probably cost twenty thousand dollars; now, thanks to the desirability of Greenwich real estate, they were worth twenty times that.

A one-way street took us down a hill before we were able to double back. Completing the maneuver, I realized that the same car had been behind us virtually since we'd left the school. It was a dark Acura Legend, the kind of pricey, yet understated car that I think of as the typical Greenwich sedan. It was far enough behind us that I couldn't see the driver.

"There!" said Jane, directing me to a small,

white clapboard Cape. Unlike most of its neighbors, the house didn't boast any recent renovations, but the yard was neat, and the porch looked freshly swept.

I glanced in the rearview mirror again. The Acura was gone. I pulled in along the curb and rolled the windows down for Faith.

"I'm telling you this isn't necessary," Jane said, jumping out of the car.

I didn't bother to argue. Instead, I followed as she headed past the front porch and down a narrow driveway that ran along the side of the house. Two concrete steps led to the back door. Jane tried the door and found it locked.

She produced a key from her pocket, opened the door and stepped inside. "Gran?"

A waist-high picket fence separated the house from the one beside it. Next door, a man who probably spent his weekdays toiling in a small office was spending his weekend toiling in his small backyard. March in Connecticut means spring cleanup. He was raking vigorously while a baby, sound asleep and bundled against the cold, swung in an electric swing.

"You looking for Mrs. Gaines?" he called. "She's not home. I saw her go out earlier."

Jane reappeared on the step. The man frowned slightly, as if trying to decide whether or not he recognized her. "You're the granddaughter, right?"

"Right," I said. "Jane wants to spend the afternoon with me. We were hoping to get permission from Mrs. Gaines."

"Can't help you there. But I don't imagine she'd object. Why don't you leave your name and telephone number with me? I'll give her the message when she gets back."

The solution pleased all of us. I scribbled the information on a piece of paper and gave it to him.

Back in the car, Jane made no attempt to hide her excitement. "How far is it?" she asked, then kept talking before I had a chance to answer. "Will we be there soon? Wow, eight dogs in one house. I can't even imagine that. Does your aunt have any other animals? She doesn't have any ponies, does she?"

"One question at a time," I said, laughing. "We'll be there in ten minutes. And no, she doesn't have any ponies. But I think the dogs will be enough to keep you busy."

"Are there going to be lots of people?"

"No," I said. "Aside from my aunt, just one. Sheila is my fiance's ex-wife. She moved here recently because she's hoping to get back together with him. Aunt Peg thought the two of us should meet."

"Wow," said Jane. Just like a soap opera. This is going to be a blast."

That was what I was afraid of.

☙ Twenty ☙

Before the Volvo had even rolled to a stop in Aunt Peg's driveway, Jane had her seat belt off and her door open. She jumped out of the car, with Faith right behind her. I could hear Aunt Peg's Standard Poodles barking inside the house; predictably, the door opened a moment later and the herd came streaming out.

Mine was the only car in the driveway, so Sheila had yet to arrive. It was just as well. One look at the manic greetings going on in front of the house and any sane person might have been tempted to run for her life.

Aunt Peg and I both reached the foot of the steps at the same time. Jane had thrown herself into the milling canine throng with glee. The Poodles, always eager for a new playmate, were happy to return her enthusiasm.

"Interesting child," Peg said, as Jane lifted her nose to the sky and howled like a wolf. "I like her already."

As the Poodles careened around us in wide circles, Faith came flying past. I heard Aunt Peg gasp. "Dear Lord! What on earth has happened?"

"We had a bit of an accident—"

"I'll say." Peg was not amused. She snapped her fingers and Faith immediately turned and raced back to her. My aunt has that effect on dogs and people alike.

Briefly she ran her fingers through the Poodle's neck hair, flipping it one way, then another, as she inspected the damage. "Do you have any idea what you've *done?*"

"Yes, but—"

"You've put her out of the show ring for six months. And now, of all times, with five good judges coming up on the Cherry Blossom circuit. With any luck she'd have finished there."

I shut my mouth and let her rant. After a minute, Aunt Peg realized I wasn't responding. "Well?" she demanded. "What do you have to say for yourself?"

"At least she's alive."

"Of course she's alive—" Peg stopped abruptly and narrowed her eyes. "Was there any question she might not be?"

"There was a fire yesterday at the school. Faith and I were trapped, and I had to hand her out through a window. Her hair got caught on a piece of glass and ripped out."

"I read about the fire in the paper. The article said it was small and contained in one area. It didn't say a thing about people needing to be rescued."

"Mr. Hanover preferred to downplay the event, and I agreed. I know the hair's a problem." More mine than hers, I thought. I was the one doing all the maintenance on the coat. "But it couldn't be helped."

"I suppose I should be grateful that everything turned out all right," Peg said grudgingly.

Was I the only one who noticed that she hadn't inquired after the state of *my* health?

"Where's Sheila?" I asked.

"She'll be along in a few minutes. In the meantime, why don't you introduce me to your friend?"

I called Jane over. She stared at Aunt Peg in awe, then carefully wiped her hand on her jeans before holding it out to shake.

"Ms. Travis said you had eight dogs," she said. "I only see five."

"The other three are back in the kennel. Maybe we'll visit them after lunch. Are you hungry?"

"Sure." Jane grinned.

"You just ate," I mentioned.

"Pish," said Aunt Peg. "A growing girl like Jane needs all the food she can get. Let's go inside and have a drink while we're waiting for Sheila, shall we?"

Peg looped an arm around Jane's shoulders and they climbed the steps side by side. I worked on ignoring a small, unworthy, stab of irritation. The first time I'd met Jane, she'd barely let me come within arm's length.

No sooner had we reached the kitchen than

the canine alarm system went into full cry again. Aunt Peg was getting a pitcher of iced tea out of the refrigerator. Jane was lining up glasses on the counter. It was left to me to go greet Sheila.

Aunt Peg is one of the world's great manipulators, so I figured it hadn't been an accident that things worked out that way. But now that the time was finally at hand, I found myself incredibly curious about the woman who'd been Sam Driver's first love. Perhaps she and I had more in common than falling for the same man. Maybe we'd even turn out to be friends.

The first words out of her mouth shattered that illusion to bits.

"You must be Melanie," she said. "I must say, you don't look like much."

"Pardon me?" The smile froze on my face.

I tried not to notice that the car she'd just climbed out of was a metallic blue Mercedes Benz. People who show big dogs need practical cars, like Volvos. At least that was what I told myself. You could probably stick a Pug or two just about anywhere.

"The way Sam talks about you, I thought you were some sort of wonder woman. I guess I was expecting someone . . ." Her gaze raked up and down. "Taller."

Considering that my height topped hers by several inches, I figured Sheila was hardly one to talk. Then again, while I've always wanted to be tall and statuesque, Sheila looked like the kind of woman who was thrilled with herself just the way she was.

Her clothes—black jeans, a white turtleneck, and a black leather bomber jacket—fit her small frame impeccably. Their lack of color formed the perfect backdrop for her sleek dark hair, creamy skin, and big blue eyes. Everything about her screamed confidence.

If I wasn't careful, I might find myself screaming right back.

"I hope I'm not underdressed," she said, glancing at my dark suit. "Peg said it was casual."

"It is. I just came from a memorial service; otherwise, I'd be wearing pants myself."

"Oh, that's right." Sheila's eyebrows arched. "Sam mentioned that your friends seem to make a habit of dying."

I choked back the first response that sprang to mind, quickly covering the word by clearing my throat. Even though one hears it all the time at dog shows, most people find it objectionable in polite company.

I guessed that meant the battle lines had been drawn.

At the door we were met by the mob of Poodles. Sheila, as the newcomer, received the bulk of the friendly assault, but she didn't seem to mind. Aunt Peg looked on approvingly as Sam's ex-wife made sure that each of the dogs got a moment of individual attention.

"They're gorgeous," she said. "I don't know how you find the time to keep them all so beautifully groomed."

"I make the time," Peg replied pointedly, and I knew the dig was directed at me.

"Well, I admire your dedication. I'm not sure I could do half as well. Luckily, my Pugs are pretty much wash-and-wear."

Suck up, I thought.

Aunt Peg glared.

Good grief, I hadn't spoken aloud, had I? If so, Sheila didn't seem to have heard. Jane, however, was grinning. I took that as a bad sign.

She hung back as Aunt Peg and Sheila headed for the kitchen. "So that's the competition."

"Sheila and I are not competing."

"Try telling that to her."

The girl's radar was way too accurate.

"Besides," I said. "Even if we were, this is neutral territory."

"All's fair in love and war," Jane quoted. For a child who didn't spend any time in school, her education wasn't half bad.

You know how time seems to speed up when you're having fun and slows when things are going badly? That afternoon passed with an excruciating lack of velocity. By the time coffee was served, I must have checked my watch a dozen times.

Aunt Peg kept scowling at me. Jane couldn't seem to stop giggling. Sheila, meanwhile, was the perfect guest. She complimented Aunt Peg on the food, the decor, and, most importantly, the Cedar Crest Poodles.

It was clear from the depth of her knowledge about the dogs that Sheila had done her homework. Peg was, I could tell, simultaneously surprised and flattered. The way to her heart is through her Poodles. In no time, she and Sheila were well on their way to becoming buddies.

Aunt Peg's usually pretty sharp. I'd trust her judgment in almost any situation. Now, however, Sheila had her completely hoodwinked. The woman sitting across from me was a totally different person from the one I'd met outside, and Peg was falling for the entire, nauseating performance.

The way I saw it, Sheila Vaughn was either a hypocrite or schizophrenic. I was hoping for mental illness myself.

Dessert is the most important part of any meal at Aunt Peg's, so I didn't dare make an escape until after it had been served. Mocha cake from the St. Moritz bakery is my favorite. It would hardly have been gracious of me not to eat a piece. Or two.

When my plate had been cleaned for the

second time, I laid down my fork, and said to Jane, "You wanted to see the other Poodles. Why don't I take you out to the kennel and we'll have a look?"

"Don't be silly." Peg rose from her seat. "Jane and I will go. You and Sheila can use the time to get to know one another better."

If what I knew so far was an indication, getting to know Sheila any better was going to completely ruin my day.

Aunt Peg never gave me a chance to disagree, however. She simply left the dishes on the table, scooped Jane up, and off they went. The silence after their exit was like a vacuum.

I stood and began to clear the dishes. Sheila got up to help.

"Please sit," I said. "This won't take long."

Sheila wasn't the only one who could lie through her teeth. If I had my way, I'd be in the kitchen until it was time to leave.

The sink was already full. I left the dessert plates on the counter and put the cake in the refrigerator. When I turned around, Sheila was in the doorway. She'd crouched down beside Faith and was scratching beneath her chin. Grudgingly, I noted that she wasn't disturbing the Poodle's precious show coat.

"I guess you don't like me very much," she said.

I shrugged, turned on the hot water, and began rinsing plates.

Sheila stood up. She had to raise her voice to be heard above the running water. "You see me as a threat."

"No, you see yourself as a threat. I think you're more of an inconvenience."

I glanced back over my shoulder to see her reaction. The barb had hit home. Sheila looked seriously peeved.

"Don't underestimate me," she said, crossing the kitchen to stand by the counter. "Sam loved me once. I think he loves me still."

"He may love you, but he's not in love with you."

"Did he tell you that?"

"He didn't have to. If he were in love with you, he wouldn't be engaged to me. Sam's a good man, better than anyone I've ever met. You should have realized that sooner, though I can't say I'm sorry you didn't."

"I was young, I made a mistake. Now I know enough to want to undo it."

I slipped the stack of plates into their slots in the dishwasher. "It's too late."

"We'll see about that, won't we?"

If that had been my line, I might have thought it made a fine parting shot and stormed out of the room. Not Sheila. Since I was filling the dishwasher, she took my place at the sink and started rinsing glasses. As if helping out was the most natural thing to do.

I hate it when people refuse to be consistent.

"That's a pretty Standard," she said, inclining her head toward Faith. "Did you breed her?"

I'd been thinking of Sheila as a Pug person. Now it occurred to me that, having lived with Sam and his Poodles, she was, of course, entitled to have an opinion. "No, she's one of Peg's."

"It figures. Her dogs are gorgeous. Do you show her yourself?"

It's hard to remain prickly when someone wants to talk about your dog. "Yes, with Peg's help. Faith has ten points, including a major. I was hoping to finish her next month, but now she's lost a big hunk of hair, so I guess it'll have to wait."

"You can work around that, you know. People do it all the time."

"You mean switches?"

Some people call them wiglets. They're made from actual Poodle hair, taken from dogs that have finished their championships and had their coats cut down. The long hair is banded or sewn together at the base; then that knot is secured to the existing shorter hair with more rubber bands. Some dogs wear switches for length; others, to give their coats more fullness.

Usually they're attached to a Poodle's topknot, but putting them in neck hair is not uncommon. Of course, the A.K.C. frowns on their use.

Properly applied, however, only one judge in fifty will even know they're there.

Sheila nodded. "Especially with a coat as good as hers is, nobody would even suspect."

"I'd know," I said quietly.

"Don't tell me you're one of those moral types."

"There's nothing wrong with following the rules."

"Except that it hardly ever gets you where you want to go."

The back door opened. "See?" Aunt Peg said, beaming at the two of us. "I knew you'd find something to talk about. Jane and I had a fine time outside. Now we're ready to consider having another piece of cake."

This must be what it feels like to die in slow motion, I thought.

Luckily, Sheila begged off, claiming that she had to get home to her dogs. It was the sort of excuse Peg could understand, so for once, she didn't argue. After another sliver of cake apiece, Jane and I said good-bye, too.

Aunt Peg walked out with us. "So now you've met Sheila. What do you think?"

"I think I'll make Sam a better wife than she did."

"Good for you."

"The two of you seemed to get along pretty well," I mentioned.

"I was the hostess. That made it my job to get along. Besides . . ." Her eyes glinted wickedly. "Haven't you ever heard that old saying, 'Know thine enemy'?"

Good old Aunt Peg. She hadn't disappointed me after all.

"Thank you for everything," Jane said to Peg. "I'll think about what you said."

I glanced at Aunt Peg, but she shook her head. "That's between Jane and me, right?"

"Right," the girl said firmly. She climbed into the car and called Faith up onto her lap, like she'd been doing it all her life.

"That girl needs a puppy of her own," Peg said as I closed the door after them.

"Don't start. You can't fix the entire world."

"Says who?"

Far be it from me to argue with a force of nature. It was time to make a graceful retreat, so I did.

❧ Twenty-one ❧

Jane was quiet in the car on the way back to her house.

"Is everything all right?" I finally asked.

"Yeah." Her head turned deliberately away from me, she stared out the window.

"Your grandmother's not going to be mad at you for coming with me today, is she?"

"Nah, she won't care."

I drove in silence for a few more minutes, watching in the rearview mirror as Jane's hand methodically stroked the length of Faith's body from neck to tail. Clearly something was bothering the girl. I wondered if it had anything to do with the secret she was keeping with Aunt Peg.

"The other day when you came to my classroom, you said there was something you wanted to tell me," I said. "But then you never got the chance. Feel like talking about it now?"

"I guess."

"Was it something important?" I prompted when she didn't continue.

"Maybe. I don't know. It was about Krebbs."

This time I let the silence grow until Jane felt ready to end it. I knew how much the whole situation had upset her, and I wasn't about to push. After a few minutes, Jane made eye contact in the mirror.

"Remember last Monday when we met in the basement at Howard Academy? The reason I was down there was because I was following Krebbs."

"Following him? Why?"

"I don't know. At first, it was just a game. You know, something to do. And Krebbs blew his top whenever he saw me, so I had to be smart about it, and sneaky, too. It was kind of like being a spy . . ."

Her voice trailed away, then came back stronger. "Anyway, Krebbs wasn't going down to the basement because of anything he had to do for his job. He was looking for something. He'd been going down there a lot recently, and he was searching the place."

"For what?"

"How should I know? It's not as if I was going to ask him."

I thought about that as we reached the traffic circle at the bottom of Lake Avenue, continued up past the library, then turned left at the light and headed east on the Post Road. What could Krebbs have been searching for? And why now, when he'd been at Howard Academy for decades? I wondered if his behavior had anything to do with the marijuana the police had found in the shed.

"Are you sure he was looking for something?" I asked. "Maybe he was looking for a place to hide something."

"Like what?"

"Drugs . . . ?" I let the thought dangle.

"Krebbs? You've gotta be kidding."

Obviously the girl didn't read the newspaper.

"Was he searching anywhere else?" I asked. "Or just in the basement?"

"That's the only place I saw him, but I wasn't around all the time. He was interested in that storeroom that had all the records. Krebbs didn't bother reading them like you did. He just pawed through the boxes."

No wonder the records had been such a jumbled mess by the time I'd gotten to them. "Do you think he found what he was looking for?"

"Nah. Right up until the day he died, he was still going down there."

Abruptly, I realized what Jane wasn't saying; what she'd wanted me to know all along. I turned onto a side street, pulled the Volvo over to the curb, and turned in my seat to face her. "That's why you were the one who found Krebbs after he'd been stabbed. You were looking for him, weren't you? You were going to follow him again."

"Yeah." A small, silent tear rolled down her cheek. "It was just a stupid game. I didn't think anyone would get hurt."

"Oh, honey." I reached over the seat and gathered the small girl into my arms. "Krebbs didn't get hurt because of you, or your game. None of this is your fault."

Jane sniffled. "That's not what Brad says."

"What?" I drew back. "What does Brad say?"

"That I never should have gone over to Howard Academy in the first place. That I should have minded my own business. When I found Krebbs, I should have just left him there rather than shooting my mouth off about what I'd seen. He says now we're both going to end up in big trouble, and it's all my fault."

"You're not going to get in any trouble," I promised.

"Try telling that to my grandmother. Before she thought I was doing okay. Now she's really pissed about all the school I've been missing."

"You didn't honestly think you were going to be able to keep that charade up forever, did you?"

Jane shrugged.

"A full semester of mono?"

She jutted out her chin. "I might have developed complications."

I fought the urge to smile. "And then what?"

"Who knows? I'd have figured something out."

I eased back into the front seat and turned on the car. "You know Brad's wrong, don't you?

You didn't do anything you shouldn't have done. Well, except cutting school."

"Gran's fixed that now. I have to go on Monday. She's going to drive me to Central Middle School and walk me to the classroom."

"I'm glad to hear that. It will be good for you to start going to classes. You'll make some new friends, too."

"It'll be boring." Jane sounded sulky; but also, thank goodness, resigned. Hopefully that meant she wasn't planning to find another dodge.

We pulled up in front of her house and parked beside the driveway. She took her time unfastening her seat belt, and stopped to give Faith a long hug good-bye.

"Do you want me to go in with you? I'd be happy to explain to your grandmother where you were."

"No, it'll be okay." She climbed slowly out of the car and shut the door behind her.

"Now that you'll be busy with school, I guess we won't be seeing each other as much."

Jane shrugged as if she didn't care, but it wasn't hard to read the expression in her eyes. Like the other people who'd come and gone in her life, she thought I was abandoning her.

"Wait," I said. I fished in my purse for a piece of paper and a pen. "Here's my phone number. If you need anything, call me. Or even if you just feel like talking, okay?"

Jane folded the paper carefully and put it in the pocket of her jeans. I hoped she remembered it was there before the pants went through the laundry.

Faith pressed her nose against the window and watched the small, slender girl walk down the driveway toward the back door. The Poodle looked as bereft as I felt. You can't fix the whole world—hadn't I just told Aunt Peg that?

Yes, but I could sure as hell work on my one small portion of it. I'd be seeing Jane again, I was sure of it.

When I got home, it looked like half the neighborhood was at my house. Lights were on, the front door wasn't quite closed, and several cars, including Sam's, were parked in the driveway. After my recent experiences at Howard Academy, my first thought was that some sort of disaster had occurred.

I parked by the curb and hurried across the yard with Faith. As I reached the front steps, the door opened. Alice Brickman stood in the doorway, looking mortified. Behind her, I saw my next-door neighbor, Mrs. Silano, pass through the hall. She waved to me gaily and continued toward the living room. Loud music was coming from that direction.

"I am so sorry," said Alice.

I raced up the steps. By the time I reached the

top, we were eye to eye. Alice has strawberry blond hair, pale, luminous skin, and a wonderful smile. Unfortunately, she takes those assets for granted and spends too much time worrying about the fifteen pounds she never lost after her daughter, Carly, was born three years earlier.

"What's happened?" I asked, trying to fit past her. "Is Davey okay?"

"Sure." Alice blinked. "He's fine. At least he was a few minutes ago, the last time I saw him."

Mothers of little boys learn that tactic early: never make promises unless the child in question is within view.

"He and Joey are playing Nintendo," said Alice. "I'm afraid that's how this whole thing got started."

"What whole thing?" I had to raise my voice; someone had turned up the volume on the CD player. Two men I'd never seen before were manning the controls.

"This gathering. Whatever. This afternoon I ran out of things for the boys to do. Carly was having a play date, and they were bored. You know how it goes."

I could imagine. One bored six-year-old boy could make a nuisance of himself; two could drive a mother to distraction.

"So Davey got this idea that everything would be all right if they could come over here and play Nintendo, which annoyed the crap out of me because you know perfectly well that Joey has a Nintendo set of his own, except that Joe is an idiot."

Joe was Alice's husband, an attorney with one of the big firms in Greenwich. He'd recently decided that playing video games would stunt his children's intellectual and emotional growth. Consequently, he'd unplugged the Nintendo system and consigned it to the attic.

As we were speaking, the idiot in question strolled down the hallway from the kitchen, beer in hand. For no reason that I could see, he was wearing tennis whites. Sam, who was also holding a cold bottle of Bud, was right behind him. He was grinning broadly.

"Most men are idiots," I said sweetly. "It's to be expected. Then what happened?"

"Well, you know how you gave me a key in case of emergencies? I figured this was sort of close, except I didn't want the boys to be here all by themselves so Tina and Carly and April and I came with them . . ."

Tina and April, I surmised, were the mother-daughter combination that formed the other half of Carly's play date.

". . . and then Sam showed up because he was looking for you and seemed to think you had this long-standing agreement that the two of you would get together on Saturday nights even though he hadn't called to confirm or anything, and there was no reason he should expect you to be here . . ."

There we were, right back to that idiot thing again.

". . . then Joe got home from playing doubles. Apparently he'd invited the other three guys back to the house for a beer, but we didn't have any, so he saw my note saying where I was and came over here to yell about the beer thing, except that you had plenty once Sam showed him where the spare case was in the garage. And you know how men are, they had to make a big production of putting some in the fridge and some in the freezer and by the time they got that all figured out, Joe had forgotten what he was mad about in the first place . . ."

By now, my eyes were beginning to glaze over. If Alice didn't stop and take a breath soon, she was going to pass out on the floor.

"Mrs. Silano?" I asked weakly.

"Who?"

"Edna Silano? My neighbor?"

"Oh, right. I guess we were causing somewhat of a commotion and she seemed to know you weren't here." Alice shielded her mouth with her hand, and whispered, "I think she watches from behind her front curtain."

She did. I was surprised Alice hadn't realized that sooner. Some days I think we entertained her better than television.

"So she came over to make sure that the house wasn't being burglarized—"

"By four kids, two mothers, and a team of racquet-wielding doubles players?"

"Something like that. Anyway, Sam gave her a beer and invited her to join the party and she's been here ever since. I hope you don't mind, we've ordered pizza."

Mind? By now, I was frazzled enough to think that was a delightful idea.

"So everyone's okay?" I asked.

"Just dandy." Alice grinned. "Come on in and join the party."

Faith trotted into the house and went in search of Davey. Before I'd even had time to hang up my coat, Sam reappeared with a second, icy bottle of Bud. Unlike Aunt Peg, he immediately noticed the bandage on my arm.

"I was going to call you last night," I said. "But I fell asleep instead." I took a minute to bring him up-to-date on what had been happening at Howard Academy.

Sam looked appalled when I got to the part about Faith's and my close call. I decided to distract him by mentioning where I'd been all afternoon.

"You and Sheila and Peg, all together in one place." He gulped, considering the implications. "Did everything go all right?"

"No furniture got broken. No breakables were thrown."

"What about unbreakables?" Sam muttered under his breath, looking far from reassured.

"Sheila's an interesting woman," I said. "I can see why you might have married her."

"You can?"

"Sure. She's smart, she's attractive, she's sexy." I trailed my fingers lightly down his arm and let them brush across the front of his jeans. Then I turned and walked away. "And you were obviously young and deluded."

Sometimes, there's nothing quite so satisfying as having the last word.

❦ Twenty-two ❦

It was after nine o'clock before Sam and I got the house all to ourselves. When beer and pizza both ran out, my impromptu guests finally began to drift away. Davey fell into bed, exhausted, shortly after the last one left.

I'd wanted to think that my son had missed me as much as I'd missed him during the day we'd been apart, but the welcome-back hug I tried to deliver shortly after my arrival had been firmly rebuffed.

"Mom!" he'd wailed, his voice floating through two octaves. "You made Mario fall off the cliff!"

Beside him on the couch, Joey chortled happily. I guessed that meant it was his turn at the controls now.

Alice tried to reassure me by saying that my son's reaction meant he was well-adjusted. That sounded like a large dose of psychobabble to me, and I made sure I got my hug later that night when Davey went to bed.

My son was drowsy and warm, and his hair smelled like popcorn. He was wearing his favorite superhero pajamas, the ones that came with a cape. He'd been too busy to notice the bandage on my arm, and I'd declined to bring it up.

Reticence about things like that comes naturally

273

to single parents. You want your little superhero to feel secure, so you try to make him think you're invincible. Some days, the charade is harder to pull off than others.

Usually Faith sleeps on Davey's bed. Tonight, however, she left his bedroom as soon as I did. It wasn't hard to figure out why. In all the commotion, I had yet to make her dinner.

Being a dog lover himself, Sam didn't take it personally that he wasn't next on my list. Standing behind me while I mixed Faith's food, however, his hands roaming, his lips nuzzling my neck, he did his best to ensure that his needs were moving rapidly up the agenda.

"I've got something to show you," I said, when Faith had eaten and been let outside.

Sam's eyebrows waggled. "I'll show you mine, if you show me yours."

"Not that kind of something." I laughed.

His hands moved up my sides, fingers caressing my breasts. A familiar warmth began to spread through me. I placed my palms on top of his. Talking could wait.

Bodies, mouths, pressed together, we edged toward the stairs, shedding clothing as we went. We only made it as far as the living room. Luckily, Sam had the presence of mind to draw the curtains.

Afterward, I had a crick in my neck and a rug burn on my hip. It was worth it.

"We're getting too old to behave like teen-agers," I said with a sigh.

"Speak for yourself." Sam chortled.

"Easy for you to say, you're on top."

He rolled onto his side, pulling me with him. I rested my head on his shoulder and settled my body along the hollow of his hip. I was floating contentedly between sleep and wakefulness when he said, "It was never like this with Sheila."

My eyes snapped open. My body stiffened. Sam was blissfully oblivious.

"What?" I asked, just to see if he'd be dumb enough to say it again.

He was.

"It was never this good with Sheila," Sam reaffirmed. He seemed to think I'd be happy to hear that.

I sat up and gathered my clothes.

"What's the matter?" he asked.

"Sheila."

"What about her?"

"My point exactly."

"You're not making any sense."

"I guess that makes us even then, because you don't seem to have any sense. Did you actually think this was a *good* time to compare me to your ex-wife?"

Sam screwed up his face and thought about that. Belatedly, he realized that anything he said might have the potential to blow up in his face. "It was a favorable comparison," he managed finally.

"We just made love."

"I know," Sam said slowly. "I was there."

"And you were thinking about Sheila."

Finally it hit him. I hoped it felt like a ton of bricks.

Sam began to scramble furiously. "No, I wasn't. Honest. At least not during . . ."

His cheeks turned a dull shade of red. He was probably hoping I'd step in and rescue him. Not a chance.

"It was after. Briefly. And I wasn't even thinking about her, I was just—"

"Making comparisons." I turned away.

"No." Sam reached for my shoulders and pulled me back. "I was thinking about how lucky I was. About how much my life has changed since we met. You and Davey are the best things that ever happened to me. That's all I was trying to say."

My lower lip trembled, half-ready to smile, half-ready to cry. "Apology accepted."

"Is that what I was doing?"

"It's what you should have been doing."

Always a fast learner, Sam nodded. He looked relieved, like a man who'd peered over the edge of a precipice and been pulled back at the last minute. Having regained his balance, he was quick to change the subject.

276

"Didn't you say there was something you wanted to show me?"

Sam's always been good at thinking on his feet. I like that in a man. "Right. It's something I've been working on for school. I just have to find it."

He went to let Faith inside and turned on the coffeemaker while I searched through the clutter in the living room for Ruth's diary. Ten minutes later, we met at the kitchen table. Sam had already poured the coffee into two big mugs and added milk to mine. He picked up the leather-bound book I laid on the table between us and looked at it curiously.

"This looks old."

"It is. More than half a century. It belonged to one of the teenage daughters of Joshua Howard, the school's founder. I'm on the committee for the spring pageant, and we've been looking for ways to celebrate the school's beginnings. That's why I was down in the basement. I was going through the archives."

"That's where this came from?"

I nodded. "I found it a couple days ago and brought it home to read. It's lucky I did because just about everything else in the storeroom was destroyed yesterday."

Sam sipped his coffee, flipping carefully through the pages as he waited for me to continue.

"This afternoon, Jane told me she'd seen

Eugene Krebbs snooping around in the basement before he died. She said he was searching for something."

"Like this diary, perhaps?"

"Maybe. Although according to what Russell Hanover told me, those records have been sitting untouched for decades. So why the sudden interest now?"

"Maybe he had some new information," said Sam. "Have you read this?"

"Part of it. I thought we could look at the rest tonight. I have to take it back on Monday. When I mentioned to Russell Hanover that I had the book, he insisted I return it to the school as soon as possible."

"Interesting."

"I thought so, too," I said, opening the diary to the page I'd marked.

At the point where I'd stopped reading before, Ruth had begun a relationship with a neighborhood workman, Jay Silverman. Earlier pages in the book had offered tidbits of information about other facets of her life; but the last third was devoted solely to her feelings for Jay, feelings which only intensified after Honoria discovered the relationship and forbade Ruth to continue seeing the young man.

Aunt Honoria says he's a totally unsuitable prospect for a girl of my upbringing, Ruth had written. The pages were brittle, and blotted, and several of the words were smeared. I suspected Ruth's tears had caused the damage. *She doesn't understand that I don't care about such things as wealth and position. Jay and I are in love. That's all that matters!!*

"She sounds so young," said Sam.

"She was." I glanced at the date. "Sixteen and a half when she wrote this. I feel sorry for Ruth, but at the same time, I can see Honoria's point. Ruth had clearly formed an attachment to Jay, but I'm not sure she had either the experience or the maturity to recognize what true love was."

"She's a fighter, though," Sam said admiringly, as we read on together. Ruth had defied her aunt's edicts and continued to see Jay behind Honoria's back. "I wonder what ever became of her."

"So do I. I asked Russell about it, but he didn't know. There were six siblings. Apparently none had an interest in continuing an association with the school. I thought I might go over to the Greenwich Library tomorrow and see if I could dig up any information there."

Eagerly, we returned to the story. Though Ruth came alive through her own words, Jay continued to be an enigma, seen only in black and white, depending on whether Ruth was describing her aunt's response to him, or her own. As the days grew shorter and winter set in, tension in the household grew. Ruth became increasingly distressed about the deception she was perpetrating. And about something else, as well. Jay was pressuring her to give herself to him physically, and Ruth wasn't sure she was ready.

"Poor thing," I said. "She was only a kid. She needed someone to talk to, someone she could confide in."

"What about the brothers and sisters?" asked Sam. "There seemed to be enough of them."

"Yes, but Ruth was the baby of the family. By this time, the other siblings were out of the house. Her two brothers were in college. Even if they came home for vacations, she would hardly have talked to them about something like this. Her sisters were all married and running households of their own."

"Keep reading," said Sam, as caught up in the drama as I was. "Let's see what she decided to do."

Tonight is the night I became a woman, Ruth wrote proudly several pages later. *Jay seemed so happy it made my heart swell with joy. Now he truly knows how much I love him and that I will always be his.*

"Notice anything?" asked Sam. He was frowning.

I nodded. "She talks about how happy Jay was, but she doesn't say a thing about her own happiness."

"Somehow I suspect this isn't going to end well," Sam mused. "Do you suppose an innocent like that knew anything about such things as birth control?"

"I doubt she even knew it existed."

A handful of pages later, our fears were confirmed. Ruth's confident script deteriorated to a shaky scrawl as her troubles poured out onto the lined page. *I am pregnant with Jay's child, and I do not know what will become of me. Jay says we will run away and marry. He is making plans, but he worries we will not have the resources to manage on our own.*

I have reassured him on that account, though I fear he does not believe me. Mother revealed the secret of her treasure to me before she died, and I have kept it safe, just as I promised I would. I will take it with me when the time comes, and everything will be all right.

"Treasure?" Sam stopped reading.

"It was a game," I said thoughtfully. "At least I thought it was. Ruth mentioned it earlier in the diary. She talked about her mother hiding things for the children to find. I thought she meant trinkets."

"Even during the Depression, it would have taken more than trinkets to finance what Ruth had in mind."

Our mugs of coffee sat, cold and untouched, on

the table. Sam and I bent over the small book and continued to read avidly. Only a few pages of writing remained.

We are discovered and my life is over. I have never seen Father so angry. Aunt Honoria says I must be sent away. She has offered Jay a sum of money never to see me again or contact me in any way. I know he will not accept. We're going to be married, he's told me so. I must believe in him. I must. But why does he not contact me?

Night after night, Poupee and I wait for Jay to come. The little Poodle is my only solace in these terrible times. And yet, Aunt Honoria would deny me even his small comfort. She screams when she finds him in my room and makes me put him outside. Why does Jay not come? I need him now, more than ever.

"Bastard," Sam muttered. "Do you think he ran out on her?"

"It looks that way." I turned to the last page. Like several before it, it was blotted with tears.

Jay finally came to me tonight. I knew he would not desert me! I held him to me and could scarcely keep from crying, so great was my relief at seeing him again. Right away, I knew something was wrong. He wouldn't put his arms around me. He would not return my kiss.

"I knew you'd come," I told him. My voice was shaking. "I've been waiting and hoping

that every night would be the one. I've packed a small bag—"

But Jay was shaking his head. He would not look at me. "I've come to say good-bye," he said.

The next few lines were indecipherable. When Ruth's script grew legible again, the spirit that had enlivened the diary's pages seemed to have deserted her.

Jay said it was for the best, she wrote. *But he was wrong. This is not the best solution, but the worst of all possibilities. Without him, my life is meaningless. I do not care if I live or die."*

"Oh no." I exhaled. "Are we reading a suicide note?"

"No, thank God." Sam was skimming faster than I was. He'd already finished the last half page.

My aunt says I'm to be sent away until the baby is born and placed for adoption. I am to take nothing with me from home, not clothing, not pictures, nor dear little Poupee, who has been my most faithful friend. I must even leave my diary behind. I can only pray that someday I shall return. And that life will seem brighter than the terrible gloom that surrounds me now.

I closed the book gently, more moved than I cared to admit by a story that had taken place over fifty years earlier. "I wonder if she ever came back."

"I wonder what happened to the child," said Sam. "And to Jay. Do you think he and Ruth ever saw one another again?"

"I doubt it. Honoria saw to that. She treated her niece abominably."

"Times were different then," Sam said. He was more of a realist than I. "A child born out of wedlock was a huge disgrace, a situation that needed to be dealt with quickly and quietly. It was the way things were done."

"And what about the treasure? Ruth didn't take it with her, after all. What do you suppose happened to it?"

"Good question." Sam carried our two mugs over to the sink and emptied them. "It certainly makes you wonder. Is that the reason Krebbs was killed? Because someone was hot on the trail of Mabel Howard's long-lost treasure?"

"But Krebbs didn't have it," I pointed out. "He'd have hardly kept working at the school if he did."

"Maybe there never really was a treasure. It's quite possible something that could have seemed priceless to a sheltered sixteen-year-old might have turned out to have very little value in the real world."

"And maybe the murder had nothing to do with the treasure at all." I stared at the small, leather-bound book, hoping for inspiration. It didn't come. "This whole thing is giving me a headache."

"Then stop thinking about it." Sam walked over and wound his arms around me. "I have a much better idea. Let's go to bed."

"All the way to bed, this time?"

He grinned. "I'll race you."

He won, but just barely.

☙ Twenty-three ☙

Sunday morning, I awoke to the sound of my son's shrieks.

Any mother of a six-year-old boy can tell you, that's not necessarily a bad sign. I got one eye open in time to see that the screams in question were supposed to be war whoops, and that Sam and I were in imminent danger of attack by a pair of wild Indians, namely Davey and his cohort in crime, Faith.

The superhero pajamas had been exchanged for a buckskin vest and pants; remnants, I seemed to recall, from an old Halloween costume. Faith sported a long red feather sticking out of her topknot. I was quite certain Aunt Peg would not have approved.

The two of them landed on the bed with enough of a thump to shake the floor beneath us. Luckily, the bed frame held.

"Time to wake up!" cried Davey.

I glanced over at the bedside clock. It was barely seven. On Sunday morning, no less.

Sam rolled over, grabbed Davey, and seated him on his chest. They were both grinning at the arrangement. If I didn't love Sam, I think I'd have to marry him anyway, just because he looks so damn good first thing in the morning.

It takes me longer to become coherent, and that first cup of coffee never hurts. "Has Faith been out?" I managed.

"Sure. We've been up for *hours*. We made you breakfast."

That got both eyes open. "You did?"

"Yup. I did most of it, but Faith helped."

I was sure she had. The Poodle was an expert at licking up spills. "What are we having?"

"Peanut butter and jelly sandwiches and chocolate milk."

"Sounds great," said Sam. Carrying Davey easily, he slid out from beneath the covers, stood up, and headed for the door. "Let's eat."

After breakfast, Sam took Davey and Faith and drove to Redding to check on his Poodles. Whenever he's going to be away for the night, he has a pet-sitter come and stay with them. The arrangement has always worked out well, but that doesn't stop him from worrying. In his place, I'd have felt the same way, and usually I'd have been happy to ride along.

Today, however, I used the time to drive over to Greenwich and see what I could find out about the Howard family. Perched on a busy corner near downtown, the Greenwich Library is a wondrous place. Renovated and significantly enlarged in the seventies, it's a haven where I could happily lose myself for hours.

I started my quest at the Information desk. The

local newspaper is the *Greenwich Time*, but Miss Abbott, the librarian, looked through the files and informed me that before 1937, the town had had another paper, the *Greenwich Press*. Records for both were stored on microfilm. Since I wasn't sure what I was looking for, I began by simply browsing through editions from the early to mid thirties. It was slow going, with very little reward.

It quickly became obvious that the Howard family was not the type to make front-page news. I was reminded of the old adage declaring that a proper member of society should appear in the newspaper on only three occasions: at birth, at marriage, and at death. With that in mind, I began to devote most of my scanning to the social pages. There, I finally had some luck.

I found the birth announcement for a daughter, born to Florence Pickwick (née Howard); and an engagement notice for Matthew Putnam Howard, Ruth's older brother. As I skimmed through the decade, all the Howard siblings eventually made an appearance, except Ruth. There was no mention of her anywhere.

After two hours of reading, my eyes were beginning to grow bleary. I'd reached the conclusion that I was going to have to track Ruth through other means when Miss Abbott appeared beside my chair.

"I'm glad you're still here," she said. "I was

thinking about your request for information on the Howard family, and it jiggled something in the back of my mind It just took me a little while to figure out what it was. Maybe this will help."

The book she handed me was large and heavy; a coffee-table book with thick, glossy pages entitled, *The Great Estates of Early Greenwich.* I set it down on the desk and opened to the table of contents.

"The Howard family home is one of those profiled," Miss Abbott said, peering over my shoulder. Her finger traced quickly down through the list of chapters. "Not the building that houses the current school. That mansion was actually constructed by the founders for the purpose it now serves. The Howard home in Deer Park, however, was once one of Greenwich's finest showplaces. Ah, there it is. Page one seventy-eight."

Together we flipped through the heavy pages. I gasped softly when the picture appeared. Even in black-and-white, the home was gorgeous.

"Wow. I'm impressed."

"You were meant to be. Joshua Howard was a man of some standing in the community, and I'm sure his house was built to reflect his position."

There were two columns of text opposite the photo, and the story continued over the next several pages. "I'm more interested in the family than the house," I said. "Especially the youngest daughter, Ruth."

"I wouldn't be surprised if there's something here. It's been a while since I've had an occasion to flip through the book, but the histories are pretty detailed."

According to the text, Joshua Howard had commissioned the plans for his house from a prominent architect of the time, then overseen the construction himself. He and his wife had moved into the mansion a few years into the new century; and all six of his children had been born there.

"The historian who wrote this was more interested in Joshua Howard's business accomplishments than his family," I said, skipping on ahead. Toward the end of the piece, I finally found what I was looking for. The last several paragraphs explained why I hadn't been able to find any mention of Ruth earlier.

This grand house was the scene of a tragedy in 1936 when Joshua Howard's youngest daughter Ruth, committed suicide in her second floor bedroom. She was only eighteen years old at the time.

The Howard family sold the mansion the following year. Much of the furniture and artwork from the vast estate was donated to the eponymous private school,

Howard Academy. During the next several decades the mansion changed hands regularly as rumors of ghostly sightings abounded. Ruth Howard was said to haunt the back stairs and the gardens below her bedroom where, according to legend, she'd once sneaked away to meet with her lover.

Plagued by superstition and bad luck, the house was allowed to fall into disrepair. It was demolished in 1960 to make way for new construction. By all accounts, the spirit of young, beautiful Ruth Howard vanished with it.

"That's some story," said Miss Abbott.

"I wonder whatever happened to her baby," I mused.

"What baby?"

"Ruth Howard got pregnant when she was seventeen. Her lover was paid off and her family sent her away to have the baby and put it up for adoption. That's why I wanted to look through the records. I was hoping to find out what happened next."

"Now you know." The librarian picked up the book. "I'm sorry your story didn't have a happier ending."

"Me too."

Back at home, I found I still had some time to kill before Sam and Davey returned. On a hunch, I pulled out a Greenwich phone book and ran through the listings, looking for the names I'd copied from the newspaper accounts. There were a number of Howards listed, but none with the first names I was looking for.

By now, at least one more generation would have passed, maybe two. It was theoretically possible that everyone listed could have been related to Joshua's family. It was equally possible that none of them were.

Grumbling, I put the phone book aside and wandered into the kitchen to pour myself a soda. The house around me was still and empty. I couldn't remember the last time I'd been home alone; with no child to distract me, no Poodle to bring me a soggy tennis ball. Most days I could only dream of peace and quiet. Now I had all I could possibly want, and it was driving me crazy.

Too bad my little Cape had been built too recently to come with such amenities as ghosts, I mused, thinking back to the story I'd read in the library. Something about that tale had struck a familiar chord. But what was it? Someone else had been talking about ghosts recently . . .

I was staring out the window into the empty back yard when it came to me. Shawna and Bobbi, the two girls who worked in the kitchen —that was who I'd been trying to remember. Each had mentioned something about Howard Academy being haunted. At the time, I'd thought they were just being dramatic. Now I wondered if they were aware of the old family legends.

Despite what I'd told Russell, I was coming to the conclusion that it wouldn't hurt to ask a few questions. Cover some bases that hadn't been covered. Prick a few consciences and see what kind of information turned up.

Especially after what had happened on Friday, I could hardly be blamed for wanting the whole process to move along. Somebody had to get to the bottom of this mess.

Monday morning, I dropped Davey off at school early again. He'd enjoyed playing doughnut delivery boy so much that he didn't mind a bit. Especially after we swung by the bakery for the second time in less than a week.

I'm not going to make a habit of this kind of behavior. I swear.

Faith's trial period was going so well that that morning I was bold enough to bring in a dog bed for the corner of my classroom. It was big and round; filled with cedar chips and covered with fake sheepskin. Faith loved it, and it smelled divine. It made a fine addition to the room, not to mention a good place to leave her for a few minutes while I went down to the kitchen.

"Uh-oh!"

I heard Shawna's high-pitched voice as soon as I entered the dining room. She and Bobbi were working together, setting the tables. A handful of silverware clattered to the floor at Shawna's feet.

"Girl, watch out!" she said to her friend. "Here comes more bad news."

"I don't have any bad news," I said. "What makes you think I would?"

" 'Cause that's what you bring around here, don't I know it?" Shawna nodded vigorously in support of her question. "First time, a man's dead. Second time, you got that runaway kid with you. She's another one who's up to no good. And Lord knows we got plenty of that around here."

I pulled out a chair and sat down, hoping to look less threatening. Hoping to indicate my intention to stay a while. Bobbi smoothed a tablecloth, snapped her gum, and looked perfectly pleased to watch the show. Shawna bit her lip and looked worried.

"What makes you think Jane is a runaway?" I asked.

"I got eyes, don't I? That child needs somebody to take care of her." Shawna stooped down and hurriedly gathered up the cutlery she'd dropped. "Ain't nobody's mama lets them go out looking all raggedy like that. Besides, she don't belong here, that's for sure. So why's she hanging around all the time? If you ask me, that's the trouble with this place. There's entirely too much of that going on."

"Nobody asked you," Bobbi said, casting her friend a warning look.

"Too much of what?"

"People running around where they're not supposed to be. Some days, it's enough to give me a heart condition."

"Shawna doesn't know what she's talking about," Bobbi said.

"I do too!"

"Does this have anything to do with Howard Academy being haunted?" I asked.

"Saints preserve us!" Shawna quickly crossed herself.

Bobbi rolled her eyes. "You get her started, it's your own fault."

"Don't tell me I'm going to have ghosts to contend with, too. Don't you tell me that!"

"Wasn't that what you were talking about?"

"Not me," Shawna said firmly. "I've never seen a ghost, and I'm not planning to neither. I got enough trouble with the here and now, without looking for somebody from the here-after to come and take me away."

"I told you not to get her started," said Bobbi.

Ignoring her, I concentrated on Shawna. "Then who are you talking about? Who's been running around where they shouldn't be?"

Shawna shook her head. "I work in the kitchen, okay? I get my job done. I do what I'm supposed to do."

"Of course you do. But that doesn't mean you don't see things. You and I both know that something strange has been going on around here. I want to find out who's behind it."

"I'm outta here," Bobbi said, striding across the room. "Girl, you can put your own butt in the fire, but you ain't taking me with you." The door to the kitchen swung shut behind her.

Shawna glanced at the door as it continued to swing. Then she looked back at me.

"You won't get in trouble from anything you tell me," I said. "I promise."

"Maybe that's not your promise to give."

True, but I could probably convince Russell to back me up. "I won't let you down."

Slowly, Shawna walked over to where I sat. "I been working here four years," she said. I patted the chair next to me, but she didn't sit down. "I like my job, you hear what I'm saying?"

"Yes."

"My job is just fine with me. But recently . . . things began to change around here. There's stuff going on that never used to happen."

"What kind of stuff?"

Shawna's voice lowered. "People running around where they got no business being. Sneaking like they think nobody can see them. So I ask myself, why would anybody be prowling around like that unless they were up to no good?"

"People like Krebbs?" I asked.

"He's one. First three and a half years I work here, I barely even saw the man." Her teeth flashed in a smile. "Mrs. Plimpton, she runs this place like a drill sergeant. She tells Krebbs not to be coming around bothering us in the kitchen, and he don't dare. Not until recently, anyway."

"What did Krebbs want in the kitchen?"

Shawna scowled at my lack of comprehension. "It wasn't the kitchen, it was the stairs. You can get down to the basement from here. You can get up to the second floor, too."

As far as I knew, the second floor contained only a few administrative offices and some storerooms. I'd never had occasion to venture up there, but I knew perfectly well that there was a wide staircase in the front hall and I said as much.

"A place this size, you don't think it has back stairs?" Shawna scoffed. "Front stairs are for people who want to be seen, back stairs are for people who don't. That's exactly what I'm talking about."

"Who else have you seen using the back stairs? The girl, Jane?"

"She's another one. Upstairs, downstairs. She's been all over the place. We keep some extra supplies down in the basement, so when I go down, I got a reason. But that don't tell me what everyone else is up to."

"Who else?" I pressed.

"That new teacher, the drama guy. He's another one who's been poking around like he thinks he's got a right."

"Michael Durant?"

"That's the one. Half the time, he don't even care if I see. He looks right through me like I don't even exist."

"Do you think he's looking for something?"

"How should I know?" Shawna sounded angry. "Man can't see me, I think maybe it's just as well if I can't see him."

Krebbs, Jane, and Michael. Apparently, Shawna had noticed all of them behaving in ways she found suspicious. But so what? Nothing she'd told me so far was enough to send Bobbi running from the room. There had to be something more.

"Who else?" I asked.

"Isn't that enough?" Shawna shrugged. I didn't need my teacher's skills to know she was being evasive.

"Not if you've got more names to give me."

She drew in a deep breath. "I guess there's another guy. I don't know his name. He wears those stupid tweed jackets with elbow patches. He heads up there to have a smoke. Like nobody can smell what he's up to."

Ed Weinstein. It had to be.

"Sometimes he isn't alone." She paused, waiting to see if I'd grasped her meaning.

I hadn't. "So?"

"So he meets somebody up there, sometimes. And maybe they do a little business together."

"Business?" I thought quickly. "Are you talking about Brad, that kid from town? Is that who Ed meets?"

Shawna glanced around the room, satisfied herself that we were alone, then nodded warily.

"Is that everybody?"

Shawna was squirming again. She'd already blown the whistle on Ed and Brad. What could possibly be left to make her nervous?

"Shawna?"

"You promised me I wouldn't get into trouble," she reminded me.

"You won't," I said firmly. "A man has been murdered. This is important, Shawna. You have to tell me what you know."

She sat for a moment, weighing her options. Judging by the expression on her face, she didn't like the conclusion she came to.

"There was someone else who's been sneaking around," she whispered.

I waited, letting her take her time.

Shawna's eyes darted from side to side. I've seen rats in a maze that looked happier.

"It was Mr. Hanover," she blurted finally. "You know, the Big Guy. The headmaster."

❧ Twenty-four ❧

I guessed that meant I needed to have a chat with the Big Guy. You know, the headmaster.

While I'd been trying to mind my own business, it seemed like half the school had been acting suspicious. Russell made as good a place to start as any. Besides, I'd brought Ruth's diary to school with me as he'd requested, and I wanted to place the book in his hands personally.

The bell to announce the start of first period was ringing as I left the dining room. Already late, I stopped in the office and grabbed the mail out of my box. Aside from the usual batch of Monday morning memos, there was a terse note from Michael canceling the pageant committee meeting he'd scheduled for noon. No explanation was offered. Just for the heck of it, I bumped his name up to second place on my list.

When I got to my classroom, I found Willie Boyd sitting on the floor beside Faith's bed. He was telling her about the Poodle that had belonged to his aunt. I knew that boy had potential.

Seeing me, Willie leapt to his feet and brushed off his pants self-consciously. "Just checking out your guard dog," he said, unsure how much I'd heard. "I guess she'll do."

"She likes to be talked to." I put my things down on my desk and walked over to where he stood. "I do it all the time."

"You do?"

"Sure, Faith makes a great listener. Besides, she understands almost everything I say."

"Nah, she's not *that* smart."

"Want to bet?"

Willie's gaze narrowed. "This is a trick, right?"

I shrugged innocently. "Some people look at Faith and can't see past the silly hairdo. They think she must be some kind of circus dog with mush for brains. That's their mistake. Luckily, Faith's way too intelligent to let other people's ignorance bother her."

"Don't tell me. We're having some kind of life lesson here, aren't we?" Willie pulled out a chair and sat down. "You're using that dog to make a point."

"You catch on pretty quick for a kid who got a C- on his last Latin quiz."

"Latin's a dead language. I'm saving my energy for things that can do me some good."

"College is going to do you plenty of good." I took a chair on the other side of the table. "And top grades are what's going to get you where you want to go. I know you've had some trouble fitting in here, and things aren't going to get any easier when you go to Brunswick for high school next year. A lot of kids in Greenwich get everything they want handed to them. I guess that makes you luckier than most."

"Luckier? How do you figure that?"

"Because you've already learned how to work hard and think for yourself. Some of my students will spend the next decade trying to figure out things you already take for granted. You have tremendous gifts, Willie, but it's up to you to use what's being offered. Slacking off isn't going to make you popular. In the long run, the only person you'll hurt is yourself."

Willie leaned back in his chair, frowning. "You sound just like my mother."

"Good."

I figured that meant I was getting my point across. Besides, I'd met Willie's mother on parents' night. Emma Boyd was every bit as smart as her son, plus she had a wicked sense of humor. I didn't mind the comparison a bit.

"You know, as teachers go, you're not half-bad."

"Thanks. Now let's dig out your Latin book and have a look."

"Sure." Willie reached for his backpack. "But first there's something you ought to know. Brad Jameson, remember you asked me about him?"

"I remember. What about him?"

"He's gone."

"What do you mean?"

"Just what I said. He's gone, left town. Cleared

out over the weekend and took his business with him."

"What business was that?" I asked carefully.

"You know." Willie frowned. "We talked about it before."

"And you said you didn't know anything about what Brad was up to."

"No," Willie corrected me. "I said I didn't *need* to know. I wasn't interested, and I didn't have any use for his services. But that doesn't mean I can't see what's right under my nose. Anyway, it doesn't matter now because he's out of here."

That was an interesting wrinkle I wondered if Detective Shertz had been keeping tabs on Brad's whereabouts.

"Any idea why he left?" I asked.

"Maybe I heard a few things. People say Brad thought Greenwich was getting a little hot. Like maybe he needed to find a new place to set up shop where he wasn't so well known."

"Thanks for the information," I said. "I'll pass it along."

Willie nodded and opened his book.

The tutoring session with Willie was followed by three others in quick succession. It was lunchtime before I had a chance to slip out and run over to Russell's office; and when I got there, he wasn't in. Now it was Harriet's turn to look smug.

"Perhaps if you'd made an appointment," she said primly. "You know how busy Mr. Hanover can be." Her hand hovered above a pink note-pad. "I'll tell him you stopped by. Is there any message?"

"Just tell him I need to talk to him, okay?"

I left her scribbling on the pad and went off in search of Michael. No luck there either. Rather than waste the entire period running around in vain, I consoled myself by going to lunch.

The kitchen was serving chicken Florentine with chocolate chip brownies for dessert. I went back for seconds, then carried the extra brownie with me to eat while I took Faith outside for a run. Back inside ten minutes later, it was time to teach some more.

This is why Kinsey Milhone doesn't have a day job.

At quarter to three, my intercom buzzed. Russell was in his office and would see me as soon as I was available. I gave my last student short shrift and made myself available immediately. Don't forget, I still had Davey's bus to meet.

Did I mention that Kinsey doesn't have children either?

No matter what else is happening at Howard Academy, Russell Hanover's office is usually an oasis of calm. The headmaster prides himself on setting an example worth following. His veneer of imperturbability is meant to inspire us all to keep a similarly stiff upper lip, and usually it works.

Not today. Today all hell was breaking loose. Even the unflappable Harriet looked frazzled

"What's up?" I whispered under my breath, as she shooed me past her desk and into the inner sanctum.

She shook her head slightly and pulled the door shut behind me.

"Mr. Hanover?"

He was standing at the window, staring off down the driveway. His back was to me, and even when I said his name, he didn't look around.

"Is something wrong?"

Finally, he turned and walked over to his desk. "Is there anything that's not wrong? In the last seven days, we've had a murder, a fire, a funeral, and a discovery of drugs on campus. I've been trying to hold things together, but regrettably, it may only be a matter of time before even I lose my grip. And those barbarians at the gate aren't helping matters any."

"The media?"

"Who else?" He shoved his hands in the pockets of his pants, ruining the elegant line of his suit. "I was asked to make a statement to the press, chastising the police for not solving the murder with more dispatch. When I refused, the reporter implied that perhaps the police were being hampered in their investigation because Howard Academy was stonewalling.

"It's been a week, and they want a story. If one isn't available, they're not above inventing one to suit their purposes. Howard Academy has flourished for half a century. It saddens me to think the school may not survive my tenure as headmaster."

I'd never seen him so morose. "I think you need a drink," I said. A small bar was set up on a cart in a corner of the room. I assumed it was there for the benefit of visiting parents. Certainly, I'd never seen anyone make use of it. "Scotch?"

"In the middle of the afternoon?" Russell smiled slightly. "Is this how low we've sunk?"

"I'd say so."

I opened a bottle of Chivas and poured him a double. Russell didn't protest when I placed the glass on his desk. I put Ruth's diary down beside it. He glanced at it, then flipped through the pages idly, not really looking at them.

"This must be the diary you told me about on Friday."

I nodded.

"Did it contain what you were looking for?"

"A theme for the spring pageant? No. Ruth's story didn't turn out to be suitable."

Russell shrugged, his demeanor clearly conveying the thought: another setback, what else is new? Much as I'd always wished that Bitsy would use a little less starch in his shorts, I wasn't sure I liked being confronted with the headmaster's more vulnerable side.

Had he been this worn down by the past week's events? I wondered. Or was something more going on? I was beginning to think that Russell looked like a man with a guilty conscience.

"There's something I've been wondering about," I said.

He picked up the drink I'd poured and took a hefty swallow. Good for him. I'd have pictured him as a sipper.

"What's that?"

"Michael Durant was hired mid year. Isn't that unusual?"

"No." Russell's voice was firm, but his eyes shifted away. "Not if there's a need."

"And Howard Academy developed a sudden need for a drama coach?"

"It was hardly sudden. I'd been thinking about making such an addition for a while."

"And about adding a spring pageant to the school's program? I understand this is the first year such an event has been held."

"So?"

"One of the other teachers mentioned that Michael's credentials were not as high as Howard Academy might normally be expected to demand."

"They were perfectly adequate for the position he was being asked to fill." Russell did not look pleased by my questions. "I'm not sure why you consider this to be any of your business."

"It's been hard not to notice that a number of people have been behaving oddly since Krebbs was murdered." I decided it wouldn't further my cause to mention that Russell's own name was on the list. "Most have been associated with the school for years. Michael only arrived six weeks ago. Detective Shertz said he didn't believe in coincidence. I'm not sure I do either."

A minute passed while Russell sat and said nothing. His drink remained untouched. His fingertip traced an aimless pattern on the blotter.

"Howard Academy is a private institution," he said finally. "Serving the best interests of our students is our first priority. In this day and age, that seems to be a somewhat idealistic notion. Unfortunately, one sometimes finds that idealism must be set aside in the face of practicality."

"What does that have to do with the drama coach?"

Once again, Russell was silent.

"Is there something you know that you haven't told the police?" I prompted. "Do you know who murdered Eugene Krebbs?"

The question shocked him out of his reverie. "Certainly not. I would never conceal such a thing. There has been something preying on my mind. A business transaction—perhaps a regrettable one—but nothing more than that."

I didn't believe him. There was something here. I was sure of it. "A business deal between you and Michael? Did it have anything to do with the drugs that were found in the cottage?"

Russell's face suffused with color. "What sort of a person do you take me for?"

"One with secrets, apparently. I know how you feel about Howard Academy. You'd do anything to protect the school—"

"Quite right. And that's precisely what I have done."

"You made a deal with Michael Durant to protect the school? I don't understand."

"Of course not. There's no reason you should."

"Mr. Hanover, whatever you're hiding—"

"Is hardly germane to what happened to Krebbs."

I pulled a chair up to his desk and sat down. "Perhaps Detective Shertz should be allowed to decide that."

"It's not a matter I wish to have made public. Indeed, that's how this whole sorry business got started." Russell looked at me and sighed. "May I depend on your discretion?"

"Certainly, unless—" His look silenced me. I waited to hear what he had to say.

"As it happens, the circumstances surrounding

Michael Durant's employment were a bit unusual."

"In what way?"

"He came to us. To me, rather, with a proposal. Howard Academy has long been proud of our position in the Greenwich community. We set an example. We uphold our traditions. And we always take care of our own."

"Like Eugene Krebbs?"

"Exactly." Russell stood up and walked back to the window. Once again, he was staring outward. I wondered what, if anything, he saw. "And like Michael Durant."

Now I was confused. "How did Michael become part of Howard Academy's family?"

"He was born that way," Russell said quietly. "Not in the official sense, but his proof was compelling enough. For as long as I've been at Howard Academy, I'd heard the stories. Rumors, really, of an illegitimate child born to one of the family members."

"Ruth," I said. "The youngest daughter."

Russell turned to look at me. "Don't tell me you're another family connection."

"Hardly. I learned the story over the weekend from Ruth's diary. She became pregnant and was planning to elope. Honoria paid off the boy and sent Ruth away to have the baby. She implied that it was put up for adoption."

"Maybe that was the plan, but it isn't what

happened. The boy's family took the child and raised him. He grew up to be Michael Durant's father."

"You're kidding!"

"I wouldn't dream of it," Russell said irritably. "Michael has possession of letters and photographs that back his claim. While the Howards were determined to keep the whole incident quiet, the Silverman family was rather proud of their association with one of Greenwich's leading names. From the time Michael was a child, he'd been told stories about his grandfather's dalliance with Ruth Howard."

"So when he came to you and asked for a job, you didn't feel you could turn him away?"

"I'm afraid it was a bit more complicated than that. Michael came to me with his grandfather's mementos and a story that he planned to sell to the highest bidder. It may have happened a long time ago, but the tale still possessed everything the tabloids dream of—money, sex, the suicide of an innocent young girl. Michael Durant was in need of money, and he seemed to think that the Howard family owed him for the wrong that had been done."

"The family and the school aren't one and the same," I pointed out.

"It would hardly have mattered, would it? We'd all have been tarred by the same brush. Michael had been struggling to make his living

311

as an actor in New York. That's where 'Durant' comes from. It's his stage name. I gather he found the profession rough going. Last December his agent dropped him, and he decided he was ready to make a career change."

"He threatened you with blackmail and you hired him?" I asked incredulously. "Please tell me there was more to your decision than that."

"There are always outside considerations that enter into any such decision." Russell's brows lowered ominously. Clearly he didn't like my tone. "I wouldn't have hired Michael if I hadn't felt he was equipped to do the job."

"If he was equipped to do his job, he'd be doing it," I said, getting to my feet. "And Howard Academy would have a spring pageant that was already in rehearsal instead of—"

"Melanie?" Russell's voice was calm. "Sit."

I sat.

"In a perfect world, one's decisions would always remain unbiased. In the reality in which we operate, however, it is often necessary that compromises be made. My first consideration must be the good of the school—"

"And you think it's a *good* thing to expose the students to a man who'd stoop to blackmail to accomplish his goals?"

"I think it was an abhorrent necessity, but a necessity nonetheless. And as you are determined to argue about this, you force me to point out that your own hiring might not bear up under the closest scrutiny either."

For a moment, time seemed to stop. The room went perfectly still. I wasn't sure I'd heard him correctly. I couldn't have.

"Excuse me?"

Russell sighed. "Melanie, how many applicants do you think we had for the tutoring position you assumed last fall?"

"I have no idea." There was a loud buzzing noise in my ears. It was difficult to concentrate on what he was saying.

My confusion must have shown on my face because Russell's voice gentled. "Nearly a hundred. Probably a dozen had qualifications as good as, or better than, yours."

So help me, I didn't want to know the answer. But I knew I had to ask. "Then why did you hire me?"

"It was strictly a financial decision, made for the good of the academy. Yours was the application that came contingent with a sizable donation from one of our alumnae."

"Aunt Peg," I whispered.

Russell nodded. "You didn't know?"

"I had no idea." My head was spinning. It wasn't a pleasant sensation. "I'm sorry. I'll tender my resignation at the end of the semester."

"It won't be accepted. And you have nothing to be sorry about. You've been an excellent addition to our staff, just as I knew you would be. The donation was only one small factor in the decision-making process. I only brought it up to try and make you understand how things work."

Oh I understood, all right. Suddenly, I understood everything. That the job I'd coveted, worked for, and thought I deserved, I'd never truly earned. Even if I had been good enough to make it on my own, I'd never had the chance, because dear, conniving Aunt Peg had taken the matter out of my hands.

I slumped in my chair, feeling defeated. What a hypocrite Russell must have thought I was, denouncing Michael Durant's hiring when mine had been every bit as suspect. No wonder he'd been self-righteous in his own defense.

Was this truly the way the world operated? Was I the only one who didn't know?

The intercom on Russell's desk buzzed. Still watching me, he pushed the button, and said, "Not now, Harriet."

"I think you better take this," the secretary's voice was audible through the speaker. "Detective Shertz is on the phone, and he says it's important. That young girl, Jane? He says she's missing."

✿ Twenty-five ✿

Missing?

Russell picked up the phone and spoke into it briefly. His end of the conversation consisted mostly of one syllable words, and when he hung up, he didn't look happy. "Detective Shertz is on his way over. He'll be here in five minutes."

There was no way I was going to leave now. As soon as Russell put down the phone, I picked it up, connected to an outside line, and called Alice Brickman. Once again, she agreed to cover for me. If this kept up, I was going to be indebted to her until the boys were in high school.

That done, we still had a few minutes to kill. "There are a few more things you need to know," I said to Russell.

"Oh?" He looked like a man who was braced for bad news, which was good, because I couldn't imagine he'd be happy to hear what I was about to say.

"Ed Weinstein."

"What about him?"

"You know he smokes?"

"Of course. I don't like it, but I can hardly dictate my employees' personal habits. He takes his cigarette breaks outside."

315

"Or in the boys' bathroom. Or on the back stairs." I watched Russell's lips tighten and felt like a tattletale. "Unfortunately, that's not all. Two days ago, I ran into him outside. He smelled of marijuana."

"Are you sure?" His tone was sterner than I'd ever heard it.

"Yes. I'm also pretty sure that Jane's friend, Brad, has been dealing drugs on campus."

"To Weinstein?"

"Probably. And maybe others as well. Brad has a reputation as a supplier, and it would explain why he's been hanging around the school."

"What about Jane?"

"I doubt she has any idea. She looks up to him, kind of like a big brother. I would imagine he was the one who brought her over here in the first place. For some reason, he fashioned himself as her protector."

"Interesting concept," Russell mused. "Do we know who she felt she needed protection from?"

"Possibly Krebbs. I know he tried to run her off on several occasions. She retaliated by spying on him. It was a game to Jane, only Krebbs didn't find it funny at all.

"Jane seemed to think that he was searching for something around the school. Then earlier today, one of the kitchen girls told me that Krebbs, along with several other people, had been sneaking up and down the back stairs."

"The other people being who?" Now Russell looked disgruntled. I doubted anything I said could surprise him anymore.

"Ed for one, looking for a place to smoke. Jane, for another. She was probably following Krebbs. Brad Jameson, doing business. Michael Durant . . ." I paused, watching his face. "No explanation there, unless you have one."

"Me? What would make you think I know what Durant was doing on the back stairs?"

"Because the other person Shawna saw was you."

Russell's frown deepened. "I do not sneak."

The man had a point.

"As headmaster, I am in charge of the entire school. Anywhere I choose to go falls well within the scope of my duties. Which brings me to a point I feel bears discussion."

Uh-oh. That didn't sound good. "Yes?"

"You seem to have acquired quite a lot of information about the goings-on at the school. I believe the last time we discussed this, I had your assurance that you would stay out of it."

"You did, but . . ."

I was hoping for divine intervention. Amazingly, it showed up. Detective Shertz wasn't exactly what I'd had in mind, but his timing was impeccable.

"Mind if I come in?" The door pushed open,

and Shertz entered the room. "Your secretary doesn't seem to be at her desk."

Harriet off-duty? That had to be a first. Maybe she was sick.

"Please, join us." Russell rose and waved the detective to a seat. He glanced out the door toward his secretary's empty desk and shook his head slightly. "I can't imagine where she's gotten to. Then again, everyone seems to be behaving oddly these days. Why should Harriet be any different? I believe you wanted to talk to us about Jane?"

"Right. According to her grandmother, the girl has disappeared. I gather she often spends a fair amount of time here, so I figured this was the logical place to start. Has either of you seen her today?"

Russell and I both shook our heads.

"A question?" So help me, I almost raised my hand. I've got to get out more.

"Yes?" Shertz swung his gaze my way.

"Since Jane came to live in Greenwich, she seems to have spent a great deal of time unsupervised. For the most part, I don't think her grandmother's had any idea where she was. What makes today any different? Why does she think Jane is missing?"

"It's not just today," said Shertz. "Mrs. Gaines hasn't seen her grand-daughter since midday yesterday."

"And she's just now getting around to doing something about it?" I asked incredulously.

"She thought Jane would turn up. Like you said, the girl is pretty independent. I gather there have been some control problems. The mother pretty much let Jane run wild, and she's having trouble adjusting to her grandmother's rules. Mrs. Gaines was concerned last night, but she didn't want to turn to the authorities until it was absolutely necessary."

"She's afraid Jane might be taken away from her," I guessed.

"Probably," Shertz agreed. "Anyway, by this morning, her fear for the girl's safety was enough to override the other concerns. Today was to have been Jane's first day back in school. But when Mrs. Gaines went to wake her up, the bed was empty, and it didn't appear to have been slept in."

"Jane talked about going back to school over the weekend," I said. "She wasn't delighted by the prospect, but she seemed resigned. I certainly didn't get the impression she was thinking of running away."

"Runaways usually take their gear with them. At the very least, they take their money. Everything Jane had was still where she'd left it. That was another reason why Mrs. Gaines didn't contact us right away. She assumed the girl would be coming back."

That didn't sound good. "Do you think some-thing's happened to her?" I asked.

"Right now I'm not forming any theories, I'm just gathering information. When was the last time you saw Jane?"

"Saturday, early evening. We'd met at Krebbs's memorial service here that morning. I was going to spend the afternoon with my aunt and Jane ended up coming with me. I dropped her off at her house around five-thirty."

"You?" Shertz looked at Russell.

"That day, as well. I saw her briefly at the service. To tell the truth, the only reason I even noticed her presence was that I was somewhat surprised by it. I certainly haven't seen her since."

"There's something you should know," I said to the detective. Russell winced slightly, wonder-ing no doubt which piece of dirty laundry I'd be airing. "Brad Jameson is missing, too."

"How do you know?"

"One of my students told me earlier that Brad left town over the weekend."

Shertz's eyes narrowed. "Any particular reason your students would be bringing you informa-tion like that?"

Russell was glowering, but I didn't have a choice. If Jane's safety was at stake, I had to share everything I knew. "After what you told me about Brad's reputation, I became curious about what he was doing on campus. I also wanted to find out if Jane was being exposed to a bad influence. So I asked a few discreet questions."

"Last time you asked a few questions, I seem to recall you ended up with a bump on your head and a murderer on your hands. I thought we agreed you'd stay out of it."

"I tried," I said honestly. "But circumstances kept dragging me back in."

The detective's lips twitched. He did not look entirely convinced by my explanation. "Since I seem to have acquired a partner whether I want one or not, mind letting me in on what else you've found out?"

"Brad was dealing drugs on campus. In all likelihood, he numbered one of the teachers, Ed Weinstein, among his customers. By the way, nobody I've spoken to can connect Krebbs with the stash that was found near his body."

Shertz nodded, encouraging me to continue. Russell walked over to the bar and poured himself another drink.

"The long-lost relative mentioned in Krebbs's will, who stands to inherit a sizable amount of money, is also a teacher here."

"We're aware of that," said the detective.

Russell looked up. "I wasn't."

"Sally Minor. Krebbs was her father's cousin. She was embarrassed by the family connection and made him promise never to reveal it. I suspect he phrased the bequest the way he did as a sort of revenge. Nevertheless, Sally intends to step forward. She's desperate for money."

Russell looked as though he was about to protest. "A mother with Alzheimer's," said Shertz, forestalling the interruption. "Anything else?"

I glanced at Russell and lifted a brow. My vow of discretion was about to be broken. Fortunately, he seemed to agree that Jane's disappearance had raised the stakes, because he nodded.

"Michael Durant, the drama coach is new at school this semester, which means he arrived on the scene about the same time that everyone began behaving suspiciously. Like Krebbs, he had a connection to Howard Academy's founding family."

"Born on the wrong side of the blanket," Russell explained. He looked pleased finally to have something to contribute.

"Another thing," I said. "Jane was convinced that Krebbs was searching for something here at the school."

"Any idea what?" asked Shertz. He'd pulled out his pad and was making notes.

"Only a really vague theory." I sat up in my chair. There was something I'd been pondering since Russell had filled in the blanks about Michael's family history. "More of a wild guess, really."

"You may as well go ahead and spit it out. At the moment, I'm taking anything I can get."

"I spent part of the weekend reading Ruth Howard's diary. Joshua Howard founded the school seventy years ago, and Ruth was his youngest daughter. She fell in love with a boy who'd been hired to do some work at the family home, got pregnant, and was planning to elope with him."

Shertz made a spinning motion in the air with his hand, asking me to skip over a few facts and bring the story up to the present. I couldn't, though; the middle was too important. I began to talk faster.

"In her diary, Ruth mentioned a hidden treasure. It was something her mother had set aside before her death. Ruth was going to use it to finance her getaway."

"Did she?" Shertz asked, but it was clear he was fast losing interest.

"No. Honoria Howard paid the boy to disappear and sent Ruth away to have the baby. A year after her return, she committed suicide. The child was raised by the boy's family and grew up to be Michael Durant's father."

"Let me get this straight," the detective said skeptically. "You think there's a treasure buried somewhere at the school and that Krebbs was trying to find it?"

"Possibly." I frowned. "I told you it was only a hunch. And I doubt if the treasure is actually buried. But when the mansion in Deer Park was sold shortly after Ruth's death, most of the family's possessions were brought over here.

"Ruth had every intention of running away with Jay Silverman. He was a laborer, I doubt that he had any money of his own. Ruth was in love—"

"Wait a minute!" Shertz cried. "What did you say?"

"Ruth was in love—"

"Before that!"

"She was planning to run away with Jay, but he was—"

"Poor. Right. Who cares? Back to Krebbs. His family had worked for the Howard family for years. That's where he grew up, right?"

"Correct," said Russell. "Krebbs's father was Joshua Howard's butler. They lived on the estate."

"Think about it," said the detective. "Kids get into everything. Krebbs must have known about Ruth being sent away. He probably knew why, too. Chances are, he'd seen Ruth's lover—"

Suddenly I realized what he was getting at. "Do you think Krebbs recognized Michael? He must have figured out who he was. That's what he was trying to tell Jane. The name she heard him say wasn't Jason. It was Jay's son."

"Strictly speaking," Russell pointed out. "Michael Durant was Jay's grandson."

As one, Shertz and I turned and glared. Having come this far, neither one of us was about to debate the technicalities.

"Where's Michael Durant now?" asked Detective Shertz.

"I can check his schedule," said Russell. "Harriet must be back by now."

She was. "Mr. Durant called in sick," she said, lips pursed in disapproval. She was the kind of administrator who found all Friday and Monday illnesses automatically suspicious. "I would imagine he's at home."

"Thank you, Harriet," Russell said distractedly. "That's all."

The secretary remained standing in the doorway. One by one, we turned to look at her.

"Well?" said Russell.

"Jane isn't here," Harriet said. "I mean, she's not on the campus. I went and checked just as soon as the detective called."

"What do you mean, you checked?" I asked.

Harriet smiled slightly. "Did you think you were the only friend that poor child had here? I've discovered Jane has a fondness for Twinkies. It's something we have in common."

The woman's cheeks took on a rosy hue, but

she was determined to finish her explanation. "That's how we met, actually. I caught her red-handed slipping my midmorning snack out of my desk drawer. Jane didn't look as though she'd had many treats in her life. It was just as easy for me to bring two as one. Every morning, I'd leave a Twinkie for her in a cubbyhole by the back stairs.

"Most afternoons, it was gone. Not today though. I'm sure Jane hasn't been on campus. If she had, she'd have taken it."

Detective Shertz was looking skeptical again, but I thought Harriet's explanation made perfect sense. A Twinkie connection, indeed. Obviously the secretary had hidden depths.

I suddenly remembered something. "Michael knows that Krebbs wasn't dead when Jane found him. I was sitting right there when she told him so on Saturday."

Shertz flipped back quickly through the pages of his notebook. "One problem," he said. "Durant had an alibi for the time of the murder. Said he was at some sort of committee meeting. Everybody grabbed lunch and ate it there. Two of the other teachers backed him up."

"No," I said, thinking back. "I was at that meeting, and Michael came in late. He didn't eat lunch. He hadn't been to the dining room with the rest of us. He was drinking coffee from the pot in the lounge. There was at least fifteen minutes, maybe more, when he could have been anywhere.

"If Michael's using the pageant committee meeting as his alibi, he's lying."

🐾 Twenty-six 🐾

Shertz flipped his notebook shut. "You got an address on this guy? I'm going to head over there now."

"Harriet?" Russell glanced toward the door.

"Coming right up."

I thought of something else. "You keep records on the teachers' cars, don't you?" I seemed to recall a question to that effect when I'd filled out forms upon my arrival the previous fall.

"I believe so," said Russell. "It's a security precaution, so we know which cars belong in our back lot and which don't."

"Harriet?" I called after her.

"I'll bring that, too."

A minute later, she was back, a file folder in her hands. She skimmed quickly through the information. "Acura Legend, 1991 model, color dark blue."

A pit opened up in the bottom of my stomach. "That's the car that was following us."

"When?" asked Shertz.

"Saturday, when Jane and I left the memorial service. It was right after she'd talked to Michael about finding Krebbs. Jane and I drove to her grandmother's house. I kept seeing the same car behind us, but I thought I was just being paranoid. I couldn't imagine why anyone would care where we were going."

"I don't like that," said the detective.

Neither did I. Michael had needed to know where he could find Jane, and I'd led him straight to her home.

"I'm coming with you," I said, as Harriet read off Michael's address.

"No, you're not." Shertz picked up Russell's phone, dialed police headquarters, and requested backup.

"If Jane's in trouble, it's my fault."

"If Jane's in trouble, she doesn't need you barging in and making things worse."

"Maybe I could help," I said desperately.

"How?"

Good question.

"Look," said the detective, his voice softening. "This is my job, it's what I've been trained to do. Nobody's going flying across town like a knight on a white horse. If Durant is there, we'll bring him in for questioning. We'll do things nice and quiet. You won't be able to help, Ms. Travis. You'd only be in the way."

Before I could protest again, he was gone. A minute later, we saw his car speed down the driveway. No lights, no sirens. Not in Greenwich.

I stared out the window and frowned mightily. Always before, I'd managed to beat the police to the punch. Well, to be perfectly honest, sometimes I'd stumbled upon the solution a few steps ahead of them. Once or twice I'd ended up putting myself in danger. But I'd never missed the big finish entirely.

I hated being left behind.

Russell crossed the room to stand beside me. "He knows what he's doing," he said.

"I know. But I still want to be there. I want to see for myself that Jane is okay."

"Ms. Travis?" Harriet was back. "There's a phone call for you."

I hurried over to the desk. I'd never gotten a call at school before. Nobody would bother me here, unless it was an emergency. I hoped Davey was all right.

I picked up the receiver and pressed the flashing button. "Hello?"

"It's me," said Aunt Peg. "I've been calling all over trying to find you. What are you doing still at school?"

"It's a long story."

Russell was looking at me quizzically. I looked back and shrugged.

"You can tell me about it when you get here. And make it quick. It seems I have an unexpected visitor. She's eating my food and playing with my dogs . . ."

Jane? My heart leapt.

". . . and I haven't a clue why she's here, except that she seems to think she's on the lam, her words, not mine. How this slip of a girl could possibly be in trouble—"

"Just hold on to her," I said quickly. "Don't let her out of your sight, okay? I'll be right there."

I slammed down the phone, and turned to find Russell waiting for news.

"Has our prodigal child turned up?"

"She's with my Aunt Peg."

"Good, then she's in safe keeping." Russell smiled slightly. "A formidable woman, your aunt."

Apparently they'd met. Perhaps on the occasion of the bribe cum donation, that had gotten me my job. I pushed the thought aside for now. I'd iron that problem out when the others had been taken care of.

"Aunt Peg will keep Jane safe until I get there. If Detective Shertz calls, would you tell him what happened?" I scribbled down Peg's address and phone number. "This is where we'll be."

I left Russell's office at a run. Luckily, the halls were nearly empty, and I was able to convince myself that I wasn't setting a bad example. Otherwise, I'd have had to put myself on report.

I stopped by my classroom, fetched Faith, and headed out to Peg's. It was a straight shot out Lake Avenue to Round Hill, and we made good time. Less than ten minutes after hanging up the phone, I was turning into Peg's driveway.

She must have been watching out the window because she met us at the door. For once, Peg's house dogs didn't seem to be doing their duty as guardians. Even with Faith on the step, I didn't hear a single bark.

"Jane has them with her in the kitchen," Peg informed me as we headed that way. "They're all besotted with her, the entire lot of them." Judging by her tone, she couldn't decide whether to be disgruntled at the Poodles' lack of loyalty, or pleased that she'd found a kindred spirit in Jane.

"What's she doing here?" I asked, hurrying to keep up.

"I have no idea. I found her out in the kennel about an hour ago. She'd used some dog beds to make a nest for herself and fallen fast asleep. I think she may have spent the night.

"Poor girl, she seemed to think she's in some sort of danger. I wasn't able to convince her otherwise, or I'd have returned her straightaway to her grandmother. I'm hoping you'll have better luck."

"She's been missing since yesterday," I said. "And she may be right about the danger. Let's hear what she has to say."

"Ms. Travis." Jane looked up and smiled as I entered the kitchen.

She was sitting on the floor, surrounded by Aunt Peg's house dogs, who tried, belatedly, to muster a halfhearted welcome. Faith received the lion's share of the greeting, while I was mostly ignored. It probably says something about the state of my life that this didn't seem unusual to me.

"I'm glad you came," Jane said. "I'm in big trouble, and I didn't know where else to go."

I sat down on the floor beyond the ring of Poodles. "What's up?"

"For starters, Gran is probably going to kill me." Jane toyed with the nearest dog's topknot, her fingers sifting through the hair.

"She's been very worried," I said. "She called the police, and they're out looking for you. Why did you run away?"

"I didn't know what else to do. Ever since Krebbs died, strange things keep happening. And then yesterday, a car started driving up and down my street. Back and forth, back and forth; it went really slow in front of my house. I think somebody's watching me."

Aunt Peg brought out a plate of freshly baked sugar cookies, offered them around, then pulled up a chair and sat down to listen.

"A dark blue Acura?" I asked, even though I already knew the answer. Jane nodded. "That's Michael Durant's car. Remember him?"

"The drama teacher. He called me."

I was chewing, but I swallowed fast. "When?"

"Yesterday. He said he needed to talk to me.

He wanted to come to my house and pick me up. He said we could go for a ride. Like I would do that with some guy I barely knew. How dumb did he think I was? I told him to buzz off."

"Good for you," Peg said to Jane, then turned to me, "Who's Michael Durant?"

"A new teacher at Howard Academy. He signed on this semester. It turns out that he's related to the school's founder. Joshua Howard's daughter, Ruth, had an illegitimate son who grew up to be Michael's father."

"Did Russell know that when he hired him?" asked Peg.

"That's apparently why he was hired. Michael said he'd sell his story to the tabloids, otherwise."

"I'm surprised," Peg mused. "I thought Russell was made of sterner stuff than that."

I shot her a look. "When it comes to Howard Academy, I gather Russell is open to all sorts of persuasion."

Peg's face paled slightly. Her gaze slid away, and she developed a sudden need to get up and pour us all something to drink.

"That's not all," said Jane.

Somehow I'd known it wouldn't be.

"I didn't tell you everything before. I wanted to, but Brad wouldn't let me. He said it was a bad idea."

"Brad's gone," I said.

"I know." Jane's head drooped. "He came to see me before he left."

Peg handed around glasses of milk, then broke a cookie into pieces and divided it among the Poodles. "This is the boy you told me about?" she asked Jane. "The one who was looking after you?"

"Uh-huh."

"He took care of Jane," Peg said to me. "He couldn't have been all bad. By the time you reach my age, you realize that nobody's perfect. Everybody has their little faults. Sometimes you just have to try and be understanding."

Were we still talking about Brad? I wondered. Or was Peg referring to herself; justifying her relentless need to take charge of things that were none of her business? I'd find that out later. Now I had more pressing things to attend to.

"What didn't Brad want you to tell me?" I asked Jane. "What happened that made you feel you needed his protection?"

"It was when Krebbs died," the girl said softly. "I told you about finding him there, but I didn't tell you all of it. He talked to me. Not just the name, but other stuff, too. I think he knew he was dying. He told me to watch out for Jason. Krebbs said that Jason was looking for something valuable, and that it was important he didn't find it."

335

"Did he tell you what it was?"

"No." Jane bit her lip. "I'm not sure he knew. He was kind of babbling about things. You know, like maybe he was delirious? He wanted me to bring him some paint."

"Paint?" Aunt Peg frowned.

"That's what it sounded like. There were a couple of cans stored in the shed. I figured that was what he meant."

Hmm, I thought, ideas igniting like sparklers. Not paint . . . not exactly. I bet I knew what Krebbs had been talking about. Things were finally beginning to make sense.

"Why didn't you tell anyone this before?" Aunt Peg asked.

"I was afraid to. Krebbs told me to watch out for Jason, but how could I when I didn't know who he was? All I could think of was that guy in the horror movies. The whole thing was giving me nightmares."

Poor child, I thought. It was a wonder she hadn't run away sooner. "What about Detective Shertz? You talked to him. Didn't you think you could trust him?"

"A cop," Jane sniffed. "Brad told me *never* to trust a cop. They say they're going to help you, but in the end they turn things around and make it all your fault."

"Did you really believe that?"

"I told Shertz about Jason, didn't I? I figured

that was enough. If he was going to help me, he would find Jason, and then I wouldn't have to be scared anymore."

"He did find Jason," I told her. "The man Krebbs was talking about was Michael Durant. And you were very smart to have nothing to do with him."

"What about the thing he was looking for?" Aunt Peg asked. "What was that?"

"I'm not positive about this part," I said. "But I have a pretty good idea. There's a painting at the school of Honoria Howard, one of the academy's founders. I've thought all along that there was something odd about it."

"Like what?" asked Jane.

"For one thing, it's a terribly unflattering likeness. I wondered why anyone would commission such a monstrosity. Or having done so, why would anyone keep it?"

"Maybe its very valuable," said Peg. "Who was the artist?"

"It wasn't signed by a name, only initials. R.W.H. The same initials belonged to the author of a diary I've been reading recently, Ruth Winston Howard. She was Joshua Howard's youngest daughter." I filled in the details of Ruth's story. "The portrait was dated 1936. Ruth must have painted it shortly before she died.

"At that point, she probably blamed her aunt

for much of what had gone wrong in her life, hence the unflattering depiction. She also placed the family pet in the painting, a Poodle named Poupee. I thought at first that he must have been Honoria's dog, but he wasn't. According to Ruth's diary, Honoria didn't like him at all. Clearly, Ruth was up to something."

"Yes," said Aunt Peg, beginning to sound exasperated. "But what?"

"Ruth talked about a hidden treasure in her diary. She said it was something that had belonged to her mother, and she was planning to use it to finance her escape. When Ruth first began painting, Honoria told Joshua that the girl had inherited her mother's interest in art. I think that's where the treasure lies. Somehow that painting is the solution to the mystery."

"Well done, Melanie. I thought you might figure things out eventually. I'm glad to see my faith in you wasn't misplaced."

I'd been so caught up in the explanation that it took me a moment to realize that the voice had come from the hallway behind me. A man's voice. Beside me, Jane's eyes were wide as saucers. The Poodles leapt up and began to bark, but their warning came too late.

Michael Durant was already in the house, and the gun he held in his right hand was trained unwaveringly on the three of us.

🐾 Twenty-seven 🐾

"Call off the dogs," he said.

Aunt Peg hesitated. Beau, a big male, was standing beside her chair, barking as though he meant business. The Poodle wouldn't attack, but Michael didn't know that. He shifted the barrel of the gun slightly to point it at Beau's head.

"No," Peg said quickly.

She laid a reassuring hand on the dog's shoulder. Immediately, Beau quieted. She stared at the rest of the group, and they followed suit, settling back on the floor.

"What are you doing here, Michael?" I asked.

"I was looking for Jane," he said, his gaze settling on the girl. "I suspected she had information I needed. And I was right, wasn't I?"

Aunt Peg glared. "You have a lot of nerve bringing a gun into my house. Is that the way your mother raised you to behave?"

Michael inclined his head. "I was raised on stories of great wealth that should have been mine, but wasn't. I was never allowed to forget, even for a moment, that my grandmother was one of the Deer Park Howards. You're right, however. My mother would be appalled at my manners. I apologize for the necessity of barging in this way. You must be Melanie's Aunt Peg."

"Peg Turnbull." She stood and extended a hand "And you must be the drama coach."

"Quite right." Michael eyed the hand, but declined to shake. "Please sit down, Mrs. Turnbull. I have no desire to use this gun, but I assure you, I will if I have to."

"Aunt Peg," I said, "don't be a hero."

She frowned in my direction and sat.

"Now what?" I asked. "I assume you've heard what Jane had to say."

"And your conclusions as well," said Michael. "I hope you're right about the painting. I wouldn't have suspected it myself, but Krebbs seems to have agreed with you."

"Even if it does contain a treasure of some sort, it won't have been worth killing for."

"I quite agree." Michael nodded. The gun remained steady. "What happened to Krebbs was an accident. He realized who I was not long after I arrived. I look just like my father. He looked just like his father. Krebbs couldn't have been more than a kid at the time, but he remembered Jay Silverman. After that, it didn't take him long to figure out why I was there."

"So he tried to beat you to the treasure."

Michael shrugged slightly. "Growing up, he'd heard the same rumors I had. The difference was, he didn't believe them. Not until I showed up, anyway. At first, I thought he was just a dotty old man. I figured he'd stay out of my way."

340

"He wasn't as dotty as you thought." Jane laughed. She didn't seem unduly alarmed by the gun that was pointing in our direction. For once it seemed like a good thing that today's kids have been so desensitized to violence. "He figured things out before you did."

"So it appears. Even so, I never meant to hurt him. I went to the shed to try and reason with him. The way I saw it, the Howard family owed both of us. They destroyed my grandmother. They threw my father away like he was nothing.

"And look what they did to Krebbs. Seventy years old and still breaking his back for them. The Howards owed us. I proposed that we work together and split the money."

Listening to him, I was reminded of the fact that Michael was an actor. He sounded thoroughly convincing. Obviously Krebbs hadn't been fooled, though.

"Must be hard to stab someone with a pitchfork by accident," Peg commented.

"Krebbs wouldn't listen to me. I only picked the pitchfork up to threaten him with. I was trying to make a point."

He'd done that, all right.

"Crazy old man," Michael spit out. "He said I had no right to anything of the Howards. That my grandfather had taken a payoff years ago and run away, leaving Ruth to shoulder the blame for everything. Krebbs blamed my grandfather for her death.

"Before I could think what to do next, Krebbs charged at me. I guess he thought he could overpower me. He ran right into the pitchfork. It wasn't my fault."

I glanced around at Peg and Jane. None of us believed him; none of us dared argue.

"What about the drugs the police found?" I asked. "Who did they belong to?"

"Nobody. They were supposed to be, what do you detectives call it . . . a red herring? I bought some stuff from Brad and stashed it in the shed. Then I called in a tip and waited for everyone to go running in the wrong direction."

"How did you get into the shed? The police had it sealed up tight."

"Nothing about that place was tight," Michael said. "Every damn window had a chink in it. I'd just killed someone. Do you honestly think I was going to worry about breaking into a crime scene?"

Now that he mentioned it, no.

"What about the fire?" Aunt Peg demanded. "Was that your doing, too? You nearly burnt my niece to a crisp. Not to mention Faith."

At least for once she'd given me top billing.

"You were getting too close," said Michael. "At first I thought it was a good idea that you were searching through the archives, too. I

342

figured you'd bring whatever you found to me."

"Michael was head of the pageant committee," I explained to Peg. "We were supposed to be doing a program to commemorate the school's founding."

"That was convenient," she said.

"Perfect," Michael agreed. "I couldn't have planned things better. But then you told me you had a diary that Ruth had been keeping when she knew my grandfather. There was no way I wanted that whole story to come out."

Of course not. He'd been using it for leverage to insure his job.

"I had nothing against you personally, Melanie," Michael said sincerely. "I wasn't trying to harm you. I set the fire to destroy the book."

Pardon me for not appreciating the distinction, I thought.

"The book wasn't in the basement," I told him. "I'd left it at home that morning. But it doesn't matter now anyway. Plenty of people know who you are and what you're up to, Michael. The police are looking for you."

He shrugged, looking unconcerned. "They won't find me. By the time they track me down here, I'll be long gone. After I stop at the school and pick up the painting, I'm going to disappear. Ruth planned to use her mother's treasure to run away. After all these years, it seems fitting that her grandson finish what she started."

"Is this the point where you threaten to shoot us all because we know too much?" asked Aunt Peg.

I sent her a look. So help me, she seemed to be enjoying herself. For my part, I'd be enjoying things more if she didn't go putting any ideas in his head.

"Don't be melodramatic." Michael sounded annoyed. "I'm not going to shoot anybody. All I need is a head start. I'm going to tie you up and leave you here. Later tonight, when I'm safely on my way, I'll call and tell the police where you are."

"For a murderer, you're very accommodating," said Peg.

I shot her another look. What was she up to?

"I'm not a murderer," Michael snapped. "I told you what happened. The whole thing was Krebbs's fault."

"Just like the fact that you grew up poor was the Howards' fault?" Peg goaded.

Michael glared at me. "Shut her up," he demanded.

"I've often wished I could," I said wistfully.

"It looks to me like you're the sort of person who always needs someone to blame," said Peg. "Even if Ruth's treasure still exists after all this time, do you honestly think that finding it will change your life?"

"It better," Michael said through gritted teeth. He reached around behind him and produced a roll of duct tape he'd left on a table in the hallway. "You first," he said, motioning to Peg. "Stand up, walk over here slowly, and don't try anything stupid."

"Stupid?" Peg sniffed "I'd say that was your department." Unaccountably her voice rose. "When I walk, the dogs will come with me. You're going to be mobbed."

"Tell them to stay."

"They never listen to me," Peg said blithely, a blatant lie if ever I'd heard one. As she started toward Michael, I distinctly saw her give Beau a nudge with her toe. The Poodle leapt up; immediately, the others followed. "Don't worry. They're a big distraction, but they don't bite."

Subtle, Aunt Peg wasn't. Obviously she had a plan, but what was it? Was I expected to take part?

Beside me, Jane was grinning. Just my luck, I was the only one who didn't know what was going on. Unfortunately, it wasn't the first time.

Dogs milling around her legs, Peg walked toward Michael. She held out her hands obligingly, a sure sign that something was up. Peg never does anything she doesn't want to do without an argument.

Maybe Michael was fooled by her age or the

submissive demeanor she seemed to have adopted. He stuck the gun in his belt before yanking at the roll of duct tape and tearing off a strip. Looking down to see what he was doing, he didn't see what Peg had in mind until it was too late.

Both hands outstretched, she shoved hard against his chest. If Beau hadn't been behind him, Michael might have stood a chance. Instead, his balance already compromised, he tripped over the big Poodle and he went down in a heap.

Duct tape tangling in his fingers, Michael was struggling to get to his gun when Jane and I jumped up to join the fray. The Poodles were running around us, barking maniacally. First they'd gotten in Michael's way; now they were in mine. I knew I wouldn't reach him fast enough.

It didn't matter. Aunt Peg had everything under control. Calmly she picked up the chair she'd been sitting on and hit Michael over the head with it.

I'd barely had time to assimilate that before the back door burst open. Guns drawn, a band of police officers led by Detective Shertz came flying into the room. The Poodles looked as stunned by this turn of events as I was. Aunt Peg was grinning.

Shertz skidded to a stop and looked down at Michael, out cold on the floor.

"Aren't you going to yell 'Freeze!'?" asked Jane. She was grinning, too.

The detective didn't look amused. He turned to Aunt Peg. "Who do you think you are, John Wayne?"

"I didn't expect to have to do the whole thing myself. I thought you were going to back me up." She didn't ask what-took-you-so-long? but the sentiment was clear in her tone.

"We were getting into position," said Shertz. "You were supposed to wait for us to make our move."

Obviously he'd never met my aunt before. Anyone who had would know that waiting patiently is not her style.

"That was cool," said Jane.

"Wasn't it?" Peg agreed, beaming. "I haven't had that much fun in a long time. Melanie, next time you track down a murderer, I want you to promise to take me with you."

If there was a suitable answer to that, I had no idea what it might be. Aunt Peg and Jane were congratulating themselves on their fine adventure. Meanwhile, my knees felt weak.

"You could have gotten yourself shot," I said, as one of the officers used the phone to call for an ambulance.

"Oh pish," said Aunt Peg. "He'd put the gun in his belt. If it had gone off, the only thing he'd have harmed was . . ." She glanced at Jane, who was listening avidly, and let the thought dangle.

Be careful what you wish for, I told myself darkly. I was the one who hadn't wanted to miss out on the grand finale.

"Besides," Peg said brightly, "all's well that ends well. I seem to have worked up an appetite. Would any of you gentlemen like some cake?"

Shaking my head, I turned to Detective Shertz. "How did you know that Michael was here?"

"We didn't. But by the time we'd checked his house and found out he wasn't home, Russell Hanover had called the station. He said you'd located Jane, and we followed you here to pick her up."

Jane sat down beside the table. Beau climbed up to put his front legs in her lap. Her fingers tangled in the silky black topknot, and her gaze was distant. "He killed Krebbs," she said.

"I know," Shertz's voice was gentle. "We heard him tell you."

"He was looking for me."

"We wouldn't have let him hurt you," I said firmly, staring at Detective Shertz.

"Ms. Travis is right. Durant was making too many mistakes. We were already on his trail."

By the time the ambulance arrived, Michael was moaning as he began to wake up; several of the officers were enjoying cake; and Peg and I were anxious to get back to Howard Academy.

I'd called Russell as soon as the excitement died down and he was waiting for us. Detective Shertz was going to take Jane and deliver her to her grandmother, but I promised to call later and let her know what we'd found.

"Me too," said Shertz, handing me his card. "I'll be at the station a while tonight."

Ten minutes later, we split up and headed in three different directions. Speed limits in Greenwich are low. I broke a few laws on the way to the school, but I was pretty sure I could get Shertz to fix a ticket if I had to.

Night comes early in March but from the road, Howard Academy was a blaze of light. I pulled up to the front door. Russell had it open before the Volvo even rolled to a stop. I'd explained much of what happened over the phone, but I hadn't told him everything about Honoria's portrait.

That was purely selfish on my part. If there really was a treasure, I wanted to be on hand for the unveiling. I set out for the faculty lounge at a jog. Peg, Russell, and Faith matched my pace.

"Don't get your hopes up," I said, opening the door and flipping on the light. "After all this time, it may be nothing."

I might as well have saved my breath. Despite the odds, I knew we were all hoping like crazy.

Together, Russell and I lifted the painting off the wall. Though I peered at it closely, the front looked the same as ever. From the back, there was nothing to be seen but the wooden frame and stretched canvas. I'd been hoping there would be paper across the back, perhaps with room to tuck something inside, but there wasn't. Everything was exposed; no hiding place existed.

I ran my fingers around the edges of the canvas, holding my breath as I probed for something, anything. Russell and Peg watched anxiously. I shrugged.

"There's a screwdriver around here some-where." Russell opened several drawers and rifled through them. "Maybe if we remove the painting from the frame . . ."

We undid the clasps and gently pried the canvas free. Now we had two pieces, and still nothing out of the ordinary. Our collective disappointment was palpable.

"Wait," said Peg. "Let me try something. I read about this in a book once."

She grasped the canvas and began to work along the edges with her fingers. It wasn't a single piece as I'd thought. Slowly, Honoria's portrait began to come loose and peel away. A swirl of color took shape behind it.

The frame had held two paintings, one on top of the other. One worthless. The other . . .

We all stared. Russell was the one who thought to step back. When I joined him, my vision cleared. The two of us began to grin like we were demented.

"What?" Peg demanded, holding the canvas. The last of Honoria's portrait lifted off, and she uncovered the signature in the corner. Her breath escaped in a whoosh.

Eugène Delacroix, it said.

🐾 Twenty-eight 🐾

I guess you could say I got off lucky.

Russell hadn't been pleased about the way I'd defied his edict not to get involved, but once the Delacroix was discovered, he decided he could overlook a few transgressions on my part. The painting was a minor work, one of the artist's later street scenes, but an appraiser at Christie's assured us that it was valuable enough to fund Howard Academy's scholarship needs until well into the next century.

I never did find out why the headmaster had been sneaking around the back stairs, and any hints I dropped in that direction were firmly quashed. For the sake of the new equanimity in our relationship, I let the matter drop. Everyone's entitled to have a secret or two.

At least that's what I'd been telling myself since I'd made the recent discoveries that two of the most important people in my life had been holding out on me. That didn't mean I was going to be as lenient with them as I had with my boss. Are you kidding? I wanted a showdown.

During the week, I called and invited Sheila and Aunt Peg to join Sam, Davey, and me for lunch on Saturday. Faith had been entered in a dog show that weekend, but with the damage to her coat, I'd be lucky to have her back in the ring by summer. Instead I decided to use the unexpected day off to hold the first barbecue of the year.

Sheila seemed a little surprised by the invitation. When she hesitated, mumbling something about having a Pug entered on Sunday and preparations to make, I mentioned that Sam was going to be there.

"Really?" Her interest level climbed a notch. "I'm surprised he can spare the time. He's been so busy lately."

"I hadn't noticed," I said sweetly. The gauntlet hit the ground with a thud. "He's always able to make time for me."

I thought I heard a growl coming through the phone line. Maybe Sheila had stepped on one of her little dogs. In any case, the lure of her ex-husband's company proved irresistible, and Sheila promised to come.

And what did Sam think of the fact that I was dangling him in front of his ex-wife like a juicy marrow bone? He didn't exactly know about it. I may be sneaky and underhanded, but I'm not dumb.

The last time—the only time—I'd seen Sam and Sheila together, he'd run from my side to hers without giving it a thought. Though he'd said all the right things since, it was time for him to back up those words with action. Throwing them together unexpectedly was, I figured, the best way to elicit an honest response.

Sam and I were in the backyard when Sheila arrived. The weather was a little chilly, but the sun was shining and you could unfasten the top button of your coat without fear of frostbite. Davey and the Poodles had gone inside to look for a Frisbee. Sam was removing the tarp from the grill and checking to see how much damage the winter had done.

I heard a car pull into the driveway and walked to the gate on the side of the house. In deference to the brisk temperature, Sheila had bundled up. The Sherpa vest looked very chic, but I thought the gloves and furry earmuffs were overkill. I was wearing Polartec myself. Lots of warmth, little bulk. Someone as tiny as Sheila ought to look into a product like that.

"Is that Peg?" Sam asked, looking up from the grill as Sheila sailed past me and into the yard.

"No, honey, it's me." Her smile was wide and confident. She strode to Sam's side. "Nice to see you again."

Sam leaned down to peck her chastely on the cheek. His eyes found mine over Sheila's shoulder, and he didn't look pleased. "I had no idea you were coming."

"No?" Her eyelashes fluttered. "I knew you'd be here. That's why I came."

"I hope not," Sam said, as Aunt Peg walked

through the gate. "Melanie, can I see you inside for a minute? Peg, perhaps you wouldn't mind keeping Sheila company? Mel and I will be right back."

Meekly, I followed him into the kitchen.

"All right," Sam said, when he'd closed the door behind us, "what are you up to?"

"Me?" I tried that fluttery lashes thing. It didn't work nearly so well for me as it had for Sheila.

"Yes, you." Sam seemed to be fighting the urge to smile. "Do you see anyone else in the room?"

I checked behind me, just in case, then shook my head.

"This is a test, isn't it?"

"Well . . ."

"I thought so. Then, here's my answer. Did you see the way I kissed Sheila out there? Take that as a measure of my feelings for her. This is how I feel about you."

Sam's arms wrapped around me and pulled me to his chest. His lips closed over mine. Our mouths opened, our tongues met. I felt as though my bones were melting. The world around me faded; nothing mattered except Sam.

When he released me a minute later I had to catch myself to keep from falling. My Polartec jacket felt like an oven, and I fumbled with the zipper. My fingers felt numb; my heart pounded in my chest. I wouldn't have been surprised to find that I had smoke coming out of my ears.

Sam leaned back against the counter and gazed at me. "Well?"

It took a moment for my eyes to focus. "A+," I managed finally.

"Am I going to have to keep proving this to you?"

"I sincerely hope so." I grinned shamelessly. After a minute, Sam joined in.

Carrying a tray holding hot dogs, hamburgers, and rolls, we went back outside. Sam was looking smug; I was still unsteady on my feet. Sheila glared at us both.

I was almost tempted to feel a little sorry for her; but I gave it a moment, and the feeling passed.

After we ate, Sam and Davey started a game of Frisbee. Vying for the good-sport award, Sheila joined in. I took the opportunity to pull Aunt Peg aside. From the way her gaze had been shifting away from mine all afternoon, I knew she knew what was coming.

"Go ahead and spit it out," she said, crossing her arms implacably over her chest. "You're mad."

"Wouldn't you be? You *bought* me a job."

"I did no such thing. You deserved that position. You had the education, the experience, the credentials. All I did was help the process along."

"You bribed Russell Hanover into hiring me."

"Don't be silly," Peg snapped. "The money I offered was a donation, that's all."

"It came with strings."

"Bequests often do. It's the way the world works."

She didn't have a clue, I realized. She honestly didn't understand why I was upset.

"All right," I said. "Suppose you had a very pretty bitch, one you were really proud of. You took her to a show and she won the points, deservedly so in your eyes. Then later you found out that I'd bribed the judge to put you up."

"That's highly illegal!"

I shrugged.

"And immoral."

"But not impossible."

"Not under some circumstances," Peg conceded grudgingly. There aren't many crooked judges at dog shows, but human nature being what it is, one can never rule out the possibility.

"How would you feel?"

"You know perfectly well I'd be livid—" Aunt Peg stopped and frowned. Bingo. I let her stew for a minute, hoping she was feeling guilty.

"I might let you make it up to me."

She didn't jump at the chance. Instead Peg looked decidedly suspicious. "How?"

I gestured to the game. "Keep Sheila out of

Sam's and my way until she goes back to Chicago."

"That's nearly three months from now!" She didn't sound pleased by the size of the task.

"Maybe that will teach you not to butt into my life."

"I doubt it," said Peg.

We'd barely gotten that settled when she dropped another bomb shell. "I went to visit Jane and her grandmother this morning."

"Oh?" Now it was my turn to be suspicious.

"I had an idea. Jane and I spoke about it last weekend. She's an inordinately clever child. I thought it seemed a shame that nobody'd ever taken the time to channel all that intelligence and energy in a worthwhile direction."

"So you decided to step in." For once, I couldn't fault her intentions. "And?"

"I'm told the girl spends most of her time at Howard Academy anyway, so legitimizing her presence seemed like a logical idea. When I offered to pay her tuition, Russell decided that under the circumstances, a midsemester enrollment could be made.

"He's already lined up some sessions with the Howard Academy therapist. I believe she'll be starting Monday. And, of course, she's missed a great deal of schoolwork." Aunt Peg's gaze slid my way. "That's where you come in."

"Me?" I asked faintly.

"You'll have less than three months to complete a semester's worth of work so she can go on to eighth grade with the rest of her class. Think you can handle that?"

If anyone could manage, it would be Jane. By the end of the year, she'd probably be running the place. I looked forward to watching her take Howard Academy by storm.

One last thing. With Michael and Ed both having been terminated, Russell appointed two more teachers to take their places on the pageant committee. After all the recent turmoil, the headmaster decided it was more important than ever that the school proceed with its plans. He did request however that, in light of recent developments, the committee choose a new theme.

We got together and voted. *Pirates of Penzance* won by a mile. One teacher abstained.

I was too busy laughing to raise my hand.

Center Point Publishing

600 Brooks Road ● PO Box 1
Thorndike ME 04986-0001 USA

(207) 568-3717

US & Canada:
1 800 929-9108
www.centerpointlargeprint.com